A FATAL FACADE

A CRIME THRILLER

A Fatal Facade

A Crime Thriller

Linda M. James

Winchester, UK
Washington, USA

First published by Roundfire Books, 2013
Roundfire Books is an imprint of John Hunt Publishing Ltd., Laurel House, Station Approach,
Alresford, Hants, SO24 9JH, UK
office1@jhpbooks.net
www.johnhuntpublishing.com
www.roundfire-books.com

For distributor details and how to order please visit the 'Ordering' section on our website.

Text copyright: Linda M. James 2013

ISBN: 978 1 78279 102 7

A CIP catalogue record for this book is available from the British Library.

Design: Stuart Davies

Printed and bound by CPI Group (UK) Ltd, Croydon, CR0 4YY

We operate a distinctive and ethical publishing philosophy in all
areas of our business, from our global network of authors to
production and worldwide distribution.

Note Of Thanks

The initial idea for the plot of this book came from many discussions with my friend Ann Woods and although the plot has changed since we spoke about it, I would like to thank her for her invaluable help.

I would also like to thank another friend, Margaret Charrington, for her help with proof-reading.

"Man is not what he thinks he is, he is what he hides."
André Malraux

"All things in the world are two. In our minds we are two, good and evil. With our eyes we see two things, things that are fair and things that are ugly... We have the right hand that strikes and makes...for evil, and we have the left hand full of kindness, near the heart. One foot may lead us to an evil way, the other foot may lead us to a good. So are all things two, all two." Eagle Chief (Letakos-Lesa) Pawnee

For Ann Woods

CHAPTER 1

Paolo Cellini's slim, naked body lay on his marbled-bathroom floor covered only with a small, white towel. All the serenity and beauty of Montgomery's *Tancred* was revealed in his face, but Jack Bradley knew he wasn't serene. He'd seen too many dead bodies to be deceived by the illusion of serenity. This man was young. He shouldn't have died. Jack moved carefully over to the large free-standing bath in a corner, took off one of his gloves and dipped his fingers into the red-stained bathwater and tasted it. A hint of red wine. Paolo Cellini liked decadence; there were two empty wine bottles and glasses on a marble table near the bath. Obviously he'd been bathing with someone before he died. Jack put his glove back on and opened Paolo's bathroom cabinet and was confronted with a wealth of toiletries: Bvlgari, Ralph Lauren, Nino Cerruti, Contradiction, Pacoxs… it went on. A bottle of Metoprolol and the usual vitamin supplements that people seemed to be obsessed with these days stood on one side of the cabinet. He'd have to ask Matthew Stanford what the Metoprolol was for; then realized he couldn't. He shouldn't even be in this room.

From outside the bathroom door, Jack heard the grating tones of Alan Saunders, his ex-colleague. Within two strides he reached the door. That's when he spotted the cream silk panties, half hidden behind a radiator. He picked them up and two white tablets rolled over the marbled floor. Jack automatically put them in his pocket, his attention focused on the silk panties – they were exquisitely embroidered; not that he was an expert on embroidery or panties. This was the first time he'd ever fingered ones as expensive as these. The panties disappeared into his pocket as the door opened. Alan Saunders stood there with the usual lopsided smirk on his face; a smirk which had always made Jack want to punch him in the face. So far, he'd resisted the urge.

'Jack – what the hell are you doing in here? You haven't touched anything, have you?'

'Of course not,' Jack answered curtly. He'd been this man's boss for ten years and now *he* was telling *him* not to touch anything!

Alan smiled and Jack knew what he was thinking. *Jack Bradley isn't my superior any more.* He stared at Jack's uniform. 'What force is that, then? Don't recognize it.'

Alan's derisory tone made Jack's stomach contract. If Alan was a plant, he'd be ivy, Jack thought. Strangling everyone with ambitious tenacity.

'I'm working for someone in the apartment block. The dead man's neighbor.' Jack was surprised that he managed to keep his tone so flat.

'Did you find the body?'

'No, the maid did. She's with my employer next door, having the British answer to trauma.'

Alan raised his eyebrows quizzically.

'Tea,' Jack said.

There was a small uneasy silence as the two men stared at each other with years of mutual dislike.

'I see,' Alan said, not seeing anything at all.

'I'll get out of your way.' Jack moved swiftly out of the bathroom as two forensic experts filed into the room; they smiled at him briefly as he passed them; he knew them both.

'How's Lucy?'

The unexpectedness of the question hit Jack hard. He turned slowly to face Alan before saying. 'If you ever came to see her, you'd find out.' Jack closed the door and took several deep breaths as he walked into the dead man's lounge. In the winter sunlight it looked like a treasure trove of Medieval and Renaissance Art. A large triptych covered one wall: three panels depicted heaven, hell and purgatory. Jack had a passion for art; he became mesmerized by the consuming flames of hell. Suddenly he was back in that house the night of the siege and the woman's screams were piercing his brain as she burnt in front of him.

A hand on his shoulder made him jump. 'Hallo, sir – where were you?'

Jack turned and saw Jamila Soyinka smiling at him.

'Not a place you want to be and...it's not "sir" any more...remember?'

Jamila flushed with embarrassment. She studied the painting. 'Who'd want that in their lounge?' Her nose wrinkled as she saw the devil roasting a foot.

'A Catholic,' Jack answered curtly, turning away from her.

There was a small awkward silence. Jamila glanced around the room in amazement; priceless art works, accumulated over five years, covered every surface.

'This place is more like an art gallery than a home. Wouldn't like to live here myself.'

'You couldn't afford it on your salary.' Jack turned to smile at her. They had always worked well together at the Met. 'The owner was an art dealer. A very successful one, according to my new employer...she's got the apartment next door. His maid Carla discovered the body.'

'What do you think, Jack?'

'About what?'

'Come on, you've always had a theory.'

Jack was just about to answer when Alan came out of the bathroom talking to Matthew Stanford, the police doctor.

'Time of death?' Alan asked.

'You know I can't be certain,' Matthew answered.

'Well, give me an expert guess,' Alan persisted.

Matthew hesitated before saying, 'Roughly between 2 and 4 am.'

Alan's face tightened as he saw Jack in the corner of the room. 'You still here? Obviously can't keep you away from death.'

The silence in the room was unnerving as everyone stared at Jack.

'I'm just leaving.'

'Jack... good to see you.' Matthew rushed over to shake Jack's hand warmly. 'I'm almost certain the dead man had a heart attack. He was taking Metoprolol, a beta blocker used to control the rhythm of the heart.' He was speaking to Jack, not Alan.

'If you remember, Matt – Jack's not one of us anymore.' Alan's face flushed with anger.

Another tense silence before Jack started towards the door.

'A heart attack?'Jamila queried. 'But the guy was only 30, wasn't he?'

Jack closed the door on Matthew's answer. He was walking down the corridor to his new employer's apartment when Jamila ran after him.

'What do you think, Jack?'

'I don't any more. You heard Alan.'

Jamila blocked his path. 'Come on – tell me what you think!'

'I think Paolo Cellini was murdered.'

Jamila stared at him in surprise. 'But Matthew found heart tablets in the bathroom cabinet. The guy had a heart condition.'

'You asked what I thought. I've told you.'

He could hear Mrs. Montgomery's voice in the distance talking to Cellini's Italian maid, trying to comfort her; she was crying. Her screams on finding Paolo's body had brought Jack running to his apartment.

'I've got to go.'

Jack started to move away from Jamila when she said, 'Why did you leave the force? Nobody wanted you to.'

'Go back to Alan, Jamila. He needs you.'

'No, he doesn't. You know he likes to take the credit for everything.'

'Not my problem anymore. I've got a new life now.'

'You call being a chauffeur a new life for one of the best DCIs in the Met!' Jamila called after him.

Jack carried on walking towards Mrs. Montgomery's apartment wishing he hadn't heard the anger in her voice.

CHAPTER 2

7th December 2012

Federico Batas pulled his short, thick overcoat closer around him. A fierce December wind scoured his face as he battled towards Cellini's Chelsea art gallery. He'd had appalling dreams last night, reliving the accident over and over, but he still had to work. He was carrying the week's takings from the Blue Notes nightclub in a large black briefcase. Rico had repeatedly told Cellini what he thought about carrying such a large amount of money through the streets of London, but the bastard had simply said, 'No one is going to mug you, Rico, are they? Not with your face.' Rico had always wanted to ask him what he meant, but he never had. He was too afraid of the answer. He turned into Lower Sloane Street and saw a large sign in the gallery window. *Gallery Closed Until Further Notice.* Rico frowned. The gallery manager had said nothing about any closure last week. Stamping his feet against the cold, he waited for the manager, Edmondo Pourani, to open the door. Edmondo's usual serious expression had been replaced by an even more somber one. It made Rico nervous. He walked past him into the gallery full of expensive and exquisite art acquisitions Cellini had bought, mainly from Italy.

'What's the matter? Why's the gallery closed?' Rico asked him.

Edmondo stared at him in surprise. 'You haven't heard? Mr.

Cellini died early this morning. A heart attack at thirty! It's unbelievable.' He patted his forehead with an immaculately laundered handkerchief while Rico stared at him in confusion.

'What do you mean – dead? He can't be dead. He was in the club last night.'

'The police rang me at 6 a.m. He had a heart attack a few hours before. I've only just returned from the mortuary. I had to identify his body. They couldn't find a trace of any family. It was simply…' His voice trailed off as he patted his forehead with his handkerchief again. 'It's been a terrible shock.'

Rico tried to think quickly, but nothing came.

'You'd better come through, Rico.'

Rico followed Edmondo's immaculate figure into the store-room at the back of the gallery. 'What shall we do with the takings?'

He frowned at Rico. 'We'll deposit them in the safe as usual…it's still Mr. Cellini's money whether he's alive or dead.'

'Of course,' Rico added hastily, looking around the storeroom for the crate. *It's not here!* Rico had to hang onto a nearby table for support. *Jesus Christ – they'll crucify me.*

Edmondo was depositing the money in the safe, so missed the panic on Rico's face.

'So…where's the shipment Mr. Cellini was expecting from Italy, Mr. Pourani?'

Edmondo locked the safe and turned in surprise to Rico. 'It's very strange, but he asked for it to be taken straight to his apartment. The police have been there all night, most probably desecrating some of the most priceless works of art in the world. One of them came to the gallery just before you arrived – he must have had all of four brain cells. The dear Lord only knows what the rest are like. If only Mr. Cellini had told me what he was shipping… I can't understand it.'

Rico could feel the room swaying. He had to sit down.

Even after an hour's walking, he still couldn't think what to do. How could he get access to Cellini's apartment? What if he'd left the crate lying around? Rico was a frozen wreck by the time he walked into the club, but all thought of the crate disappeared from his mind when he saw Bianca sitting at the bar, drinking heavily. It was the middle of the afternoon.

'I was with him last night, Rico. How can he be dead?' She knocked back a glass of whisky without looking at him. Rico corked the bottle and put it under the bar.

'That's not going to help, Bi.'

'It is. Don't want to feel anything...why'd he rush off like that? We were going to get married next year.' Her convulsive crying had made her mascara black-lead her eyes.

'Married!' Rico couldn't disguise his disbelief.

Bianca glared at him. 'We were! We just didn't want anyone to know – not yet.'

'Oh, come on, Bi – you know what he was like.'

'What's that mean?'

'You know what he was like with women.'

Bianca slid off the bar-stool and shouted into Rico's face. 'What do you mean? Was he seeing someone else?' She shook Rico so hard his head hurt. 'Who was she, Rico? Tell me, you bastard or I'll kick your fucking nuts in! Tell me!' She started to hit him.

'Bi – he wasn't worth this.' He held her arms tight until, at last, she suddenly slumped against him, moaning. 'Shhhhhh,' he said gently, stroking her hair and breathing in the chamomile shampoo she always used. Gradually, she stopped shaking. 'Come on... I'm taking you home.'

She leaned away from him – her panda eyes trying to focus through the alcoholic haze. 'I'm never going to see him again, Rico...how am I going to live with that?'

He stopped her collapsing onto the floor. At that moment, Rico wanted Cellini to be alive again; just so he could kill him – very slowly.

CHAPTER 3

7th December 2012

Jack stared at the man in his bathroom mirror, amazed at his reflection. A tired, forty-eight-year-old stranger stared back at him with a face so crumpled it looked as if people had been drying their hands on it. How had it happened? He used to jog every morning before work; he'd start again; he had to keep fit for Lucy. He swallowed some sleeping tablets quickly and had a pee. *Worry, that's what's aged me. Why should I care about the death of one more man? What does it matter if Paolo Cellini was murdered or not? So why can't I stop thinking about a naked body lying on the marble floor, covered by a small white towel?* He snapped the light off and stumbled out of the room, exhausted. But the question kept circling his mind as he walked up the corridor towards his son's bedroom: *who covers himself with a small white towel when he's having a heart attack?*

He glanced into Tom's room that was covered with posters from Batman films. His duvet was half off the bed. Jack entered the dimly lit room. Even though Tom was nearly 13 he still wanted a night light on to keep the demons away. If only a light could do that, Jack thought, covering his son's vulnerable body with his Batman duvet. Tom looked much younger than twelve. Not much older than in the photos by his bed. Jack picked up his favourite picture of Lucy and Tom on holiday in Snowdonia three years ago. They were climbing Cader Idris. It was a hard climb, but Lucy was determined to get to the top before either of them. Her face was turned towards the camera, smiling. Jack could see the determination of a fighter in her face. Of course, that was before her illness. His hand trembled as he placed the photo carefully back on Tom's cupboard and smiled at his son. He looked so peaceful sleeping; if only he could look like that when he was awake. Jack closed Tom's door quietly and crept into their bedroom. Lucy was propped up with four pillows, obviously finding it difficult to breathe, but at least she was sleeping. Jack climbed into bed and lay there listening to her heavy breathing. They'd had a night-light in their bedroom too, since Lucy's illness; in case something happened. They often spoke in euphemisms now; it helped them all to cope. The ominous oxygen cylinder waited on Lucy's side of the bed. Would he have the courage not to use it when the time came? Jack thought, before the sleeping tablets took effect.

He woke the next morning to find the bed empty and momentarily panicked. Then he remembered Irina, Lucy's full-time carer. Throwing his woolen dressing gown over his pyjamas, he padded into the kitchen to have breakfast with Lucy and Tom. Irina was feeding Lucy who sat passively in her wheelchair. Jack bent and kissed her before sitting down opposite Tom. He was doing some forgotten homework as usual, but Jack had stopped telling him off. There were more important things to worry about than forgotten homework, he thought. *God, it's taken me years to work that out.*

Jack smiled at Lucy and had his usual small shock. Each day her face seemed a little more deflated, like a balloon with limited air. Muscular dystrophy had almost paralyzed her completely now, except for her fingers, her eyes and her brain which was still agile. Jack didn't know whether the latter was a blessing or not. Her wheelchair had a voice stimulator attached to it, but she hated the disembodied sound, so she typed messages via a small laptop attached to her wheelchair. She started typing, then looked up at Jack. He glanced at her message *tried to stay awake last night*

'Sorry, Luc. I didn't get in until late. I had to drive Mrs. Montgomery home from the theater. She's a theater fanatic.'

lucky she can go Lucy typed.

Jack cursed himself for his insensitivity. Lucy used to love going to the theater before she was ill. 'Better get dressed or I'll be late for work.'

Tom made a dismissive sound under his breath as Jack got up and walked out. It had taken him a few weeks to get over the embarrassment of the uniform; each day it got a little easier. He studied himself in the mirror. He actually looked smarter than when he was working at the Met. He steeled himself and went back into the kitchen to kiss Lucy goodbye.

He stopped at the door, trying to make a joke. 'What d'you think of the uniform, then, folks?'

Irina smiled at him. 'You look nice, Mr. Bradley.'

Tom carried on writing in his tiny scroll as Lucy typed *handsome*

He smiled at her, then turned to his son. 'Come on, Tom – we'll be late.'

Tom carried on writing, his feet twisting awkwardly under the table.

Jack desperately wanted his son to look up at him and smile. 'So what do you think of my uniform, Tom?'

Tom studied his father for some time before saying. 'You look *really* sad.'

Jack drove through the heavy morning traffic without swearing once, while Tom sat beside him, staring rigidly out of the window at the tawdry Christmas decorations in shop windows. Jack couldn't remember a time when he was dreading Christmas so much.

After ten minutes he couldn't stand the silence any more. 'Mrs. Montgomery's got a Daimler...fancy a spin in it? It's a beautiful car.'

Tom carried on staring out of the window as if the silence was still intact. The school entrance was swarming with boys when Jack drove up. He turned to Tom and smiled, but Tom was out of the Ford, running through the school gates before Jack could say a word. No one spoke to Tom as he ran into the school and he spoke to no one. Jack started up the car, his face creased with pain.

Chapter 4

8thDecember 2012

The annual Christmas party was a loud and boozy affair. Hal Morrison and Peter Marshall, two of the most experienced reporters on *The Daily Reporter*, were standing in an isolated corner of the newspaper office, studying the milling throng of younger reporters and secretaries chatting animatedly to each other. People were starting to pair off for the night.

Hal leaned drunkenly towards his equally drunk friend. 'Bloody early for the Christmas do, Pete. Not that I'm complaining.'

'That's what I like about you, Hal – you never complain. Bet it's because our Führer is swanning off for an early Christmas holiday.'

Hal patted his friend on the shoulder affectionately. 'Bet you're right, Pete. You usually are. Have I told you you're the best friend I've ever had and I've had a fucking shag every Christmas party for thirty years?'

'Only every party, Hal. All over you like ringworm, aren't they?'

Hal's bloodshot eyes narrowed as he considered Peter's words. 'Ringworm? Don't think that's the right er...' He looked up at the neon ceiling with his mouth open, as if hoping the right word would drop in. 'Can't understand it...what's happened this year?'

Peter stared at him with all the seriousness of a drunk. 'You said that last year.'

A small wave of excitement oscillated around them as the editor of the newspaper, Mark Logan, strode past them, followed by a small entourage of women; all determined he was going to be theirs for the night. Mark was everything Hal and Peter weren't: dynamic, attractive and slim.

'The bastard's only forty, Pete. What's he know?' Hal slurred.

'About what?'

'About women.'

They stared at Mark's retreating figure as he disappeared out of the door, pursued by three young women.

'Absolutely nothing, Hal,' Peter said reassuringly.

Mark hadn't meant to stay so late. He sped down the corridor away from the women. When had they become so predatory? he thought, dashing into the gents before they saw him. He stood behind the door until he could hear their retreating voices shouting – 'Where'd he go?' He waited a few more minutes before opening the door and creeping out. Then he saw Lavinia, his new trainee. She was wearing a tight pelmet skirt and her low-cut blouse had a sprig of mistletoe nestling between her breasts. She tottered towards him on six-inch heels.

'I hate office parties, don't you, sir? They're always full of drunks.'

Mark lost the power of movement as she pinned him against the wall and gyrated her body against his.

'Happy early Christmas.' Her kiss held all the promise of a woman who was completely focused on getting promotion fast.

At that moment, Hal and Peter staggered down the corridor and saw Mark being buttressed against the wall.

'Didn't invite the wife this year, then, Mark!' Hal shouted.

He'd never felt so happy in his life. Lavinia had given him the opportunity for hours of enjoyable blackmail.

Mark broke away from Lavinia and ran towards the lift, jamming his fingers repeatedly on the button. Hal and Peter went to join him, wanting to sink the sword of Damocles a little deeper.

'We're not blaming you, Mark.'

'Christ, no!' Peter added. 'Hal would be right in there if she'd give him a sideways glance, but she never has.' He paused. 'Understandable, of course.'

Hal leaned forward to breathe stale whisky over Mark. 'It's all in the tits,' he said enigmatically.

At last, Mark could hear the lift moving up towards their floor. 'Look – I'm not interested in other women. I'm a reformed man since I married Angelica.' The lift opened. Mark stepped inside gratefully as the door closed on Hal's words.

'I want some of that reformation, Pete.'

Mark hunched up against the cold as he hurried away from the office, thinking about the party. He'd meant what he said. He *was* a reformed man. Why would he want to be in a room crowded with drunks with a wife like Angelica waiting for him? He wished she'd have come with him, but she'd hated their Christmas party last year. He hailed a passing cab, but it drove past full of people. The air was so cold it made his bones ache. He sprinted down the road, trying to get the blood flowing around his frozen body. The sudden noise of a police siren sliced the night. It was driving towards an ambulance at the other end of the road. It's late, Mark told himself, go home. But years of looking for stories forced him to sprint towards the flashing lights.

A number of pubescent girls and boys were shivering beside a large white coach as a slight body was lifted onto a stretcher. A stunned-looking coach-driver stood helplessly opening and closing his hands. Mark noticed a crowd of people watching from outside a burger bar across the street. A cordon had already been erected to keep them at bay. A man who looked like a bouncer was striding down the street, oblivious to the accident. Years of reporting stories forged this detail on Mark's mind automatically. It might be important. He flashed his press card at a young police officer as he moved towards the stretcher. Then suddenly, he stopped. He knew the Albanian child lying there. The ghastly palette of blood and ribbons of rubbish on Ramiz Agani's unconscious face traumatized him. Last year his newspaper had covered a story where Ramiz's family had been involved in a siege on a house. The police had made a serious error of judgment by starting the raid too late and Ramiz's mother had been burned alive. As the paramedics closed the ambulance door and drove off, Mark unconsciously raised his hand in a farewell gesture. He watched the lights flashing garishly down the freezing street. Beside him, the stunned coach-driver was giving a statement to the young police officer.

'I just stopped for the kids to get some food. Then this car come out of nowhere and knocked this kid down and the bastard just drove off. The bastard just drove off!' the coach driver kept saying. 'I got a kid the same age.'

'Did you get the car registration number?' the young officer asked him.

'No time, mate. Over too quick. He run from behind the coach, see, to get something from over there.' The coach driver pointed to the late-night burger bar across the road.

Mark glanced at the children who were standing motionless beside the coach. Some of them were clutching pantomime programmes. God, what a way to end a night at the pantomime, Mark thought. Suddenly, he felt very sick. It could be his daughter lying on a stretcher.

It was 5 am when Mark arrived at the hospital. He couldn't go home without knowing if Ramiz was okay. He stopped a nurse in the hospital corridor to ask which room he was in.

'Are you a relative?' she asked suspiciously.

'No, I'm the editor of *The Daily Reporter*. I'm going to run an article on hit-and-run drivers. I just wondered—'

The nurse gave him a disgusted look and walked off. Mark continued down the corridor, immune to such reactions. A trolley appeared from around the corner, wheeled by two nurses; Ramiz, being brought back after surgery. They wheeled him into a room and the door closed. Mark looked in through the window. A large group of Albanian people were gathered inside. They stood in silence as the nurses hooked Ramiz up to a life-support machine. The women started to cry. At that moment, a green-gowned surgeon entered the room to explain what had happened during the operation. Mark watched his arms gesticulating in large expansive gestures, but couldn't work out what he was saying. Suddenly, one of Ramiz's Uncles glanced up and saw Mark. His face darkened with fury as he stormed out of the room to confront him.

'What is the matter with you people? You are like vultures – preying on people's misery! Haven't we had enough pain already without you pestering us again! Leave us alone or I'll call the police!'

Mark desperately wanted him to understand. 'Look – I can't say how sorry I am about your nephew's accident, Mr. Agani. All I want to do is to find the hit-and-run driver. I've got a child myself. I'd been as angry as hell if someone did that to her. Did anyone see the car that hit her?'

Murat Agani had to restrain himself from hitting Mark. 'Didn't you hear a word I said? We don't want you here! Go away!' A number of other members of the family came out and waited until Mark had retreated down the corridor.

By the time Mark had walked home it was nearly 8 o'clock. He was swaying from fatigue as he staggered up the driveway of his large detached house. Unnerving silence greeted him. Angelica was always up early cooking something special. He went into the kitchen and saw the debris from last night's dinner littering all the surfaces. Christ, this wasn't going to be easy. He poured out a large glass of orange juice, drank it and dumped the empty carton in the bin. The remains of Angelica's curry stained the bottom of it. Shit. Where the hell was she? He glanced out of the kitchen window. She was standing motionless in the orchard; a beautiful Madonna wrapped in thought; the morning sunlight burnished her blonde hair with filaments of fire. Mark etched the scene in his mind before taking a deep breath and going out to join her.

'Hallo, Angel,' he said as he wrapped his arms around her.

She gave no hint that she'd heard or felt him; she simply received his arms without response.

'I'm sorry, I...' He stopped, searching for the right words.

'You smell stale.' She drew away from him.

Mark felt his face flushing. 'You know what our Christmas parties are like.'

'I didn't think they went on all night.' She moved towards the house before he could answer.

'I saw the victim of a hit-and-run accident near the office. He was only 12. Only three years older than Emily.'

Angelica immediately stopped walking and stood motionless.

'I recognized him,' Mark continued. 'You remember the kid in the hostage story I covered last year? Ramiz Agani – he's in a coma in hospital.'

Angelica didn't respond. Mark stared at her rigid back, wondering what she was thinking.

At last, she turned to look at him. 'Junior reporters cover hit-and-run accidents, Mark, not editors.'

Angelica walked into the house, leaving him frozen with frost.

CHAPTER 5

9th December 2012

The sizzling atmosphere at Blue Notes had gone. The punters hardly listened to Bianca singing a song that Bessie Smith wrote called *Please Help Me Get Him Off My Mind* because there was no soul in her voice. The band was playing badly too; they couldn't find the right resonance with Bianca's listlessness. Everyone was going through the motions of playing jazz without the emotion. Max, the sax player, looked across the room and glared at Rico. They'd already had words about Bianca and nothing had been sorted. The noise level in the club increased dramatically as Bianca finished the song. There was only a smattering of applause. She walked off the stage as if the audience wasn't there and meandered across the room towards Rico.

'I need a whisky, Rico,' she said, slumping onto the barstool.

'I'm taking you home, Bi – you've had enough. I've just got to organize Pierre and then we'll go.'

Rico had already warned Pierre about giving Bianca whisky, but he knew how difficult it was to refuse her anything. For once, Bianca didn't argue with him; she was too exhausted. Just as Rico was about to leave instructions with Pierre, a short, squat man hurried towards him and held his arm in a vice-like grip and moved him away from her. Rico felt sick.

'Where's the stuff, Rico? Capote's waiting for it.'

Sweat poured down Rico's body as he looked at the man. Everyone knew what Capote did to people who crossed him. 'Mr. Cellini didn't get it shipped to the gallery. Don't know why.'

'Capote knows that. We went looking for it when we heard he'd snuffed it. I just hope that the dropper didn't steal it 'cos if he did, you won't have no kneecaps. Capote thought you ought to know. You got five days to find it. He ain't happy, and remember what Capote's temper is like when he ain't happy? I'd find it if I was you. You want some more advice? – get rid of the singer, she's crap. I'll be back in five days, Rico. Cheerio. Have a nice day.'

Rico wiped the sweat off his face as he watched him disappear out of the door. *Jesus – five days!* In five days he knew they'd do more than kneecap him if he didn't find the crate. Somehow, he had to get into Cellini's apartment after he took Bianca home.

He parked his old Cortina outside a high-rise block of flats and sat there, thinking what to do. It suddenly came to him. Why hadn't he thought of it before? He turned to look at Bianca's sleeping face only inches away from him; her glossy hair shadowing her cheek. He brushed it back with the tips of his fingers; she immediately woke and smiled at him.

'Sorry, Rico.'

'What for?'

'I can't sing anymore.'

Rico's chest tightened. 'What do you mean you can't sing? You're the best jazz singer I've ever heard. Blue Notes would be nothing without you.'

'It's nothing *with* me, Rico. Come on…be honest.' Bianca touched her chest. 'You can't sing jazz without your heart.'

His chest tightened even more and for the hundredth time, he tried to work out why a woman like Bianca put up with a bastard like Cellini.

'Bi, you're a fighter like me. Just take some time off to get over...'

He couldn't say his name aloud. Rico's head fell forward onto the steering wheel as impotence flooded through him; he'd never escape from Cellini's shadow, so what did it matter what happened to him?

Bianca touched his hand in concern. 'What's up?'

It took him a long time to think of something. 'Working too hard, Bi.'

'Come on, I'll make you a coffee.'

Rico looked at her. She obviously couldn't see the irony of the invitation; this was the first time Bianca had ever invited him to her flat and it was only because that bastard Cellini was dead.

An old lift, covered in lurid graffiti, creaked up to Bianca's floor. Rico was shocked by the vandalism in the building. Why did that bastard let her live in a dump like this? But when Bianca opened the door to her flat, everything was transformed: it was colorful, artistic and chaotic. She closed the door and hung a large bunch of keys up on a green-painted key fob on the wall.

'Why've you got so many keys?' Rico asked as he walked into her sitting room.

'Three of them are Paolo's. I kept losing the one he gave me, so I had two more cut – you know what I'm like with keys.'

Rico kept his face impassive as he stared at large posters of Maltese dghajjes covering the walls. 'Those are colorful,' he said.

Bianca smiled and pointed to a vividly painted boat. 'My Uncle Joey owns that one. He used to take me out on trips around the Grand Harbour when I was a kid.' She looked depressed as she disappeared into a small kitchen. 'Have a look around. I've got lots of things from Malta,' she shouted back.

Rico crept into the hall and removed one of Cellini's keys from Bianca's key-fob. It only took him a minute and he was back in the sitting room studying the fine lace and copper jewelry cascading over wicker chairs and tables; the exquisitely colored bottles and glass ornaments dotted around. Rico smiled. He could see Bianca in every item; he could smell her Dior perfume everywhere. Then he turned to the photographs pinned to the far wall and his face hardened. Cellini stared back at him from every one: Bianca and Cellini on numerous holidays in the Mediterranean.

Bianca walked in with two cups of coffee and put them down on one of her glass-topped tables. 'That was taken two years ago when we were in Malta. We stayed at the best hotel in Valetta. Paolo insisted.'

Rico stared at Cellini's smug expression as he stood on the steps of the majestic *Le Meridien Phoenicia.* He desperately wanted to rip it off the wall.

'You should get rid of these photos. Start living again. You need a man to look after you, not cheat on you.'

Bianca spilled some of her coffee over a piece of exquisite Maltese embroidery. 'Rico – you must tell me, I won't get hysterical this time, I promise.'

Rico studied her; she looked exhausted and vulnerable. 'It'll only hurt you.'

She stared at him, waiting.

'Sometimes he brought women to the club when you weren't there.' He didn't want to say this. 'Blondes.'

All the blood seemed to drain out of Bianca's face, but her voice was strong. 'Bollocks - he wouldn't do that! Someone would have told me!'

She had to know the truth about Cellini. 'I told them not to, Bi. I wouldn't make it up – I love you too much. I don't want to hurt you like him. We're the same, you and me – we don't fit in – not like that bastard who had everything.'

Bianca knocked the rest of her coffee over in agitation. 'You know nothing about Paolo! He came from nothing, and look where he got to?'

Rico stared at her for some time. 'Yeah – a coffin.'

CHAPTER 6

10th December 2012

Mud-colored clouds prolapsed from a flinty sky. Lucy studied their shapes from the depths of her wheelchair.

'Mum?' Tom stopped hammering to look at her. 'What you looking at?'

She pointed a finger at the clouds and Tom smiled. 'They look like giant hammocks stretched across the sky.'

Lucy wanted to smile back at him; she loved the way Tom looked at things, but he was already back building his bird table. 'I've only got to put the roof on, Mum, and it's finished.' His face was full of grim determination.

Frost had glazed the garden and icicles encased the withered reeds around the pond. She couldn't tell him she was frozen because he'd wrapped two large blankets around her and she knew he wanted to please her.

Tom's clumsy hammer blows resounded around the neglected garden as Jack stormed out of the house, holding a newspaper.

'Why on earth did you bring your mother out in this cold?' he shouted at his son. 'She could have caught her...'

The unspoken word hung in the air as Tom dropped the hammer and ran into the house, his face contorted.

The silence froze Jack and suddenly all his anger was directed against himself. Lucy tried to move her chair away from him, but he blocked it by kneeling in front of her.

'I'm sorry, Luc, I always seem to say the wrong thing to Tom these days.'

Jack stared at the misshapen bird table; Tom's love for his mother could be seen in every hammer blow. 'Come on...let's get you in out of the cold. I'll go and talk to him, Luc. Make him...you know...' Jack trailed away. *Did* he know? As he pushed Lucy's wheelchair up the gravel path she pointed to the weeds which had choked her unborn flowers.

'You know I'm no good with gardens, Luc – everything dies on me.' Jack bit his lower lip, wishing he could rewind words as easily as a video recorder.

He found Tom sitting on his bed, staring fixedly at a book when he entered his bedroom. His loud agitated breathing filled the room.

'The bird table looks great, Tom...couldn't had made it better myself. Well, actually, I don't think I could make it at all. You know what I'm like with a hammer.' Jack attempted a small laugh.

Tom carried on staring at the book.

'Tom... I just wanted to—'

'I'm busy,' he snapped.

Jack stood there, watching his son's determined efforts to dam up his tears. He'd had all sorts of training in the police-force: how to deal with violent prisoners, murderers, drug-dealers, arsonists, even rapists. He knew how to deal with all these people, but not with his own son. Not when his son knew his mother was dying.

'Listen... we need to talk about... you know—'

'Leave me alone – I'm reading!' Tom yelled; his mouth contorted with pain.

Jack noticed that Tom's Batman comic book was upside down.

And in that instant, he remembered the excitement on his son's face three years before Lucy's illness. They'd had a wonderful holiday staying at a cottage near the stunning Barafundle Bay on the Pembrokeshire coast in Wales; smelling the salt-edged air; watching the greedy sea gobbling up the shore and fighting to stop the ocean demolishing the enormous castle the three of them had built. He walked out of Tom's bedroom thinking if only he could have stopped time that perfect day; the day Tom had sung as they climbed up the cliff; the day his high-pitched voice had pierced his heart; the day they had all laughed.

In his bedroom, Jack concentrated on getting his chauffeur's uniform on, his shoulders tight with tension. *How the hell am I going to cope with him when Lucy's gone?* His hand went into his jacket pocket and touched silk. He pulled the panties out in surprise. He'd forgotten them. How important was a pair of silk panties, hidden behind a radiator anyway? He went into the study, sat at the desk and logged onto the computer. Jack's fingers sped over the key board as he typed *Paolo Cellini* into a search engine. A number of sites appeared. He clicked onto one and details of Cellini's playboy lifestyle popped up: Cellini at the Opera; Cellini at the races; Cellini on a yacht. And every time he was with a blonde. Why only blondes? Jack fingered the silk panties, imagining the sort of woman who wore them – an expensive one. The sudden squeak of Lucy's wheelchair alerted him to her approach and in an instant, the panties were thrown in a desk drawer. He couldn't let Lucy see them even though she'd been a forensic scientist before her illness. Panties like that reeked of sex; a painful reminder of the past. He turned to smile at her.

'What do you think, Luc?' Her grey eyes blinked at the screen as she studied the pictures of Cellini with his variety of blondes. 'This was the man who died a couple of days ago. What do you think when you look at him?'

Lucy stared at Cellini's smiling face and typed one word
facade

'What do you mean?' Jack asked her, frowning. 'I've seen his apartment. Full of the most beautiful paintings and sculptures I've ever seen. Nothing fake there.'

Lucy made a derisive noise as she typed her mantra in the Met
assume nothing believe nothing check everything

The phone suddenly rang. Mrs. Montgomery asking him to pick up *The Times* newspaper on his way to work.

'Have a look at the site and see if you can find out anything useful, will you?'

She stared at him and typed *yre not a dci now*

Jack glanced at his watch. 'Got to go. Irina will look after you.' He kissed her quickly and rushed out.

There was chaos at Mrs. Montgomery's apartment block when Jack arrived. Frank was supervising a group of men who were desperately trying to erect an eighteen-foot Christmas tree in the foyer. Pulleys and ladders and pine needles littered the floor and walls. Workmen were shouting conflicting instructions to each other while Frank added to the chaos by shouting out even more. The tree oscillated between angles of 45° and 180°.

'Left a bit…no, right…no, not that way!' Frank shouted.

Mrs. Montgomery sat in a large armchair, watching the entertainment with great enjoyment. Frank walked over to her.

'You know something, Mrs. Montgomery – my old mum could do a better job of putting up a Christmas tree and she's nearly 90!'

Jack gave Mrs. Montgomery the newspaper, but their attention was suddenly drawn to Frank's portable T.V. set on his desk. Alan Saunders was talking to an interviewer about Paolo Cellini's death.

'Apparently Mr. Cellini had been suffering from a heart condition for many years which nobody we've questioned seemed to know about,' Alan said to the camera.

The interviewer stared at him. 'Well, having a heart condition wasn't too good for the image of one of the most eligible young bachelors in London, I imagine. Could you tell us a little more about how the body was discovered? There's a great deal of public interest in this case.'

Jack could tell that the public interest didn't spread as far as Alan; his eyes were glazed with boredom.

'I don't understand that,' Frank said to Jack. 'You'd never know he had a bad heart. I saw him bounding up those stairs the night he died.'

'So did I,' Mrs. Montgomery added.

Jack's antennae started twitching. 'Was he with someone, Frank?'

Frank shook his head. 'Not that night. Must have been expecting someone, though. He had an excited look in his eye – you know... mind you, he had strings of girls. Well, only to be expected with his looks and money – only blondes, though. Never saw him with a brunette.'

'I wonder why?' Mrs. Montgomery said, looking at Jack.

Frank suddenly noticed the Christmas tree was just about to topple over and shouted at the men who were fighting to get it upright. Wiping his forehead with his sleeve, he muttered, 'Bloody Christmas. I'd ban it.'

Suddenly Mrs. Montgomery looked into her handbag and groaned. 'Oh, no!'

'What's the matter?' Jack asked.

'I left my glasses in Paolo's apartment when I was trying to calm his maid. I can't read without them.' She looked at Jack innocently.

'No problem, Mrs. Montgomery.' Frank got a key from under his desk. 'I can't leave the foyer or I'd get them for you, but we all trust Jack here, don't we? Being an ex-copper an' all.'

Mrs. Montgomery looked only mildly embarrassed when Jack stared at her. She took the key off Frank. 'Thank you, Frank. I don't know how we all managed before you came.'

Frank beamed at her.

As Mrs. Montgomery and Jack headed towards the lift, Jack leaned over to her. 'You should have been a psychologist, Mrs. M.'

Mrs. Montgomery smiled at him. 'I've no idea what you mean, Jack.'

Cellini's lounge looked exactly as it did on the night of his death. Jack wasn't sure why he was surprised. But the smell was different. Camphor-like and musky. His nostrils wrinkled. Mrs. Montgomery stared at the paintings in amazement.

'I've always wanted to see Paolo's apartment, but I was never invited. Not a young beautiful blonde, you see.' She turned back to the paintings. 'They must be worth a fortune.'

Again, Jack was drawn to the triptych of heaven and hell; amazed that anyone could believe in a religion that frightened its believers half to death with the thought of the horrific damnation they would suffer if they sinned.

'I've never been to the scene of a murder before.' Mrs. Montgomery's comment broke into Jack's thoughts.

'It's not a murder scene, Mrs. M. Paolo Cellini had a heart attack.'

'Oh, rubbish – we both know someone bumped him off and I want you to find out who did.'

Mrs. M's walking-stick tapped on the polished floor as she hobbled towards the kitchen. Jack went into Cellini's massive bedroom and wandered around in fascination. An enormous bed was center stage, surrounded by expensive Italian furniture and a collection of Post-Impressionist paintings. Although Jack recognized the thick lively strokes of Cézanne, one of his favourite painters, he didn't recognize the paintings. *The Murder*, was written on one, *The Abduction*, on another. Interesting that out of all of Cézanne's paintings, Paolo Cellini chose two full of turbulence and violence to look at it while he was in bed.

He moved across to an antique wardrobe and opened it. Rack upon rack of designer clothes lined the inside. How could one man possibly wear all those? Jack glanced at the bed and saw four silk cords tied to the bed posts. So Cellini was into S & M. He walked over and slid his fingers slowly along one of the cords, wondering who he tied up with it.

By the side of the immense bed was a faded photograph. A middle-aged Italian-looking woman stared out at the camera. Jack picked it up and studied it. There was no resemblance to Cellini's fair coloring. As Jack stared around the room, trying to find a way to understand the mixed metaphor of Cellini's life, he took a notebook out of his jacket pocket and wrote *the murder* in surprisingly beautiful handwriting; the handwriting of a man who had studied calligraphy. Around the words he drew lines radiating away from them. At the end of the lines he wrote in italics: *guilt, hell-fire, Catholic Church, blondes, Italy, panties, tablets.* He stopped writing and delved into his pocket. Of course, the white tablets he found under the panties. He put one in his mouth and tasted it. Vitamin C. Why were they on the floor? He wrote *vitamin C* on his mind-map before closing his notebook.

'Jack!' He heard Mrs. Montgomery call him from the other room and automatically ran his fingers over the furniture before leaving. He studied them. Nothing.

He wandered back into the lounge, glancing uneasily at all the religious figures who were staring at him from the walls. Suddenly, he trod on something that crackled. He knelt down and saw some bubble wrap. He put it automatically in his pocket as Mrs. Montgomery entered the room.

'Did you find anything interesting?' Mrs. Montgomery asked him.

'Women have a tendency to leave things behind if they want to see someone again – even if it's only a strand of hair. In Paolo

Cellini's bedroom, there's nothing at all.'

'I must see it,' Mrs. Montgomery said, pulling Jack back towards Paolo's bedroom as she spoke. 'That's very odd. Every time I comb my hair, some drops out. Mind you, it might be my age, but everyone leaves some hair somewhere, don't they?' She paused. 'You know what I've found out in my long life of acting, Jack? You can fool too many of the people too much of the time.'

'What do you notice about this room, Mrs. M?'

Mrs. Montgomery's mouth opened in astonishment when she saw the size of Paolo's bed and the silk cords attached to the bed posts. 'Good God – there's enough room for four people in there and those cords...so he was into S & M.'

She saw the surprise on Jack's face.

'Look, I may be old, Jack, but I've been around. My third husband was into S & M... with other women, naturally. Anyway, I thought an ex-DCI like you couldn't be surprised by anything.'

There was a small silence before Jack asked. 'How did you know that?'

'That nice-looking sergeant told me. She said you were the best DCI she'd ever worked for. Mind you, she's very young, isn't she?' Mrs. Montgomery laughed. Jack couldn't help smiling.

'You must smile more, Jack. You look quite handsome. If I weren't—'

'You said you saw Paolo Cellini the night he died,' Jack inter-rupted quickly. 'Did he look ill?'

'No, elated. A large crate had arrived for him. I happened to hear the delivery men ringing his doorbell. Well, I'm not nosy, but I knew he wasn't home, so I went out to tell them. You ought to have seen the look on their faces at the thought of having to carry it down again. Then just as they were about to leave, Paolo bounded up the stairs. He looked just like I imagine Paul did on the road to Damascus. When he saw the crate he said "Una gioia sparge un centinaio di dolori."'

Jack frowned at Mrs. Montgomery. 'I only passed O-level

Italian, Mrs. M.'

'Paolo told me it means "One joy scatters a hundred sorrows." A funny thing to say, wasn't it? I never associated him with sorrow. I told him that he'd obviously brought something exciting back from Italy and he said another strange thing. "I've bought what God would have bought, if he had any money, Mrs. Montgomery." Then he disappeared into his apartment. I wonder what he meant.'

Jack looked thoughtful. 'So do I.'

They stared at each other, both thinking of Cellini's words, then suddenly Jack realized the significance of what Mrs. Montgomery had told him: there was no crate in Cellini's apartment when his body was found. How the hell could a crate disappear? Was there something in it worth killing for? Everything about this case was an enigma and Jack loved solving enigmas, but he wasn't a DCI anymore. He must leave the case to Alan and forget it.

'Paolo Cellini was the best-looking charmer I've ever met and I've met a lot as an actress,' Mrs. M said, breaking into his thoughts. 'Of course, he knew it, but I still liked him and so it seemed did every woman he met.' She suddenly sneezed loudly. 'Oh, no – not another cold. Let's go into my apartment, Jack. There's something I want to ask you.'

Mrs. Montgomery's lounge reminded Jack of a theatrical agency; every available inch of wall space was covered with a lifetime's work in the theater: large colorful posters advertising every Shakespearean production she had acted in. She nestled back into a large olive-colored settee, sipping a Whisky Mac before speaking.

'I was going to Paolo's funeral tomorrow, but I don't think it's a good idea with a cold, do you?' She took another sip of her whisky before adding. 'You see, the thing is…I *fear* death more than death itself. Could I ask you a big favor? Would you go as my representative?'

Jack studied her cream carpet before answering: the last thing he wanted to do was go to a funeral with his family problems, but he couldn't tell Mrs. Montgomery about Lucy.

'Of course I will,' he said.

'That's very kind of you.' Mrs. Montgomery suddenly looked much better. 'Oh, and find out all you can, will you? Do you know something, Jack? I haven't felt this excited since I played Lady Macbeth fifty years ago. That's me, over there.' She pointed to a large poster of an attractive dark-haired girl dressed in a long purple gown holding out blood-covered hands. Jack couldn't help the shock showing on his face. 'Oh yes, I know – hard to imagine that this ravaged old bag ever looked like that, but I did, Jack. Had men falling at my feet all the time. Most of them were drunk, of course.'

And suddenly, Jack was laughing. Great explosive laughter. It went on and on. Mrs. Montgomery struggled to get up from the settee and poured him a large Whisky Mac. The laughter abruptly stopped and Jack covered his eyes with his hands.

'Drink this,' she insisted.

'I've got to drive home. You don't want to employ a chauffeur who drinks and drives.'

She smiled at him. 'You know what Alan Bennet once said, Jack? – "Life is rather like a tin of sardines and we're all looking for the key."'

Jack uncovered his eyes to look at her.

She smiled at him. 'I haven't found mine either. I wonder if Paolo ever did.'

CHAPTER 7

6th December 2012

The Blue Notes nightclub was swarming with men and sexual fantasies. They were waiting for Bianca Vella to arrive; a firecracker of a woman who sang close to the mike and squeezed men's members with her vocal cords.

Federico Batas, the Filipino manager, watched the men from a contemptuous distance. What did they know about the blues? About Bianca? Nothing. He was waiting for her too. He was always waiting for her, but she never came for him.

The door suddenly opened. Paolo Cellini and a brassy blonde with theatrical make-up stood in the doorway, waiting to be noticed. Paolo always wanted to be noticed and since he owned the club, Rico always noticed him. But this was the first time he'd brought a woman to the club when Bianca was singing. Rico felt sweat trickle down the back of his dark jacket as he hurried over to greet him.

'Good evening, Mr. Cellini. Madam.' He turned to the blonde who barely glanced at him. Why would someone as wealthy as Cellini want to bring high-class hookers to the club when he had Bianca? 'I didn't expect to see you tonight.'

Paolo stared at Rico with cold blue eyes. 'Good evening, Federico. I aim to surprise. My table is ready, obviously.'

'Obviously, sir.' Rico guided them over to a table in front of the stage. The men at the club stared at the blonde's rear movements with interest. Not many women came to the club. Rico clicked his fingers at Pierre, the barman. Within seconds a bottle of Krug Grande Cuvee, Vintage 82 appeared in a bucket of crushed ice. Rico was meticulous in his organization of the club: he had to be. Pierre hurried over and showed the bottle to Paolo. He nodded and Pierre uncorked the champagne expertly and poured Cellini a glass. A small smile appeared on his face as he savored the superlative quality of the vintage. Rico watched him lean over to whisper to the woman. She didn't look comfortable. Rico wasn't comfortable either, but he had a good reason: fear. His jacket was soaked with sweat. Bianca would be arriving soon. *What the hell would she do if she saw that tart with Cellini?* Rico left instructions with Pierre and rushed out into the freezing night air. It was going to be another lonely Christmas; he was far from the warmth of the Philippines and Bianca loved a bastard called Paolo Cellini.

There she was; her glossy dark brown hair highlighted in a street light. Rico frowned as she smiled at Paolo's Porsche, parked on double yellow lines outside the club. She never smiled at him like that.

'Bianca!' Rico called from the entrance of the club. Her face turned towards him and his body tightened in anticipation.

'What are you doing out here? It's freezing.' She brushed his cheek with her lips before running towards the stage door. Rico touched his cheek and hurried after her.

'Do you fancy a walk?' he asked in desperation.

Bianca's eyes widened in astonishment. 'Are you nuts? It's cold enough to freeze your balls off.' She swung back the stage door and hurried down the dark corridor to her dressing room. 'He's back then?'

'Who?'

Bianca didn't bother replying; they both knew he hated Paolo.

She switched on the soft lights around her dressing-room mirror and saw the chaos gently reflected; every surface in her dressing-room was cluttered with make-up, bottles of Dior's *Addict*; her favourite perfume, and clothes and mementos from Paolo's travels. But Bianca knew where everything was: her life only held the illusion of chaos. Rico caught her coat as she threw it off and hung it up for her.

'What's the crowd like tonight?' She went behind a lattice screen and started to undress, knowing that Rico could see her in the mirror and not caring.

'The usual,' Rico said, looking at the soft glow of Bianca's skin in the subdued lighting in the room. 'Overweight men waiting for the most gorgeous woman in the world to sing just for them.'

Bianca smiled at him and his chest expanded – if only that smile was really his. 'Don't hurry, Bi, they can wait. I'll see you later – I've got to do something.'

'Tell the boys I'll be ready in ten minutes. I'll start with *Summertime*.'

Rico turned in surprise. 'You can't sing that –it's December.'

'No, it's not.' Bianca's large brown eyes shone as she smiled at him again, but he knew she wasn't seeing him. He turned away quickly and left.

Paolo was washing his hands in the gents, feeling immensely pleased with life. He was going to have a superb night. Not only was he with a woman who knew exactly how he liked sex, but waiting for him in his apartment was one of the most precious icons he had ever bought. Could life get any better? He glanced into the mirror and realized it could. Soon Bianca would come onto the stage and see the blonde sitting with him at his special table. He smiled as he sauntered back into the club. His smile evaporated instantly. The table was empty. He looked around for Rico and saw him strolling towards him.

'Where's the woman I came with?'

'Unfortunately, she had to leave, Mr. Cellini, but she said she might see you later.'

Paolo tried to read the subtext behind Rico's words, but couldn't. 'Are you sure she said *might*?'

Rico looked at him impassively. 'Yes, I'm sure that was the word she used. Excuse me, sir, I have work to do.' Rico strolled over to the bar, looking back at the petulance on Paolo's face as he sat down at his table and poured himself another glass of champagne. It was almost worth working for him just to be able to savor this moment, he thought.

The noise in the room gradually lessened as the drummer performed his usual drum roll. And suddenly, there she was: a voluptuous temptress in a slinky dress that highlighted every curve of her body. The men went wild – shouting and clapping. Every one of them wanted to fuck her and she knew it. She blew them kisses before she looked at Paolo, leaning back on a chair, smiling his usual sardonic smile. Her face glowed.

'Tonight, gentlemen, I'm going to sing you something wonderful for cold winter nights... *Summertime*.'

Max, the saxophonist, played a sensuous intro and the room went silent. Bianca began to sing *Summertime* to Paolo and every men in the room pretended she was singing it just for him.

An hour later, Paolo and Bianca were in her dressing room and he was unzipping her tight dress. He liked the landscape of her body, knowing exactly how it would respond to his every touch. He studied the shadow created by her large breasts in the dimmed lights. His fingers started at her shoulders and moved down to her breasts. She shuddered, but stopped him.

'Don't. I'm on again in ten minutes...when did you get back?'

Paolo poured a glass of champagne before answering. He hated being questioned. 'Two days ago.'

Bianca was stunned. 'Two days ago! – why didn't you call me?'

Paolo sipped his champagne in silence. She never seemed to

learn.

'I've bought something that will interest you,' he said at last, glancing at her face to gauge her reaction.

Bianca reached over to her dress-rail for her late-night sparkler; a tight, sequined black dress which always made the punters salivate. She didn't show any excitement. Not this time.

'Don't put the dress on yet.' Paolo reached into his pocket and placed a priceless emerald necklace around her neck. Bianca studied it the mirror. She was dazzled by its brilliance. 'It's beautiful.'

'It's flawless,' Paolo answered.

She turned and kissed him on his neck, his cheek, his lips. Immediately, Paolo began a new assault on her body; bending to lick her nipples in the circular route she loved. She moaned softly, her hands unconsciously moving in the same route over his soft blond hair. A sudden flat note from the trombonist on stage made her stiffen and she moved away from him. Music should be perfect.

'I told you – I'm on again soon. We've got plenty of time for love-making later,' Bianca murmured.

'There won't be a later – I'm busy, but I can't remember what I'm doing.'

'You *must* remember.'

She knew her remark was a mistake the moment their eyes met in the mirror. His face closed like a clam. He drank his champagne.

Bianca busied herself with putting on her black dress. It was made especially for her and followed every curve. She looked into the mirror and saw Paolo frowning at her.

'What's wrong?'

'Surely you can see.'

Bianca saw a dark-haired, sexy woman wearing a priceless emerald around her neck. She looked stunning.

'Do you know what causes that distinctive rich green?' Paolo asked her.

Bianca shook her head. She was a nightclub singer. What the fuck was she supposed to know about emeralds?

'Cromium impurities.' Paolo stared at the emerald. 'Completely flawless.' He paused for some time. 'Of course, it's all wrong.'

'What is?'

'You and the emerald. Turn around.'

Bianca obeyed him, trying not to shiver as his fingers touched the back of her neck while he undid the heavy clasp. He took the emerald off and placed it carefully in a quilted box. Her breath-control was perfect; she was determined not to show any emotion. Not this time.

'Will I see you tomorrow?' She couldn't help herself.

Paolo frowned as if he was really considering the question. 'I don't know.' He glanced at his watch. 'Maybe. I'll give you a call.' He placed the quilted box carefully in his Armani suit-pocket before saying, 'By the way, I didn't buy the emerald for you. I just wanted you to see how beautiful it was.'

He strolled out of the room as Bianca slumped into a chair.

Chapter 8

6th December 2012

The foyer of Paolo Cellini's apartment block held all the hallmarks of wealth: marble mixed with thick carpets, camouflaged traffic noises, subdued voices and two concierges. But not four weeks before Christmas. Frank, the senior concierge, was sitting at his desk working on his latest tapestry to block out the noise of a group of revelers waiting for the lift. The door of the foyer opened. Paolo sauntered in, looking elated.

'Evening, Frank.'

Frank looked up and smiled at him. 'Evening, Mr. Cellini.' He glanced at his watch in surprise. 'Only 11 o'clock, sir. You're back early tonight.'

Paolo tapped the side of his nose conspiratorially.

Frank laughed, then looked at the revelers who were singing to the lift like a football mob.

'*Come on! Come on! Come on! Come on! Come on! Come on!*'

Frank shook his head at Paolo as they repeated the refrain again. 'Bloody Christmas.'

Paolo smiled and sprinted up the stairs to avoid them. Frank, turning back to his tapestry, didn't see a woman creep past him wearing a black scarf over her hair. She hurried towards the stairs after Paolo.

Paolo placed his hand-made Italian shoes outside the door of his apartment for the junior concierge to polish. Barely glancing at Brueghel's macabre painting *The Triumph of Death* which covered one wall of his wide hall, he padded across to his lounge and opened the door onto a room which gave him immense pleasure each time he walked into it. For a few moments, he studied the musical harmony in Simone Martini's painting of *The Annunciation* before flicking a switch. Bach's *Goldberg's Variations* flooded through the room and into Paolo's soul. The fact that the music was commissioned by Count Kaiserling, the Russian ambassador at the court of Dresden, to act as a soporific when he couldn't sleep appealed to Paolo's sense of the surreal. For how could anyone sleep listening to such music? Bach obviously knew exactly what he wanted from the world. Just like him. A great feeling of joy descended on him. He poured himself a glass of scotch before looking across the room. There she was – waiting for him. He resisted walking over to her; wanting to savor the moment when he saw her face again. But soon, the desire was too strong. Holding his breath in anticipation, he strolled across the room and stared down at her. One of the most sacred icons of the Catholic Church lay below him: the Black Madonna and Christ Child. With great reverence, Paolo lifted the statue out of the crate and placed it on a priceless Italian marble table. Mother and child stared back at him; the Madonna's white eyes contrasting vividly with her black skin and red lips. For a moment, Paolo had to resist the urge to kneel in front of one of the most powerful images of motherhood in the world.

A sudden diminuendo in the music allowed him to hear the front door click open. He placed the statue carefully back in the crate and covered it with bubble wrap before she came into the room.

'Why did you leave the club?' he asked her.

'It don't matter why I left, love. I'm here now.'

She took the black scarf off her brassy blonde hair and opened her black coat. Underneath she was wearing a bright red basque and fishnet stockings. Paolo smiled. 'Perfect,' he said. 'Come into the bedroom.'

CHAPTER 9

10th December 2012

It was late afternoon when Lavinia tottered into Mark's office wearing a tiny skirt and holding some statistics he'd asked for. She leaned over his desk, revealing a small section of bright blue panties with red hearts on them. Mark glanced away and concentrated on his phone call, studiously avoiding the eye contact she desperately wanted.

'Tell Brian his football report needs to be edited by 200 words. Yeah...on my desk by 9 a.m. tomorrow morning. Bye.'

Lavinia loomed over him like a praying mantis while he concentrated on the statistics she'd been working on for days, aware of her eyes boring into his body. 'This is good research. Give it to Hal and tell him to come in, will you?'

Hal had been hovering outside since Lavinia went in. She glowered at Mark before tottering to the door and shouting into Hal's face, 'The editor wants you!' She thrust her work into his startled face. He grabbed the papers off her and squeezed past her into Mark's office. She followed him in.

'I want a two-page spread on Ramiz Agani's coma in tomorrow's paper. The kid could die at any moment,' Mark said.

Hal stared at him in surprise. 'But we won't have any space to cover Paolo Cellini's death if we do that, and he's hot at the moment. He sells papers.'

Mark's face flushed with anger. 'This is not just about selling papers, Hal! This is about finding a heartless bastard who drove off without finding out if he killed a kid or not. I'm not interested in giving a rich, spoilt mongrel like Cellini any more notoriety. He had enough when he was alive.'

Hal looked at Mark in astonishment. He obviously hated the guy. 'But a two-page spread on a hit-and-run, Mark, when a colorful character like Cellini dies!'

'You haven't got kids, have you? What do you know?'

Hal was shocked. He and his wife had been trying for kids for fifteen years.

'Could I interview the family?' Lavinia drawled.

Mark glanced at her miniscule skirt. 'Don't be ridiculous – in those clothes? They're Muslims. I want you to dig up some statistics on drunk-driving figures for the last five years, convictions, jail terms etc.'

'More statistics! God – how boring!' She flounced out, slamming the door behind her. Hal stared after her in amazement. Mark wouldn't have taken that from him.

'I want to run the story as a human tragedy, Hal.' Mark began an irritating repetitive drum roll with his fingers on his desk. 'Ten months after mother dies in domestic siege, son in coma after being knocked down by a drunk hit-and-run driver etc. etc. You know the style.' The tapping continued as Mark sat deep in thought. Hal wanted to pound his large hands down onto Mark's fingers to stop the tapping.

Instead he said: 'Yeah, yeah – short and punchy. Link it in with the mother's death. Remember my headline after the siege? POLICE BLUNDER. MOTHER TORCHED AS SON WATCHES.'

Mark stared at him. 'Yes. It sold a lot of newspapers. But I don't want to run this story just to sell more newspapers, Hal. I want an in-depth report on how our society allows such men to get away with murder.' Mark suddenly jumped up. 'I want to catch this bastard with the biggest campaign this paper's ever had on drunk drivers. I want this guy found. Start by interviewing that coach driver. He might remember something about the night Ramiz was hit. The hit-and-run driver is going down for manslaughter if the kid dies. I'll make sure of that.'

Hal stared at Mark in amazement. Why was he putting *him* on such a story?

'Well, what were you waiting for?' Mark snapped.

Lavinia didn't look up when Hal plodded past her; she just carried on stabbing her computer keys with long crimson nails. Peter stared at her in fascination.

'Mark's not giving her what she wants, then?' Peter asked when Hal reached his desk.

'No, he's cracking up. Wants me to follow that hit-and-run story. Me – his top reporter!'

'*One* of them, Hal!'

'My God, when you think what's happening in the world and he's worried about one kid. I've got to interview a coach driver and it's nearly 5.30...' Hal's voice trailed off as he puffed towards the lift. 'See you tomorrow, Pete.'

Mark could smell the candles the moment he opened his front door. His heart beat faster in anticipation.

'Angelica?' he shouted up the stairs, knowing where she'd be. In the bathroom, polishing herself. Mulled wine, peaches and cinnamon. The smell of the candles was overwhelming as he climbed the stairs, but the assault on his senses was always worth it because of what always followed.

He undressed and lay naked in bed waiting for her to finish her rituals. Everything had to be perfect when they made love.

'Angel – come on – I'm going flaccid in here.'

Angelica smiled as she polished the last section of her body – her legs. She never hurried the process. Her fingers moved in wide circles until every section of them was silk-textured. Then she brushed her hair until it formed a golden halo around her head. Now – she was ready.

She strolled into the bedroom and Mark turned to her, stunned by a slim, translucent body and a face that could eclipse Helen of Troy's.

'What have I done to deserve you?' he said.

'Nothing, but I'm still all yours, Marky.'

She started to massage his chest with perfumed oil, moving over his pectorals like a professional. Angelica had learned to play his body with all the expertise of a professional musician.

An hour later, she was lying on her stomach, biting her knuckles and Mark was above her. His thrusting hurt her deep inside her body, but she endured it because she loved him and he loved this position. At last, he climaxed and rolled over onto his back, exhausted, but elated. She lay completely still, waiting for the pain to lessen.

'Nothing happened at the Christmas party,' Mark said at last. 'Why the hell would I want another woman? Have you any idea what you do to me?'

Angelica didn't answer. She simply turned and licked his stomach sensuously.

'Jesus – she's trying to kill me,' Mark said, smiling as he closed his eyes.

Angelica got up quietly and walked out of the bedroom and down the stairs. Although the house was cold she didn't stop to put on her dressing-gown over her silk nightdress. Some things couldn't wait. She knelt in front of her Black Madonna and made the sign of the cross. Mark called from a distance, but she didn't respond. She had to pray.

'Hail Mary, full of grace, the Lord is with thee, blessed art thou among women, and blessed is the fruit of thy womb, Jesus. Holy Mary, Mother of God, pray for us sinners, now and at the hour of our death.'

Mark opened his eyes, wondering why Angelica was taking so long. Obviously in the bathroom, staring at the calendar. He stumbled out of bed and went into the bathroom, exhausted from love-making. It was empty. He walked out and sighed. Not again.

As he moved silently downstairs, he could hear her reciting her Hail Marys through the open door of her prayer room. There she was – kneeling in front of her statue, surrounded by candles and twisting a rosary between her fingers in supplication.

'Angel, what are you doing in here? It's freezing.'

She stopped her mantra. 'You know what I'm doing. Praying.'

Mark kept his voice light. 'For what?'

'Forgiveness.'

'But you hadn't done anything that needs forgiveness, sweetheart.'

'We're all sinners.'

Mark tried to control his anger. 'Christ – that's the nuns talking, not you. Come on, come back to bed.'

She shook her head. Mark wanted to pick her up and carry upstairs into the warmth of their bed, but he knew he couldn't, even though her body was trembling with cold.

'I can't... not yet.'

He stared at her for a few moments; so beautiful and so remote; already back with her Madonna. She started reciting her Hail Marys again. Mark wanted to scream that it was all an empty ritual, but he stopped himself. He reached over and touched her belly.

'Listen, sweetheart. It *will* happen – I know it will, but God won't have anything to do with it. *We* will.'

CHAPTER 10

10th December 2012

Rico had been trying for two nights to get into Cellini's apartment. He hadn't anticipated a concierge in the foyer monitoring everyone who went there. He paced up and down in the wind, opposite Palladian Place, the mansion block where Cellini used to live, praying that a crowd of people would go in. Some bastard must be having a Christmas party there, surely! He kept glancing around, terrified that they were watching him. Tonight, he had to get in. There were only a few days left before they kneecapped him or worse. He shuddered at the thought of the pain. Suddenly he heard shouts of laughter. A throng of drunken young people surged up the street; their public-school voices carrying on the wind. They were obviously intent on having a great night out. Rico couldn't remember the last time he'd had one. He smiled as they opened the glass doors of Cellini's block and ran across to join them.

The old concierge Rico had seen for hours through the glass doors looked up from his tapestry and tutted as he saw the noisy group. 'Just a minute...who are you going to see?' he asked suspiciously.

A young man with expensive vowels drawled drunkenly. 'Our old school-friend, Giles Fortesque! We're all going to his party!'

The group roared with laughter as the concierge muttered, '4th Floor. Apartment 42.'

The group surged past him and the concierge concentrated on his tapestry. Rico couldn't understand it. Why would a guy want to work on embroidery? As the partygoers waited at the lift, Rico merged with them, then separated himself by walking up the stairs as they were talking. It was five flights up and Rico could hardly breathe by the time he'd reached the top. He had no time to work out in gyms with two jobs.

He crept out of the lift and did a quick reconnaissance of the long corridor, trying to slow his rapid heart rate. He relaxed when he saw that it was empty. He hurried over to Cellini's apartment and inserted the key he had stolen from Bianca's flat, silently thanking him for putting the number 57 on the key fob in case Bianca forgot it. The key turned effortlessly. Rico pushed the door open, closed it silently and switched the lights on. He walked through the wide hall with its numerous paintings and went into the lounge and stopped short. He was stunned by the abundance of religious artifacts there. He'd expected a palatial apartment but thought Cellini only bought religious artifacts to sell, not to live with: Paolo Cellini and religion were a total contradiction. Everything in the room reeked of wealth. All the bitterness he felt against a man who had everything rose up his throat. Rico slumped into a large leather settee, swallowing back the bile. Spread out before him was a treasure trove of casual wealth; the remnants of a life that was spent in decadence at the expense of other people. He wondered why his life was spent living on the edge of society; an outsider who was always looking in on other men's lives; men who had money; men who could decide what they wanted to do with their lives; men who didn't have other people telling them how to live; men who could have any women they wanted and didn't care how many they hurt. Why couldn't he have had Cellini's life? The irony of this question missed Rico completely. He was alive: Cellini was dead.

As Rico looked around the room, the first flickering of fear twisted his gut. No crate in here. It must be in one of the other rooms. He rushed into all of them; the flickering of fear had now become a burning ulcer eating through his stomach wall – there was no crate anywhere. He slumped down on Cellini's bed and cradled his head in his hands. He only had three days left before they came for him. Suddenly the click of the front door opening. Rico jumped up and rushed over to Cellini's enormous wardrobe and hid behind a rail of expensive suits. His body was suddenly awash with sweat. He tried to slow the loud agitated beating of his heart in case the new intruder could hear it. There was no sound in the apartment at all. Rico leaned against one of Cellini's Armani suits to control his shaking. They couldn't have followed him here, could they? Then he smelt her perfume and knew who it was. Opening the door a fraction, he saw Bianca pick up a photograph of an older woman which stood beside Cellini's bed.

'Hello, Bi.'

Bianca screamed and dropped the photograph. 'Jesus Christ – what the fuck are you doing here? How'd you get in?'

'Sorry I frightened you, but I'm in deep shit. I owe a lot of money to a lot of people and Cellini owes me.'

'Paolo owes nothing to anyone and he never keeps money here.'

'I'm not looking for money. I'm looking for a Black Madonna.'

Bianca looked at him, suspiciously. 'Why?

'I was supposed to sell it for him.'

Bianca walked out of the room in disgust. 'You're such a bull-shitter, Rico. I should call the police.'

Rico followed her into the lounge. 'They'd ask what you are doing here too.'

Bianca sat down on one of Paolo's white leather settees. 'I'd show them all the keys he gave me. So that's why you wanted to have a coffee at my place. You just wanted to steal his key! You're just like all the rest, Rico. A user.'

Rico felt as if she'd punched him in the stomach. 'I've never used you. Not like Cellini.' He collapsed into the settee beside her and laid his head back. 'If I don't find out where the statue is, I'm a dead man, Bi. You'll find me in an alleyway with my throat cut.'

'What the fuck are you talking about? Paolo always sends his valuable art to his gallery, not here and why should he use you? What do you know about art?'

'Nothing, but I know about...other things.'

'What things?'

'I don't want to involve you. It's too dangerous. They can't get any information out of you if you don't know anything.'

'Jesus, Rico – you sound like a cheap Hollywood cop. You've been watching the wrong T.V. shows.'

'This is serious, Bi. You know how I feel about you. I don't want you to get hurt.'

'Why the fuck should I get hurt?' Suddenly Bianca felt her hands go clammy as she saw the sweat on Rico's white face. He was telling her the truth. 'What was Paolo messed up with?'

'How can I get out of here without being seen?' Rico whispered.

'Jesus – it's bad, isn't it?'

He wiped his hand across his sweating face and nodded.

Chapter 11

11th December 2012

Jack could see the tall spire of St Sebastian's Church from some distance away as he crawled through the traffic. Of course, he hadn't told Mrs. Montgomery about his past. 'Nothing to do with anyone else,' he said aloud. 'It should be buried.' The blue Volvo in front of him braked again, but for once, Jack was happy to stop-start along the street. The thought of a funeral was too raw. *Damn*. The traffic suddenly surged forward. He had no choice but to follow it.

St Sebastian's had been a resplendent Gothic church for centuries after it had been built in 1262, but now time and neglect had etched itself deeply into its architecture. The large traceried windows had been boarded up against vandals and an air of desolation hung around its crumbling stones. Jack stopped the Daimler near the church, wondering why anyone would want to be buried in such a desolate corner. Paolo had left explicit instructions about his funeral in one of his bureaux. Jamila had rung Jack to ask him what he thought about a thirty-year-old man who arranged his funeral details meticulously: the church must be St. Stephens; the music must be Monteverdi's *Vespers*; donations must be sent to the Children's Hospital in Great Ormond Street, instead of flowers; Father O'Brian must officiate if he was still alive. Jack found it incredible that a young man had thought about his funeral at all, let alone left such detailed instructions. He suddenly realized he hadn't even made a will. I should, he thought as he climbed out of the Daimler, sucking in great gulps of cold air to wake himself up. Not much sleep again; Lucy had been restless last night and his bottle of sleeping tablets was empty.

Jack dawdled towards the knot of people in the distance, then stopped short. Why on earth would a millionaire want to be buried in a run-down East End church? Everything about this man was enigma, Jack thought, remembering the small white towel covering Cellini's body and the lack of one female hair in his apartment. He suddenly felt guilty; not only had he missed the service, he was even late for the burial.

A large number of people fringed Cellini's open grave; nearly all were women. Jack walked self-consciously towards the scene. He hated funerals, but he hated Catholic priests even more. He stood at the back of the crowd, trying to block out the priest's depressing dust-to-dust oratory as he studied the women fringing the grave. A Mediterranean-looking woman was standing very near the grave, crying noisily as the priest spoke. Jack glanced around at the other people and suddenly noticed a woman half-hidden by an elder tree in the distance. She was elegantly dressed in an olive-green cashmere coat and a black scarf over ash-blonde hair and she was fingering a rosary. As she tilted her head the sun formed a halo around her head. Jack immediately got out his mobile and took her photo before realizing that it was totally inappropriate at a funeral. She glanced into the distance, looking startled as she saw someone she knew and suddenly she ran off. Jack was riveted by the interplay. The man followed her and Jack started to follow them, but his attention was abruptly brought back to the funeral by a woman shouting as earth thudded onto Cellini's coffin.

'You bastard! You fucking bastard! How could you leave me?'

The priest looked at the woman in horror as she started to sway. Everyone stood transfixed. Jack rushed forward to catch her before she fell on top of the coffin.

'She's upset!' Jack shouted into the priest's horrified face.

The café had the same air of decay and neglect as the church. Jack sipped his coffee and winced – it tasted of iron filings.

He and Bianca sat opposite each other in a half-empty greasy spoon café.

'You feeling better?'

She nodded. 'Yeah... thanks. It was... just a bit too much. I've been to too many funerals recently. Both my parents died last year.'

'I'm sorry. You obviously knew Paolo Cellini well,' Jack said, appalled by his hypocrisy.

'We've been going out for over two years... I thought...' Bianca suddenly looked at Jack suspiciously. 'Who are you?'

'Just a chauffeur who works for one of Mr. Cellini's neighbors. She liked him.'

'Everyone liked Paolo... well... women did.'

'It's odd that he wanted to be buried in the East End with all his wealth, isn't it?' Jack said lightly, avoiding any eye contact by staring out of the dirty windows.

'No, it's not. People didn't know Paolo. He was brought up here. Didn't want people to know. Bad for his image, I suppose, but he told me everything.'

'Did he?' Jack said, disingenuously.

'What's that mean?' Bianca sounded hostile.

'Well, it's difficult to know everything about another person, isn't it? Even if you love them. My wife once told me a French saying: *"In love there is always one who kisses and one who offers the cheek."'*

'So which one are you?' she snapped.

Jack lifted his cracked cup and sipped his coffee. 'This is the worst coffee I've ever tasted in my life.' He smiled at her and her face relaxed a little.

'Yeah, it is…sorry, I'm a bit…' She trailed off into silence.

Jack watched her repeatedly dipping a plastic spoon into the sugar and twisting it until the table was carpeted with granules.

'The French may be right,' she suddenly said, 'but we had something special Paolo and me. We were both immigrants – didn't fit in. He told me things about his past.'

'Like what?'

Her eyes narrowed as she studied Jack. 'You ask a lot of questions.'

'My grandmother told me when I was eight that if I didn't ask questions, I'd never get answers.'

Bianca smiled at him. 'My granny said that too and she was Maltese…you haven't got Maltese ancestors, have you?'

'No, only Welsh,' Jack answered, waiting for her to continue. The smell of over-cooked, greasy food in the café was beginning to make him feel nauseous.

Bianca was silent for so long that Jack thought of paying for the iron filings and leaving. Just as he was about to get up, she said, 'Paolo hated his father.'

Jack kept his voice casual. 'Why?'

'Don't know… something to do with his mother.' She looked around the café and saw a number of old men staring at her as if trying to remember the feel of firm flesh. 'Paolo didn't talk about his past much. He always liked to live in the present.'

Her face crumpled as she realized what she'd said. 'Jesus – what am I doing in a dump like this? Let's get out.'

Jack took out his wallet and a photo of Lucy and Tom fell out. Bianca picked it up and stared at it.

'This your family?'

Jack nodded.

'Your son looks like you. The same watchful eyes.'

Jack looked at the photo; he'd never seen the similarity before.

'That's about all we've got in common at the moment.'

Jack threw some coins on the table before they walked out.

They ambled around Haggerston Park, so deep in their own personal pain that neither noticed their elongated shadows creeping ahead of them towards the shelter of the trees.

The pond, a mirror of light in the summer, now lay like a sheet of unpolished lead in front of them. As they walked towards it, Bianca turned to him and said, 'Paolo was going to manage my career. He'd booked venues all over the world for me to sing in.'

They walked on in silence, then Bianca touched his arm. 'You know what you said in the café about never knowing everything about someone you love. I never knew Paolo had a heart condition. How could I? He made love as if it was last time he'd ever do it.' Her mouth suddenly twisted. 'Oh my God – that's what he thought, isn't it?'

'He must have loved you a great deal if he didn't tell you.'

Bianca hung onto these words, desperate to believe him. 'You think so?'

Two mallard ducks sliced the water with their reflections. Looking at the picture they painted almost made Jack forget the deadly conundrum he was trying to solve.

'Everything's in pairs, isn't it?' Bianca said, staring at the ducks as she unconsciously opened and closed the clasp on her leather handbag.

'Something's worrying you,' Jack said at last.

'Oh, Christ – I've got to show someone – it's driving me nuts.' She took out a small black book and gave it to him. 'I found this diary in Paolo's jacket in the club. Open it.'

The word **STELLA** jumped out from numerous pages as Jack flicked through it. He caught his breath, but Bianca didn't notice his agitation.

'The night he died he left the club early. He was seeing this

Stella... I know that now. I couldn't believe it. I'm not mentioned once.'

Jack's face was full of compassion as he looked at her. 'I'm sure there's a good reason for that.'

'I can't think of one,' Bianca answered. 'Could you find her for me?'

'I'm only a chauffeur.' Jack said quietly.

Bianca stared at him, her face mottled by the cold air. 'No, you're not.'

Jack was impressed by her intuition, but frightened by what she was asking him to do. Go to places he didn't want to go. Feel emotions he didn't want to feel. Bianca's grief was too raw for him. She stood shivering, waiting for his answer. Then suddenly she was pleading. 'Please... I need someone to help me. I feel as if I'm drowning.'

How could he refuse? 'Okay. I'll ring someone,' he said.

Bianca touched his arm, tears in her eyes. 'Thank you.' She suddenly shivered. 'Jesus – I hate English winters. Have you ever been to Malta?'

'No.'

'I remember having dinner with my parents and my gran in the garden. We had plum and orange and lemon trees there. My gran used to make me fresh drinks all summer. Funny how it always seems like summer when you're a small kid, doesn't it?'

Jack blinked rapidly against the sudden stinging in his eyes, wishing he could reverse time and be sitting on the golden sands of his favourite beach in Wales, building dream castles and the future was a million years away.

'Come to hear me sing sometime,' Bianca said, giving him a small card. 'The Blue Notes nightclub. Everyone knows it. Bye.'

Jack watched Bianca walk away from him with the same sensuality Marilyn Monroe showed in *Some Like It Hot* and wondered how often Paolo Cellini had enjoyed her body.

The Red Lion pub was almost empty when Jack arrived. He saw Jamila sitting near the 16th-century inglenook fireplace in front of a blazing log fire; its ruddy light coloring her face. She glanced at the grandfather clock in the corner as he hurried up to her.

'Sorry, I'm late. The traffic's terrible. Shall I get you something to drink?'

'Just a coffee. I've got to go back to work soon. What's so urgent?'

He looked out of the pub window. The somber aspect of the sky heralded rain. So what *was* so urgent? When he'd rung Jamila he'd made it sound as if the diary was of national importance.

'Have a look at that.' He gave her Cellini's diary while he ordered a coffee and a lemonade at the bar. He couldn't face any more coffee.

He watched Jamila flicking idly through the diary while he paid for the drinks.

'So the guy was interested in a woman called Stella,' she said when he sat down with his lemonade.

Jack took the diary off her. 'You haven't looked at it properly.'

'The coroner's verdict stated Paolo Cellini died from a heart attack, Jack. Alan's closed the case. All that diary shows was that the dead guy was seeing a woman called Stella – so he was sleeping around – that's not a crime – lots of men do it – remember my ex-husband?'

Jack's face tightened.

'Don't look at me like that,' Jamila said. 'What do you want me to do?

''Find out who this Stella is – that's all I'm asking.'

'And then what?'

Jack flicked through the diary to illustrate what she obviously couldn't or won't see.

'Stella...Stella...Stella... Her name's almost on every page. No mention of the girlfriend he'd been seeing for over two years. Don't you think that's odd?'

'Odd, maybe, but it doesn't warrant opening the case again, you know that.'

A young girl brought Jamila's coffee and put it down onto the rough wooden table. Jack and Jamila drank in silence.

'I thought you always wanted to know the truth. What's happened to you since you've been working with Alan?'

Jamila flushed. 'Nothing. It's just that I've got more important things to do than chase ghosts.'

'What the hell's that supposed to mean?' The ice in Jack's voice made Jamila flinch.

'I don't mean...' She stopped and sipped her coffee. 'Look, we're covering a big case at the moment, Jack, that's all. I'm very busy.'

Jack got up to go, wondering why he felt so deflated. 'Okay – sorry to have wasted your time, DS Soyinka.'

Jamila put her hand on his arm. 'Hey, you're not talking to a stranger.'

Jack sat down again and stared at the familiar brasses and bric-a-brac littering the walls and felt his chest tightening. He shouldn't have suggested they meet here. Jamila followed his gaze, knowing what he was thinking. She wanted him to look at her. He didn't.

'I remember the first time you bought me a drink here,' she said. 'I was a newbie and you were the big boss and suddenly, in walked this important forensic scientist who just happened to be—'

Jack's expression froze Jamila mid-sentence. She took a deep breath, knowing she was going to regret what she'd about to say.

'Okay – give me the diary. I'll see what I can do.'

Jack smiled at her, 'Thanks, Jamila.' His face was transformed into the boss who'd welcomed her into the Met and taught her so much. She leaned over to touch his hand.

'Why did you resign, Jack?'

Jack's smile faded as he got up from his seat. 'I've got to go back to work. If you find out something about this Stella woman will you ring me?'

Jamila nodded.

Jack strolled out of the pub, his hands deep in his pockets and his mind on Stella.

The police stores were in the basement of the building. Jamila hated going down there; it was damp and dingy, but she'd promised Jack. Perhaps searching for this woman was helping him in some way.

P.C. Green looked up in surprise as she walked into the outer office.

'Morning, ma'am. Don't see you down here often.'

'Morning, Barry. Just got to check something. What happened to all the items that were taken from that wealthy art dealer's apartment – Paolo Cellini?'

P.C. Green frowned. 'They're still here, ma'am.'

Jamila was surprised. 'Nobody came to collect anything?'

'We couldn't trace any family. Bit odd, him being so wealthy. You'd had thought they'd be crawling out of the woodwork.'

The phone rang as Jamila walked past him into the store room.

'You get the phone. Won't be a moment.'

Barry didn't know what to do. This was against regulations, but the sergeant was his superior. He answered the phone.

Jamila walked into the dingy room, her nose wrinkling against the marshy smell. She was glad P.C. Green was in charge of stores. Everything would be labeled exactly as it should be. She searched down the rows of Cs until she came to Cellini. On opening the polythene bags, she discovered very little for a man who was supposedly surrounded by women and wealth: cufflinks, numerous receipts, monogrammed handkerchiefs with expensively embroidered initials: A.C. As she moved the handkerchiefs, she discovered more handkerchiefs at the bottom of the pile with the initials A.M. on them. Who was A.M.? She wondered. She heard P.C. Green in the outer office trying to get off the phone. If Alan found out she was snooping about in Stores she'd be in trouble. So what was she doing down here? She searched through the pile of clothing. Nothing about Stella at all. Then just as the P.C. called out to her she saw a DVD. On the side of it, written in large black letters was the word **Stella.** Her heart thumped as she pocketed the DVD quickly as the P.C. walked in.

'Found what you wanted, ma'am?' he asked.

Jamila smiled as she walked past him. 'Unfortunately not, but I've never seen the stores organized so well before. Well done, Barry.'

Barry beamed as Jamila ran up the stairs.

Fortunately, the office was empty when she entered. She rang Jack to arrange to meet him later and give him the DVD. It was burning a hole in her pocket. It was going to be a quick call, but when Jack asked her how her daughter was, she couldn't resist telling him.

'She's rehearsing for the school pantomime at the moment which means I've somehow got to find the time—'

'Is that a personal call, DS Soyinka?'

Jamila jumped. Alan was glaring at her from across the room. She carried on talking into the phone, raising her hand in a gesture designed to stop interruption.

'Well, I hope you and your wife could still find the time to take your son to the pantomime, sir, I'm sure it will take his mind off the damage to your shop,' she smiled at Alan as she spoke. 'Perhaps you could come into reception this afternoon and I'll get a police officer to take a statement from you.' She listened for a few moments, then said, 'Yes, we certainly *do* want to catch the vandals who damaged your shop. We're heavy on crime and heavy on the people who commit crime in the Met. Goodbye, sir.'

She put the phone down and sighed, 'I thought talking about

the pantomime might help him, sir. His son has been very upset by the vandalism in his father's shop.'

'Get one of the DCs to answer such calls in future,' Alan said. 'I need you to concentrate on the drug smuggling. It's vital we catch these people before the problem escalates.'

'I'm following up a number of leads at the moment, sir. Actually, I'm meeting someone who knows a great deal about drugs later today.'

Alan's face relaxed. 'Good – I'll see you at the briefing tomorrow.'

Jamila hugged herself as Alan walked out; he *actually* looked pleased for once.

A coppery light slanted across the crystallized pavements as Jack crossed Trafalgar Square, walking towards the Sainsbury Wing. He stared at it, still uncertain whether the American architect's idea of harmonizing the neo-classical façade of the National Gallery with the asymmetrical façade of the Wing worked. As he passed the recessed glass wall he was even more uncertain, but how else was he going to see Leonardo da Vinci if he didn't venture through the Sainsbury's portals? He ran up the stairs towards his favourite room.

Jack Bradley was renowned for three things while he worked in the Met: his love of paintings, his 'nose' for uncovering the truth and his lack of interest in clothes. When Jamila entered the room, she saw him staring at a large drawing and smiled; he was wearing a shapeless overcoat that could never have been fashionable in any era. He didn't notice Jamila at all; he was too intent on studying *The Virgin and Child with St. Anne and John the Baptist*.

'Hallo, Jack,' she said when she reached him.

Jack didn't take his eyes off the cartoon. 'You see how delicate da Vinci's treatment of the Madonna's hair was. And look at the way he created one form gliding imperceptibly into another – it's breathtaking, isn't it?'

'Oh, hallo, Jamila and how are you?' Jamila said, expecting him to smile at her, but Jack still didn't take his eyes off the Madonna. She stared in fascination at the transformation in Jack's face. How could one painting affect such a change? Four shadowy figures was all she saw, but that's obviously not what Jack was seeing. She didn't know anything about art; there hadn't been time for it when she was growing up. Her parents were too busy working day and night to feed them all, but there'd always been music and laughter inside her home, even if there wasn't much outside. Her experience of art, when growing up on a tough council estate in Hounslow, was the graffiti covering the walls of the buildings as she walked to school. She'd fought her way out of the tough estate through sheer determination and hard work. But she'd been lucky too; Jack had been the one to recommend her for promotion. She'd never have got it working for a self-promoter like Alan Saunders.

'How did he make them look so...' Jamila searched around the room for a word that Jack would like. It came at last from all the long hours of studying, '...ethereal?'

Jack smiled at the painting. 'He used different glazes to create subtle transitions between tones and shapes.' He pointed to the light in the Madonna's face. 'Imagine being able to create that. I always wanted to be a painter, but I didn't have the talent.'

'So you just had to make do with being a brilliant DCI. Must have been tough.' Jamila's laughter made Jack smile at her.

'Thanks for coming. Did you find out anything about Stella?'

Jamila looked around the room before reaching into her pocket and handing the DVD she'd found to Jack. 'Alan would demote me if he found out what I've done. I don't know what's on it, but I must have it back by Monday morning. You know what happens if something goes missing.'

'Thanks.' Jack put the DVD in his pocket. 'Let me show you *The Virgin on the Rocks.*'

'If I didn't know better, Jack, I'd think you were religious.'

'You don't have to be religious to enjoy religious paintings. Come and look at this face.' He guided Jamila out of the room into another and stood her in front of a painting. 'Now look at that Madonna's face – can you see the wisdom there – not only interior, but artistic?'

'Are you giving me a lecture?'

'Sorry.' He smiled at her. 'I become a zealot when I talk about painting.'

'I wish you hadn't left the Met, Jack.'

Jack's smile faded; he moved off to another room, but Jamila wouldn't be deflected. She hurried after him.

'It's not the same without you. The chief's on his way to a second ulcer and Alan Saunders – well, you'll know what he's doing.'

'Climbing faster than ivy, I imagine.'

Jamila nodded and Jack suddenly stopped walking.

'I don't want to go back into the force, Jamila – not after…' he suddenly studied *The Last Supper* in the distance. 'That part of my life's over.'

'Then why have you got that DVD in your pocket, Jack?'

He looked at her, but didn't know the answer.

Chapter 12

12th December 2012

The candles flickered in rhythm with Jack's movements up and down Lucy's legs as his fingers dimpled her wasted muscles. Over the last year, he'd become an expert masseur through weeks of watching the physiotherapist massage Lucy. This was their last retreat; both he and Lucy knew it wasn't going to improve her circulation or her muscle tone, but they both pretended it was. Meditative music played in the background. Jack hated it, but Lucy looked relaxed as she lay on their bed, her laptop near her fingers. He smiled at her, trying to suppress the immense anger he felt when he looked at her wasted body.

She stared at him questioningly.

'I couldn't get through to him, Luc. Do you think we should get a child psychologist to talk to him?'

He moved to massage her skeletal arms; wondering how they all managed to endure such pain.

'Perhaps I should talk to Tom's headmaster and ask his advice. What do you think?' Jack's tone was light.

Lucy blinked once: her code for yes.

'All right. I'll ring him later...all done, Luc. I think I'm getting better at massage, don't you?'

Jack wiped the oil off his hands on a towel as Lucy started to type laboriously.

'You're supposed to relax after my superb massages, remember?'

Lucy carried on typing. Suddenly, she stopped to look at him. Jack's hands tightened. She waited while he wasted time, folding the towel into a neat rectangle.

'*Ac!*' His name sounded harsh on Lucy's distorted lips.

He walked towards her lap-top. Below him were words he didn't want to see.

dont let me die slowly

They had talked incessantly about euthanasia before Lucy had become paralyzed. She had argued passionately that it was immoral to leave someone with no hope of recovery to die without dignity. She had asked him to promise to take her to the Dignitas Clinic in Switzerland where they would give her voluntary euthanasia. And, of course, Jack had; the thought of his intelligent, vibrant wife being reduced to a vegetable filled him with horror. But they had forgotten Tom in their intellectual arguments. When he had discovered his mother's research about euthanasia on the Internet, he'd become hysterical. She couldn't go abroad to be killed, he'd screamed at his father. Of course not, Jack had agreed; he'd told Tom that she would stay with them. Now he had to face his wife every day, knowing he'd betrayed her.

Lucy and Jack stared at each other for a long time until he lay down beside her and rocked her in his arms, repeating over and over again. 'I can't do it, Luc, I can't do it.'

He waited until she fell into a deep sleep before going into the study to watch the DVD. He hoped it would take his mind off Lucy's words. It certainly did. A caption popped up which read: *The Nurse and The Patient.* Paolo Cellini was standing in his large bedroom wearing a small black leather thong, staring at someone in the distance. A brassy blonde, wearing a skimpy nurse's uniform walked into view, her back to the camera. Stella, Jack thought. She told Cellini that she had to take all her clothes off before she could treat him as it was so hot. Jack smiled at the banal absurdity of the scene. The camera panned slowly down her long legs as she bent over to discard black fishnet stockings, then it moved up her body as she unbuttoned her uniform to reveal a peep-hole red bra covering small firm breasts. The camera panned in onto rosy nipples, then moved down to a tiny leather thong, designed to reveal, not conceal. Cellini walked towards her and removed the bra and thong with one movement. Jack wondered how he did it; he could never do that with Lucy's underwear. Stella told him she had to remove his thong before she could take his pulse. Jack laughed as she ripped it off with the same fluid movement as Cellini's. They were both experts at removing clothes. She took Cellini's pulse and gasped with simulated shock as he rubbed his penis against her. Jack found his own stiffening, in spite of the clichéd scene being acted out in front of him. The camera played over the woman's red, painted nipples as Cellini bent his head and folded his lips around each one in turn to suck them. Both nipples stood out like luscious cherries. Stella threw back her blonde hair in a semblance of ecstasy. Jack snorted. Lucy had never been that easily pleased. Cellini picked her up as if she was a bird and threw her onto a bed. She held up her hands to cover her body in mock terror but he grabbed each hand in turn and tied her to the headboard with the silk cords. Then he rubbed his penis slowly up and down her body before thrusting it deep into her vagina; she pretended to struggle and Jack found himself becoming more and more aroused thinking how exciting Lucy and his love-making had always been. His face contorted; their old intimacy was now a mere memory. Suddenly, the woman's face appeared on the screen and Jack was shocked; her make-up was so elaborate that he was reminded of the performers in Kathakali, a dance drama he and Lucy at seen on their honeymoon in India. The performers wore intricate make-up to define the character they were playing: Stella was playing a whore. His arousal instantly disappeared as he registered the charade being acted out in front of him. He switched the DVD off and sat back in his chair, wondering why Cellini would go with prostitutes when he was surrounded by beautiful women. Just as he was going to put the DVD back into its box, he saw that Cellini had written a link to a chat-line on it. Jack typed in the link on his computer and entered a chat-line. The first name that he saw was Stella. What would he achieve by contacting her? He glanced around the room, musing on the incredible challenges life threw at people. Three years ago he was a respected DCI at Met with a witty, brilliant wife and loving son, now he was contemplating meeting a prostitute and he didn't know if it was simply for research. He typed quickly before he changed his mind and sent her a clichéd message that he hoped would get her attention.

Just seen your DVD. Hot! Tell me what lights your fire and I'll find the right matches. I'm free tomorrow night. Are you? Blade Runner.

Jack winced at his banality and went to the bathroom to have a pee. Why should she be online tonight? Most probably she'd be out with a client. But when he went back into the study, a message popped up.

Meet me in the foyer of Downs Hotel in Victoria at 10 p.m. tomorrow night and bring the matches. How will I know you? S

Jack's heart thumped hard as he typed, *I've got light brown hair, 5 foot 10 and I'll be carrying a copy of Private Eye. I'll bring lots of matches! B.R.*

Chapter 13

12th December 2012

Mark was alone in the office; he knew he should go home to Angelica, but he had to find some clue to the identity of the missing hit-and-run driver before he could. He must have missed something in the interviews Hal had done with all the numerous people who'd been on the street the night Ramiz Agani had been hit. Hal was a meticulous reporter; Mark knew he should have let him cover the problems in Israel, not a hit-and-run accident. The owner of the newspaper, Sir Thomas Keaton, wasn't happy with the amount of newspaper coverage Mark had given to the story; he wanted a result, or he wanted a big new story. Mark knew that his judgment was being eroded by an emotional connection with a young Albanian boy who was still lying in a coma; almost dead to the world. It had become his raison d'être, but if it didn't become the country's Cause Célèbre soon, he might find himself out of a job; there were far too many hungry wolves out there desperate to sit in his chair. If he couldn't find something he'd missed tonight, he'd have to move on to another big story and he didn't want to.

He got up and stretched, staring out at the expanse of London lights spread out below him. He and Angelica should be out there enjoying themselves; not separated by his quests for the so-called truth. Was anything he ever reported going to make a difference to the world at all? He shook such negative thoughts out of his mind and sat down at his desk and went through every interview again. The only thing that everyone agreed on was that the driver was speeding; the car was a blur and it sped off into the night. He waded through the others and noticed one eye-witness stated that he thought the car was black but he couldn't be sure. That was the only clue he'd found after two hours of reading. It was hopeless. Mark closed the file and swore. Two hours wasted when he could have been with Angelica. He was just about to get up and leave when he noticed the other tabloids and broadsheets that Lavinia had put on his desk; it was always good to look at the competition. The main story was the sudden death of Paolo Cellini: good-looking playboy and astute art dealer; each paper was full of his lavish lifestyle; his fabulous art collection and his donations to charity; it was nauseating how even the most respected broadsheets were pandering to the masses' obscene voyeurism. He closed the last paper in disgust and was suddenly faced with a grainy picture of Cellini's funeral; in the corner of the photo was the profile of a woman wearing scarf; it was unmistakable – Angelica! What the hell was she doing at that bastard's funeral?

Mark felt his heart thumping. He shot out of his chair just as the cleaner came in and looked at him, startled. He almost ran towards the exit.

An hour later, he was sitting with Angelica eating a prawn stir-fry that she had rustled up within minutes of him arriving home. She was a miracle, Mark thought, looking at her in the candle-light. There were none of the tantrums he'd endured from his first wife every time he was late home; Angelica knew how important his job was to him. It was always a joy to return to her. All the anger he'd felt on seeing her photo in the paper vanished the moment he saw her, but he had to know why she had gone to Cellini's funeral.

'So what were you working on tonight?' she asked, before Mark could speak, expertly lifting a small portion of stir-fry with her chop-sticks.

'Still on the hit-and-run. Been wading through eye-witness interviews,' Mark said as he tasted the stir-fry. 'Um, this is very good.'

Angelica shot him a look. 'Find anything?'

'No.' He put down his fork and stopped eating. 'Well, yes, but...' He was suddenly reluctant to ask her.

Angelica looked at him nervously. 'What?'

'You didn't tell me you went to Paolo Cellini's funeral. Why'd you go? You only met the guy once.' Mark knew he sounded petty, but he couldn't stop himself.

Angelica concentrated on her food as Mark stared at her. 'Margaret Montgomery asked me to. The elderly lady you met at the charity dinner last year.'

'Why didn't she go herself?'

'She was too ill, apparently. It was difficult to say no on the phone. I didn't stay long. Just long enough to tell her I'd been. I didn't think you'd be interested. I'm sorry if you thought I should have told you.'

She smiled at him in the candlelight and Mark was appalled with himself; she never became angry about his petty jealousies. 'I'm sorry. There's no reason why you should. It's not important.'

Later, as he lay in bed alone, completely relaxed after they'd made love, he didn't even resent the fact that she was downstairs again chanting mantras to her Black Madonna; he just thanked fate or whatever force had brought Angelica into his life before falling into a deep, dreamless sleep.

CHAPTER 14

13th December 2012

The Downs Hotel had all the anonymity of a large chain which was obviously why she had picked it. Jack sat inconspicuously in a secluded corner of the foyer, pretending to read a newspaper, while glancing at the door occasionally as people walked in. His hands were sweating and soon his fingers were black from newspaper print.

There was no sign of Stella. Jack wondered what he was going to do when she eventually arrived. He'd never been unfaithful to Lucy and now, suddenly, it seemed a monumentally bad time to be disloyal. He got up to leave only to fall back as the revolving door swung round and a seductress walked in. Every man in the foyer was instantly riveted by the sight of two long slim legs, underneath a skimpy tight skirt and a sparkling crop top. All the moisture in Jack's mouth evaporated. His newspaper dropped to the ground, forgotten. Stella searched the room for him, but he was glued to his leather chair. Her face became hostile: no one stood her up. She flounced towards the door, her long blonde hair swinging around her shoulders. A hand suddenly appeared on her arm; a man, wearing a Gieves & Hawkes suit, stopped her. Jack couldn't hear what he said, but Stella's face relaxed and her arm moved through his. They walked along the patterned carpet towards the stairs as Jack slumped down into his chair trying to be inconspicuous; there was something unsettling about her and he didn't like being unsettled. What was he missing? He took out his notebook and wrote: *Stella & Paolo = Sex and?* He still couldn't work out why Cellini went with prostitutes. Then he had a mental image of Cellini's diary. He wasn't obsessed with prostitutes, only one: Stella. So what was there about her that made a wealthy man like Cellini obsessed with her? It didn't make any sense. He almost smiled at the irony of the thought: most things people did made no sense. Why the hell was he sitting in an anonymous hotel waiting for a prostitute he was never going to have sex with?

Half-an-hour later, Jack was still in the hotel, half-asleep, waiting for her to appear. Suddenly, she ran down the stairs, glanced at her watch, and disappeared into the night. Hastily throwing some coins on the table, Jack hurried after her.

She ran towards a four-wheel drive in the distance, threw the door open and climbed in. Within seconds she was speeding down the road. Jack raced towards his car, thankful he'd started jogging again. Why the hell was she in such a hurry? He sped after her in his Ford, watching her tail-lights disappear around the corner. Shit – he was going to lose her. But for once, red lights were on his side. As he turned the corner, he saw a Mini in front of her stopping. Stella slammed on her brakes. Jack was now only two cars behind. The lights changed and she immediately leaned on her horn, trying to levitate the snail in front of her. Jack watched her overtake the Mini and race towards Quarry Road, wondering why she was taking such a lonely route. She was a good driver, but Jack was an expert, having taken every Advanced Driving Test known to the police-force. Within minutes, he was behind her. Suddenly, she slammed on her brakes and screeched to a halt. De-clutching rapidly, Jack managed to swerve around her and stopped his car a long way in front of hers and switched off his lights. When he looked back, she was being sick at the side of the road. She leaned against a nearby tree to recover. Jack wondered what the client had done to make her feel sick. Stella wiped her mouth clean before getting back into the car. Jack ducked down in the Ford in case she saw him as she drove past. Revving up fast, he raced after her.

Half a mile ahead of them was a development site; large diggers were excavating a quarry so that it could be flooded to form a picturesque lake. Jack subconsciously registered the numerous WORK IN PROGRESS signs which littered the road as he sped after Stella, thinking no one would be working at night. Suddenly, a large lorry pulled out in front of her – she skidded around it and it careered across the road towards Jack. So this is *it*, he thought. No amount of advanced driving was able to help him anticipate the trajectory of the lorry's wheels as the driver fought to control it. Snapshots of Lucy and Tom flashed repeatedly across his retina. He wasn't supposed to go first. Then suddenly, the lorry shot past him, knocking off his wing mirror and he was laughing into the darkness. A great feeling of power surged through his body as he accelerated up the road. A year of memories had flashed through his mind, but unbelievably, he could see the tail-lights of Stella's car in the distance.

Jack tailed her from a discreet distance for miles; from country lanes through to the residential streets of Hampstead, past shops, boutiques, cafes and brassieres. He suddenly realized where she was driving to – Hampstead Heath. She was going to tout her trade on the Heath in the dark! Jack was disturbed, not knowing why he was concerned about the welfare of a prostitute. He turned a corner and stared at the empty road in front of him in confusion. She'd disappeared. He speeded up, thinking she must have seen him and tried to lose him. Half an hour later, he stopped the car in an empty street and rested his head against the steering wheel, wondering what the hell he was doing with his life. He wasn't a DCI any more, he was a chauffeur. He had a very sick wife and a traumatized son and he was driving around London in the middle of the night, tailing a prostitute and he didn't know why. His mobile suddenly rang. He glanced at it in surprise. Who on earth could be ringing him in the middle of the night? He opened it and saw his father-in-law's name.

'Hello, Colin. You're up late.'

'Lucy nearly died this evening. She's in hospital. We've been trying to ring you for hours.'

Jack was instantly riven with guilt. While he was wasting his time tailing a prostitute, his wife was fighting for her life.

'Which hospital?'

CHAPTER 15

13th December 2012

Tom sat in a corridor with his grandparents. It was 1.30 a.m. and he lay asleep against Mary, his equally exhausted grandmother. Colin, Lucy's father, was pacing up and down as he waited for Jack to arrive.

Jack ran down the corridor towards them, blinking in the over-bright neon lights.

Colin's face was stony as he stared at Jack. 'Where on earth have you been?'

Tom woke up at the sound of his grandfather's voice and glared at his father.

Jack couldn't breathe. What could he say? I was following a case? What chauffeur follows a case? He couldn't explain to himself or to Tom what he'd been doing. 'How's Lucy now?' he asked Colin, knowing exactly what his in-laws thought of him after he'd resigned from the Met.

Suddenly, Mary woke up and glared at Jack too. 'She's stable now, but my God, Jack, what would have happened if Tom hadn't been there?'

Tom shouted: 'Mum would have died and it would have been *your* fault! You're never there when we need you!'

Jack had never felt so low in his life. Is that what his son really thought of him?

'Her carer left her for a minute to go to a local shop, thinking that Tom or you would be back at any minute so there was nothing to worry about,' Colin said. 'Lucy needed oxygen but couldn't reach it. Tom rushed in, saw what the problem was and gave her to it. Tom's quick thinking saved our daughter's life.'

Jack wanted to weep, remembering how many times Lucy had told him she wanted a quick death, but how could he tell them that? 'Well done, Tom. It must have been frightening for you.'

Tom stared at the floor. At last he said: 'Can I go to bed now?'

'We're taking Tom home with us.' Colin glanced briefly at Jack before adding, 'Until Lucy comes out of hospital ... because of your irregular hours.'

'Chauffeurs obviously work stranger hours than the police do,' Mary added coldly.

Jack winced at the ice in her words; he didn't know how he could cope with all the guilt that had been thrust into his life since Lucy's illness and the siege. He could hardly remember a time when he could sleep without sleeping tablets.

'We're going home now you've come,' Colin whispered in an exhausted voice. 'Lucy's in the room over there.' He gestured towards a small door near where they were sitting. 'A pity you didn't come before, Jack.'

Jack couldn't speak. He went to hug his son, but Tom moved away from him before he could touch him. 'I'll ring you tomorrow. See how you are.' Jack's words echoed down the long, lonely corridor as he watched them all trudging away from him.

A nurse left Jack alone with Lucy after showing him the alarm button if he needed it. He sat beside her, listening to her heavy breathing as she lay on the hard hospital bed, hooked up to oxygen, looking incredibly fragile.

'Hello, Luc. Been causing mayhem while I'm out again, have you?' Jack stroked her hand. 'I know you want to go but Tom and

I need you. Selfish, I know, but there it is.' And suddenly Jack was crying; crying for all the moments in his life when he hadn't told her that he loved her; crying for the mother in the siege who'd died because of him; crying for the pain that Lucy's illness was creating for their son. 'I don't know what to do, Luc. I don't know what to do.' Lucy had always been his rock when problems happened in the Met; she was always calm and looked at things from an analytic perceptive. 'How can I cope with Tom?'

There was no response and Jack didn't expect any. He leaned his head against Lucy's arm and fell asleep. An hour later he woke up with a very stiff neck and looked at his wife; she looked exactly the same as before. 'Sorry, Luc – I dropped off. Do you want me to do anything for you?' Jack didn't expect a reply, so he didn't notice Lucy's fingers moving as he did exercises to alleviate the pain in his neck. He was stunned by the sudden sound of her trying to say his name: '*Ac!*'

'What, Luc?' She desperately tried to move a finger towards her computer beside the bed and Jack rushed over to move it to her. He watched her laboriously type:

tell tom let me go!

Chapter 16

6th July 2011

Angelica struggled against the crying of a baby being baptized in a church; she fought to wake up, hating being in that dream again. Slowly, the crying baby and the church retreated and her parents appeared in a garden shouting *Where is he? Where is he?* Angelica wanted to tell them but her mouth wouldn't open. They screamed out their pain as she watched but there was nothing she could do. She could smell the oranges and lemons in the garden, but she was transfixed by her parents' pain.

Gradually the garden retreated and their bedroom formed around her. She glanced over at Mark's sleeping form and touched the nape of his neck. So solid a presence. Perhaps everything would be all right with him. The sun was fringing the curtains. She got out of bed and moved behind them so the light wouldn't disturb him. In front of her was a sky which looked as if Turner had painted it with vibrant planes of light; it glowed onto her translucent face. In the garden, a blackbird, perched on a sycamore tree, scoured the garden for food. His crocus-colored bill opened for a rapid trill and Angelica smiled. Suddenly, he flew down to the ground and the scene froze into her memory as he hopped along their garden path. How beautiful the world could be, she thought. She turned back to Mark's sleeping body.

Time to pray before he woke up.

She tiptoed out of the room and down the stairs to her prayer-room, where the Madonna was waiting for her.

All too soon she heard Mark calling her. She ignored him as she recited her Hail Marys. She couldn't be disturbed while she prayed. There was so much she must atone for.

Mark got out of bed and went into their en-suite for his usual power-shower, knowing exactly what Angelica was doing. Why was she always praying? What the hell did she have to seek forgiveness for? He couldn't understand her or her religion.

Half-an-hour later, they were having breakfast together. While Angelica had a shower, Mark had filtered their favourite Ethiopian coffee and heated up the croissants they had every morning. They sat opposite each other, smiling at the glow in the other's face from the summer sun slanting through their windows, then Angelica tensed before saying lightly:

'I thought I'd go to Sotheby's this evening. There's a special auction on.' She studied her croissant as she spoke, not wanting to see Mark's customary reaction. 'What do you think?'

There was silence in the room for a long time. She played with her croissant, littering the floor with flakes. She desperately needed Mark's approval, just as she had always needed her parents', but had got something else entirely.

'You know what I think about you buying more religious icons you don't need, but you still do it, so it doesn't matter what I think, does it?' Mark spoke as if the words were painful. 'Your parents left you a wealthy woman.'

Angelica looked at him with such vulnerability that Mark wished he hadn't spoken; her wealth had always been a barrier between them.

'But I want your approval more than anything else in the world, Marky.'

She came and kissed him. Immediately, Mark wanted to carry

her upstairs and make love to her, but a small question stopped him: *do you need my approval more than you need religious icons?* He glanced at the clock, not knowing if he was ready to hear the answer. Shit. He was late.

'Got to go. Kiss me again tonight and I'll show you how much I approve of you.'

She smiled at him with such love that he felt he was the luckiest man alive.

At 6.30 p.m., a taxi drove Angelica down New Bond Street and glided to a stop outside Sotheby's. She got out and paid the driver; ignoring his appreciative look. As she walked up to the glass doors, she saw that the foyer was packed with people. She knew why, of course. It was evening of the Old Master and British Painting Sale and every art collector in London was there. Angelica prayed that that they weren't all there to bid for the item she'd come for: Correggio's painting of *Madonna and Child With The Infant Saint John The Baptist.* No one could want it as much as her. She didn't want it as an investment, but because of the way the Madonna's right hand touched her baby's arm and cheek – there was so much love in the gesture. It mattered far more to her that mere money. She strolled through the foyer; smiling briefly at the few people she knew and went into the auction room as if she had all the time in the world and her stomach wasn't cramped with tension. The need to have the painting was so great she felt faint. She sat down quickly and took some deep breaths; determined to outbid everyone else in the room. She hadn't been to the auction house for six months, but she knew most of her potential rivals by sight, although most of the men wanted more than just the sight of her. Sitting two rows in front of her was the odious Mr. Halabi who was always trying to get her to have dinner with him. Someone at the last auction had told her that he was one of the wealthiest men in the world; oil poured out of him. If he was interested in the painting, she had no chance of buying it at all.

She opened her bag and fingered her rosary, praying that he wouldn't want it. Sitting three rows in front of him were the Norwegian collectors Mr. and Mrs. Engelson; they waved when they saw her. Angelica smiled at them, delighted by the fact that they were both atheists and never bid for religious paintings. Who else might be bidding for it? She scanned the room until she caught sight of Mr. Abramova; the Russian billionaire; why were all the wealthiest people here today? she wanted to scream.

The moment Paolo entered the auction room, he saw her and stopped walking; she reminded him of the Madonna in his favourite painting by Salvi. He had to meet her, whatever it cost him. There was a seat empty near her; he hurried to get it before anyone else did. As he moved across the row behind her, people greeted him and he smiled back at them; it was always good to have allies; you never knew when you might need them. He sat down and studied her, wondering why she sat so tensely on her chair. As she turned her face to look around, her blonde hair shone as if it had been polished and he saw her perfect Madonna profile; Paolo was mesmerized by her; he wanted to touch her hair, her face, but refrained. He looked around, wondering who could get him an introduction, but before he could speculate any further, the auctioneer started the bidding and all Paolo's attention was focused on him; he was waiting for Lot 57; the painting he was determined to have.

The auctioneer glanced over at the painting before turning to the buyers. 'Now we come to the highlight of this evening's sale – Correggio's *Madonna and Child With The Infant Saint John The Baptist*. A rare opportunity to purchase one of the most magnificent examples of sixteenth-century Northern Italian painting in the world. And I have one million pounds starting on the phone.'

One million! Angelica felt the room swaying around her. They were starting the bidding almost at the limit of her buying power. She tried to steady herself to see who was going to bid before she raised her paddle. Soon the bidding was feverish as people constantly raised their paddles from all quarters of the room as they competed with the phone bids. The auctioneer's voice was almost as feverish as the bidding.

'I have 1,10 in the room, 1,500 up front, 1,800 on the phone, 2 million from an absentee bidder, 220 up front, 230 in the room, 240 against the phone. Any advance on 240?' The auctioneer's eyes swept the room; the tension was unbearable. Angelica felt her heart race as the auctioneer looked at her; she raised her paddle. '250 in the room.' There was a lull in the bidding and Angelica felt sick; how on earth could she afford 2.5 million pounds! Suddenly the auctioneer's feverish voice was off again. '260 on the phone, 270 from an absentee bidder.' He paused, then looked around the room. 'I'm bid 270, ladies and gentlemen...any advance on 2.7 million pounds?' Another slight lull as people held their breath. Would anyone bid against Mr. Abramova? The auctioneer raised his gavel 'Going at 270.' Suddenly, someone raised his paddle. The auctioneer said: 'Nearly too late, sir... 280 in the room, 290 on the phone, 3 million pounds up front. Any advance on 3 million pounds? 320 at the back, 340 on the phone...any advance on 340? 350 in the room...350 in the room. Any advance on 350?'The auctioneer's eyes swept the room before he brought his gavel down hard onto the black lectern. Sold for 3.5 million pounds to Mr. Paolo Cellini.'

Paolo felt as if he'd climbed Everest. He'd outbid them all, even if it *had* cost him far more than he had anticipated. A number of people around him congratulated him and he smiled at them. He knew he'd made an excellent investment, but it wasn't just an investment; he loved Correggio's brushstrokes; the way he created a lasting luminescence in the Madonna's porcelain face; in the sheen of her red dress and blue cloak. The painting was a masterpiece. He glanced at the blonde woman in front of him and was surprised to see her body shaking. He wanted to tell her that she could see the painting any time she wanted, but before he had a chance, she shot up out of her seat, raked him with her eyes and stormed out. Paolo's elation punctured in a second; he realized, too late, that he wanted her more than he wanted the painting.

He looked around. A few people who'd been bidding against him frowned at him, but he ignored them. Someone must know who she was. He suddenly spotted Jonathan Cranbrook on the other side of the room, getting up to leave. Paolo found him incredibly boring, but he seemed to know the names of everyone at the auctions. He'd have to speak with him; it was going to be excruciating as the man could bore for Britain, but if he wanted the information he'd have to act fast. He hurried after him having already arranged that Sotheby's debit his account when he won the bid as he knew he would.

He caught up with him in the foyer. 'Jonathan! You're leaving early.'

He turned around to smile at Paolo. 'Things to do, places to go. Congratulations, Mr. determined-to-get-the-painting-whatever-the cost, Cellini!'

He guffawed with laughter as if he'd actually made a joke and Paolo forced himself to join in as if Jonathan Cranbrook was the wittiest man alive.

'Out of my league this evening, Paolo. Been betting too much, I'm afraid.' The man continued boring Paolo about his gambling debts while Paolo arranged his incredibly interested face until he wanted to scream *Chiudi la bocca!* into the man's face. After a few minutes, he couldn't stand it anymore. He glanced at his watch and feigned surprise.

'I'm really late for an appointment, Jonathan. Oh, before I forget, could you tell me the name of the blonde woman sitting in front of me?'

Jonathan Cranbrook roared with laughter as if he'd been

expecting this question all the time. 'I should be charging for this. You can't imagine how many fellows want to meet her. Last week it was—'

'Yes, I can, actually. Really in a hurry here, Jonathan. ' Paolo desperately tried to remain calm.

'She's called "The Ice Queen". None of the fellows have even got her to smile at them, let alone talk to them.' He guffawed with laughter again. Paolo walked off before he punched the man in his stomach.

CHAPTER 17

14th December 2012

Jack crawled through the heavy London traffic as he chauffeured Mrs. M back from her doctor.

'I hate doctors, Jack. They keep telling me that all my aches and pains are caused by old age.'

He smiled at her briefly in the rear mirror, before turning the corner into Holland Park Avenue. In front of him was another long queue created by temporary traffic lights because of more road works. He swore under his breath.

'I remember driving with one of my boyfriends through London fifty years ago,' Mrs. M said. 'It was my first night at the Old Vic. I was terrified because Lawrence Oliver was in the cast and I was a nobody. Reggie, my boyfriend, picked me up from my flat and drove like a lunatic along this very road at 70 mph. It seemed very daring then, but we hardly saw any other cars. He dropped me right outside the theater and parked his car. No yellow lines and no traffic jams. Imagine that.'

'I can't, Mrs. M – look at that bloody idiot racing through the lights on red!' Jack shouted. 'Sorry.'

'Don't apologize. As the traffic increases, the standard of driving decreases. Imagine what it will be like in thirty years.'

'Good grief, Tom will nearly be my age,' Jack said without

thinking and immediately regretted it.

'Who's Tom?'

'My son,' he said quietly.

'You didn't tell me you had a son. How old is he?'

'Twelve.' Jack didn't want to speak about Tom; he'd told his grandparents he didn't want to see his father so Jack had to ring them to find out when they were visiting Lucy so that their visits didn't clash. Talking about him brought the pain out into the open and he preferred it closed in a tight box.

'What's he like?' Mrs. M's question jolted Jack back into the present.

He didn't want to answer; didn't know how to answer. What *was* his son like? He didn't know anymore. He'd become a distant stranger and Jack didn't know how to reach out to bring him closer.

'I'd rather not talk about him, Mrs. M.' The traffic was at a stand-still so Jack delved into his pocket and gave her a photo of Tom before turning back to the road. Anything to stop her asking any more questions. 'This was taken last year when Tom was eleven.'

She took it off him. 'Sorry. You must think I'm a nosy old bat.' She watched his hands tighten on the steering wheel as the lights changed; he carried on driving in silence.

Ten minutes later, Jack turned into Royal Crescent, maneuvered the Daimler into a space outside her apartment and stopped.

'Your son reminds me of you, Jack,' Mrs. M said handing the photo back to him.

'Someone else said that recently.'

'Then it must be true.' She leaned over to touch his shoulder. 'Whenever anyone in my family had problems my grandmother used to come out with a terrible old cliché but it seemed to work: "A trouble shared is a trouble halved". Now help me out of the car and I'll see if my ridiculous arthritic hips move.'

Jack got out of the Daimler and opened the back door to help her. She got out with great difficulty. 'The doctors are right. Don't get old, Jack,' she said, smiling at him.

He gave her a glimpse of a smile before saying, 'I'll try not to, Mrs. M.'

It took Jack a long time to help Mrs. M into the lift and to her apartment. She sat down with relief and said. 'Will you join me for some tea? I have a jewel of a helper who organizes everything for me.'

'Chauffeurs don't normally drink tea with their employers, Mrs. M.'

'But I'm not a normal employer, Jack, and you're certainly not a normal chauffeur. Now go into the kitchen and get the tea. Alice will have left everything ready.'

Ten minutes later, they were sitting opposite each other. Mrs. M watched Jack's eyes roaming around the apartment, trying to avoid eye contact. 'Do you know what my biggest regret is, Jack? Not having children – three husbands but no children. You're a lucky man.'

Jack made a dismissive sound at the absurdity of her statement. 'I don't think so.'

'Is it that bad?' She watched Jack's eyes crease with pain. She knew he didn't want to talk and she also knew that if she was going to help him he must – and she was determined to help him.

'What happened between you and your son?' She finished her tea and waited as Jack stared at one of her posters.

'He blames me for his mother's illness.'

Why – did you make her ill?'

'No, of course not!' Jack snapped. 'Sorry... it's just that every-thing... everything I do or say to my son is wrong at the moment. I wasn't there when my wife needed oxygen last week and he saved her life. Only...' Jack didn't know if he could say the words out loud.

'Only?' Mrs. M said gently.

'Only she doesn't want to be saved. She wants to die.'

'Why?' Mrs. M hid her shock at his words. Life was still precious to her, in spite of her words to Jack about old age.

Jack put his cup down on a small table, leant back against the armchair and closed his eyes, feeling utterly exhausted. 'She has Muscular Dystrophy; she's dying a slow, undignified death and she hates it.'

Mrs. M wasn't prepared for such an awful revelation. She had imagined his wife as a vigorous woman. 'Oh, Jack. I'm so sorry. I don't know what to say. I make flippant remarks while you have all these terrible problems.'

Jack opened his eyes and looked at her for the first time since they'd sat down together. 'I'd prefer the flippant remarks to the reality of trying to reach out to a son who doesn't want to speak to me.'

'He obviously loves his mother a great deal.'

'We both do. Before she became ill she was the fulcrum that steadied our lives. We both want her to live and she wants to die.'

Mrs. M looked at him a long time before saying: 'Perhaps the greatest love of all is helping those we love to die, Jack.'

The words pole-axed Jack: did she know what she was saying? 'It's illegal, Mrs. M.'

'So are many things in our society, but people still do them. You just have to find the courage.'

Chapter 18

14th December 2012

After leaving Lucy lying asleep in hospital, Jack realized that he couldn't go home to a desolate, empty house that was no longer a home. He wandered around the streets of London, wondering whether going to a strip show in Soho would only make him feel even more depressed. The wind sliced through his jacket as he turned a corner and a flurry of rubbish danced along the street into his face. Where the hell could he go on a freezing night and feel human? He shoved his hands into his pockets and touched a small card. Sheltering in front of a shop-window laden with tatty Christmas decorations, he took it out of his pocket. *The Blue Notes Nightclub*. He hailed a passing taxi.

It was the first time Jack had been to a club since he had married Lucy. He'd forgotten how desperate lonely men could look. Did he look as desperate as they did? The club wasn't very full. Piped music was playing; there was no sign of a band or Bianca. Perhaps it was her night off. The place wasn't lifting his depression at all. He was just about to leave when he saw the man with the granite face he'd seen at Cellini's funeral but there was no hint of a cold smile on his face now. He kept glancing nervously at the door as if he was expecting someone at any moment as he gave the barman some instructions. Jack's depression disappeared in a second. So this man knew Cellini well enough to go to his funeral and something linked to his death was making him very nervous. Jack swayed a little as he sauntered over to him, giving an impression of relaxed drunkenness.

'Hello!' Jack took Rico's hand and shook it vigorously which threw him. 'We've met before.'

The man looked worse at close quarters; his suit seemed to be hanging off him. 'I don't think so, sir.' He disengaged his hand from Jack's. 'I remember all our customers.'

'No, we haven't met here. At Paolo Cellini's funeral.' Jack's lie slipped out as easily as saliva.' He watched Rico's eyes tighten, then immediately relax. He smiled at Jack and he knew he was dealing with an expert in deception.

'I don't remember...will you excuse me?' Rico started to move off.

'Well, I'm sure you'll remember how distraught Bianca was. I had to stop her collapsing onto Cellini's grave with grief.'

Jack knew he'd got him the moment his face darkened.

'He was a bastard! She didn't know him like I did!'

'And how did you know him?'

Rico studied him before saying smoothly. 'He owned this club.'

Jack was surprised. Bianca hadn't mentioned that when they'd met. He was just about to ask him where she was when she suddenly appeared at his side wearing a slinky black dress.

'Can you come into my dressing room?' She walked off before Jack could answer.

The man's look should have frozen Jack to stone, but he simply smiled at him and followed Bianca's oscillating rear.

'Do you often bring men in here?' Jack said as she closed the door to her dressing room. He wanted to know what her relationship with the granite-faced man was.

She turned to look at him coldly as she started unzipping her dress.

'Only Paolo.'

'What about the man at the bar?'

'Rico manages the joint. That's all. Sit down and pour yourself a whisky. It's forty years old.' Bianca nodded towards two glasses and a half-empty bottle of a whisky, then moved behind a screen to change, knowing that Jack could see her reflection in the mirror. Normally she liked men watching her, but tonight she was only interested in discovering who Stella was.

'Have you found her?' she asked as she removed her dress; she didn't have time for small talk.

'Not yet, but I will. Give me time.'

Jack glanced at her reflection in the mirror, trying not to be disturbed by her voluptuous flesh, then looked around for somewhere to sit. How much underwear did one woman need? he thought, as he moved numerous bras and panties from a chair and sat down. But none of her underwear had the same silkiness as the panties he'd found in Paolo's bathroom. He picked up the bottle of Black Bull Whisky and smelt its rich aroma: orange, candied peel and oak. He always thought he would have made a great taster. What a job. Getting paid to drink fine spirits and wine! He poured two small measures and sipped one. He was stunned by the whisky's quality; it was a perfect integration of oak and luscious lemon zest. He wished he could afford something so expensive.

'It's very good.'

'Paolo only buys the best.' Her face crumpled; she was still using the present tense. 'Oh, Jesus. I don't know how to live with so much pain.'

Jack sipped his whisky. Did she know what real pain felt like? When someone you love more than yourself wants to die and you haven't the courage to help them? He knocked back his drink and suddenly saw a half-opened letter on Bianca's dressing table. The name Giovanni Macari jumped out at him before Bianca emerged from behind the screen, wearing another tight dress. She noticed him glancing at the letter and scooped it up before he could read anything else. 'That's got nothing to do with Paolo.'

Jack knew immediately that Giovanni Macari was another link to Paolo and it was important. He mentally logged it.

She sat down opposite him, knocked back the whisky and poured another. 'So you're a copper who can't find people. I knew it when we were in the cafe and you asked all those questions, so what did you find out about Stella?'

'She's a high-class prostitute who only goes with wealthy clients.'

Bianca jumped up and shouted at him: 'Paolo wouldn't use prostitutes. Why should he? He had me!' She thumped her sternum hard. 'He didn't need other women!'

'Then why is his diary full of her name?' Jack spoke quietly.

She collapsed back onto the chair, her face twisted with grief and Jack hated the brutal way he had spoken. Lucy's illness had made him callous.

'I'm sorry. I know how you're feeling.'

'Like shit you do! You've not just lost someone you love.' She filled up their glasses again and they both drank.

'No, I lost someone I love two years ago,' Jack whispered.

She stopped drinking and looked at him. 'You're not bull-shitting me just to get information out of me, are you?'

'No, I'm not bull-shitting you.'

'Was it your wife?' Bianca's face was suddenly full of compassion.

Jack felt his eyes stinging. He nodded, not trusting himself to speak.

'How did she die?' Bianca asked.

'She hasn't died yet.'

Bianca frowned. 'I don't understand.'

And suddenly all Jack's pain came pouring out of him; he told her about Lucy's illness and Tom's alienation; he told about his failure as a husband and a father and a DCI. Once he had started talking he couldn't seem to stop. He knew it was the whisky that had opened the floodgates, but the sense of relief was enormous. He told her about his biggest fear: not having the courage to help Lucy die.

Bianca was silent for a long time after he'd finished. 'Jesus Christ, Jack – that's a lot of pain to be holding inside you.'

'Well, I've released a little of it,' Jack said.

'It makes my loss seem trivial in comparison. Have you got any photos of your family?'

Jack was surprised by her question. He hadn't thought she'd be interested in an ex-DCI's life. He brought out his mobile and scrolled down until he reached the photos of Lucy and Tom laughing as they climbed up Cader Idris.

She scrolled through the photos before saying wistfully, 'They're beautiful people, Jack. I wish Paolo and I had had a son.' She continued scrolling through the photos until her face suddenly went pale. 'Where was this taken?'

Jack rubbed his forehead; he already had the beginnings of a headache; he wasn't used to alcohol. 'Which one?'

Bianca leaned over to show him the photo she was looking at and Jack tried to avoid looking down at her cleavage. 'This one.' Bianca's voice was tight.

Jack was surprised by her tone of voice. Why was she upset? He took his mobile off her and looked down at a photo of a woman with blonde hair standing under an elder tree fingering a rosary. The unknown beauty at Cellini's funeral, but why would Bianca be interested in her?

'She was at Paulo Cellini's funeral. Didn't you see her?'

Bianca shook her head.

'She rushed off before it finished because the man at the bar was smiling at her. Very strange.'

'If that's who I think it is, Rico wouldn't know her. She was wealthy. Rico and me move in different circles.'

'But you both knew Paolo Cellini and he was wealthy, so why shouldn't the manager know her? What's her name?' Jack felt his heart beating faster. He had learned from many years of police work that waiting for answers was usually the best way of getting them. He put his drink down carefully, vowing never to drink whisky again and waited.

Bianca got up and started pacing up and down the room in agitation. 'I don't know if it's the same woman, but she looks like someone I went to school with. Angelica da Carrara. Her father was an Italian banker and her mother was an English model. She had everything I always wanted; beauty, wealth and masses of friends. All the girls had crushes on her. She was like a beautiful lily; half concealed but promising paradise, but...'

'But?' Jack was suddenly incredibly sober, realizing that this was the link he was looking for; the link to Cellini's murder.

'If you pulled away her leaves, there was deadly nightshade lurking underneath.'

Jack stared at her. If this was the same woman she'd gone to school with, why had she gone to Cellini's funeral only to rush off so suddenly? Jack had a flashback to the moment he had seen her, standing beneath an elder tree, wearing a black scarf over ash-blonde hair, frowning as she saw Rico in the distance. What was the link between them? He was missing something, but he couldn't work out what.

CHAPTER 19

27th March 1983

Angelica was sitting in the Chapel of Valsalice-Sacro Cuore in Torino with the other girls, praying to the Madonna to thank her for giving her the strength to complete her Lent Mission. She didn't think she would be able to sustain forty days' abstinence, but each prayer to her had made her stronger. Life without the Madonna would be impossible, she thought; she always made her feel she could do anything if she really wanted it enough, and most important of all, she always forgave her for everything she did.

Four weeks ago, like all the girls, she had listened to the Reverend Mother telling them of the message that his Holiness John Paul II had sent all Catholics. The Reverend Mother wanted the Pope's words to resonate in all their hearts. And they had in Angelica's. He'd told them that Lent was an earnest appeal from the Lord to undertake an inner renewal; both personal and communal: they must first beg forgiveness for others and search for an inner peace within themselves. But they must also never forget Jesus' fasting in the desert. If each of them could give up something that was important to them to help others, they should do so during Lent. And she had; something she loved; she conveniently forgot that it wasn't helping anyone else.

She opened her eyes to find Bianca Vella staring at her again from across the aisle, and sighed. She didn't mind girls having crushes on her if they were pretty; but Bianca was overweight with a muddy complexion. She was like an unwanted satellite constantly orbiting around her. *But I'm a Catholic, so I must be Christian towards her, especially at this time of year,* she thought. She smiled at the girl and Bianca's face lit up.

Her best friend Fiona nudged her and whispered. 'When are you going to tell me what you gave up, Angel?'

'When I've finished praying,' Angelica whispered back, smiling at her. They always sat beside each other; in the schoolroom and in chapel. More like a sister than a best friend, Angelica thought with pleasure. Fiona was coming to stay with them this summer in their house in London. Angelica couldn't wait. It would be wonderful to have someone to go dancing with; someone to be happy with. She tried not to think about her father sitting in the house by himself. The emptiness of the large, lonely house filled her with dread. It was saturated with memories; more like a mausoleum than a home. He wouldn't go back to their house in Italy anymore because of the trauma of the past. But he couldn't expect her to be with him all the holidays, surely? She couldn't fill all the emptiness. She was young; she was supposed to enjoy life. They were flying to London in five days. It was *so* exciting!

Fiona and Angelica put their rosaries into their pockets, made the sign of the cross and walked out of chapel together; neither of them noticed Bianca's crestfallen expression. All the light in the chapel disappeared for her when Angelica left. She got up hurriedly, made a rapid sign of the cross and followed them.

The girls were strolling towards the boathouse in the distance, arm-in-arm and Bianca was consumed with jealousy; that should be *her* arm Angelica was holding. Their heads were close together and they were laughing. Were they laughing at her? Bianca broke into a trot; both the girls had much longer legs than she had; their walking was effortless. They were already at the boathouse. Bianca hid behind one of the numerous trees on the lawn surrounding the convent as Angelica looked around. When she saw that the grounds were empty, she took a key out of the pocket and opened the door. Bianca frowned. Where had she got the key from? They weren't allowed in there; it was full of old rusty boats and machinery that was never used now; the nuns considered it a dirty and dangerous place for young ladies to visit. The girls closed the door and Bianca ran across the grass towards them. She had to hear what they were saying. *I bet they're talking about me,* she thought.

She peeped through one of the dirty windows. The girls were sitting on the floor. Fiona looked shocked. What had Angelica said to her? One of the windows was ajar; Bianca knelt down under it and heard Angelica say.

'The gardener's son.'

'You didn't! I don't believe it! When? We're never allowed out.'

'We came here. How do you think I've got a key? Every night I could.'

'What – when we were supposed to be sleeping in the dormitory? Angelica, you're *so* wicked!'

Then the girls started laughing. Bianca didn't understand what they were talking about. What had the gardener's son got to do with someone as pure as Angelica?

Then she heard her say something that made her feel sick.

'I've given up sex for forty days, Fi, but tonight I'm going to have it as many times as the boy can get it up!'

The next day Bianca was standing in the Reverend Mother's office telling her what she had heard. Her idol had fallen off a high pedestal. The Reverend Mother looked at her with incredulity.

'Ciò non è possibile! Are you telling me that Angelica da Carrara, one of the best Head Girls we've ever had at the school, is having a relationship with our gardener's son?'

The Reverend Mother often spoke a mixture of Italian and English and so the girls did the same.

Bianca nodded. She knew she was doing the right thing. What Angelica was doing was a mortal sin and had to be stopped. The Reverend Mother would help her to get back on the road to redemption.

'This is a serious accusation you're making, Bianca.' The Reverend Mother looked at her. 'Are you sure that's exactly what you heard?'

'Sì, Reverenda Madre. Angelica needs help.'

'I don't want you discussing this with the other girls. I'll speak to Angelica and Fiona and we will discover the truth. Thank you for coming to see me, Bianca. Deve essere stato difficile per te.'

'It was very difficult, Reverenda Madre. I've always admired Angelica.'

'I know that, child. Ritorno alla classe ora.'

Ten minutes later, Angelica was sitting opposite the Reverend Mother looking at her with horror. 'Lo non ci posso credre, Reverenda Madre. Why would she invent such terrible lies?'

The Reverend Mother studied her over her half-moon glasses. 'Non ho idea, Angelica. Obviously the child is unhappy. Have you offended her in some way?'

'I hope not, Reverend Mother. She hasn't many friends. Perhaps I should have spoken to her more, ma non l'ho fatto.'

'Sì, questo potrebbe essere il problema.' The Italian Reverend Mother agreed with her; she had seen this problem with young girls repeated many times over her long years as the head of the convent. Plain girls becoming infatuated with beautiful girls with lots of friends, but it didn't make her task any easier. She had to confirm that the girl was inventing a story because she was jealous of Angelica's friendship with Fiona but if she was...it was a difficult situation for her.

'Chiedete Fiona di venire a vedere me per favore?'

'Naturalmente, Reverenda Madre. I'm so sorry that these problems have been created for you.'

Angelica rushed to find Fiona. It was a study period so they were allowed to study wherever they chose. She found her in the empty art-room; a solace of quiet on the top floor of the convent.

'Fi, the Reverend Mother wants to ask you some questions about what I told you in the boathouse. If you tell her, I'll be expelled and my father will never forgive me and I have no one else. Please promise me you won't say anything. It will ruin my life.'

Then Angelica cried and so did Fiona and she promised she would never breathe a word about the gardener's son for the rest of her life.

Angelica knew it was going to be more difficult to convince the gardener's son to keep quiet; he was a simple boy who didn't like lies, but once she'd told him that he and his father would lose their jobs if he told the Reverend Mother what had happened between them, he told the Reverend Mother that he didn't even know the girl she was talking about and she believed him.

A few days later, the Reverend Mother wrote a letter to Bianca's parents suggesting that Bianca would be better suited at another school. Her appalled parents, who had beggared themselves so she could have a good education at an Italian convent, removed her two weeks later and her relationship with them was never the same; they told her she had disgraced them.

She never forgot or forgave Angelica for what she had done to her. At seventeen, she left Malta forever and came to live in London. For years she was bitter, working for little money as a waitress. Then one evening, she went to a jazz club and they asked if anyone could sing. She'd only sung in the convent choir before, but she went up on the stage and discovered she was a natural-born blues singer.

CHAPTER 20

15th December 2012

Jack tried to ignore the hammer blows in his head and the freezing wind which whipped around the forecourt of the hospital as a paramedic expertly maneuvered Lucy's wheelchair onto an ambulance. It was only ten days before Christmas and he hadn't put up one Christmas decoration up in the house. It had always been a chaotic joyful ritual they had all enjoyed and there was always laughter when Jack's decorations fell down. Jack climbed into the ambulance and sat down beside Lucy as the paramedic closed the door and drove off. He lovingly arranged the blankets around her slight body; then held her hand. She tapped it with a finger and looked at him. She wanted answers.

'I went to a jazz club and drank too much. I know what you're thinking. I shouldn't drink, but sometimes it helps, Luc. I went to speak to the girlfriend of that playboy art dealer who died. You remember Paolo Cellini? There's something very odd about his death and you know what I'm like with unfinished puzzles. I know I'm not a DCI anymore but I can't—' He stopped as Lucy started laboriously typing a message on her laptop; it took so much energy out of her and he didn't want to see the message. She waited for him to look at it. He took a deep breath and looked down, expecting the worse.

want me 2 help u?

Jack's smile was radiant. This was the Lucy he loved. 'You bet!' he said. 'Can't solve it without my lovely girl.'

She tried smiling at him.

An hour later, Lucy was lying in bed, propped up with four pillows, exhausted by the journey home and Jack was up a ladder in the lounge, desperately trying to put up some Christmas decorations before Tom came home from his grand-parents. He hadn't even thought what to buy him for Christmas; in fact he hadn't thought about Christmas at all until today. His mobile suddenly rang. He got it out of his pocket and opened it. Mrs. Montgomery's name popped up.

'Hello, Mrs. M. Is it important? I've just brought my wife home from hospital and I'm hanging up Christmas decorations.'

'It's not important at all.' Mrs. Montgomery sounded mortified that she'd disturbed him at such a time. 'I was just going to ask you to accompany me to the theater tomorrow evening to see *Macbeth*, but you certainly won't want to with your wife at home. Forget I rang. I'll see you tomorrow morning. Bye, Jack.'

'Bye, Mrs. M. Sorry I can't come.' Jack put his mobile away and carried on hanging up the decorations. All that money and no one to share it with. What a lonely life she led. Jack tried to concentrate on the positives in his own life until he heard his in-laws' car stop outside the house and his mouth went suddenly dry. The garish garland he had just hung up looked completely out of place, but there was no time to remove it as the front door opened and they all trooped into the hall. Jack got down from the ladder and went to greet them. This was ridiculous; he was frightened to see his own son.

They were gathered in a group waiting for him. He gave them all an over-bright smile. 'Hello everyone!'

Mary jumped and Jack realized his voice was too loud.

'Hello, Jack,' Colin whispered as if speaking was too exhausting.

'Where is she?' Mary's voice was just as exhausted as her husband's.

'She's sleeping. Hello, Tom.' He looked at his son, desperately wanting him to look up at him, but all he did was study the hall carpet as if it was the most interesting thing he'd ever seen. The silence was appalling.

'I've been putting up Christmas decorations but they're not very good...I need your help.' Tom still didn't answer. 'It's a bit late to be putting them up, I know, but...' There was no point in continuing. He wanted to scream at his son. *It's not my fault that she's ill! Stop blaming me!* 'Anyone want some tea?' he asked.

Colin and Mary nodded briefly as they took off their coats. Tom rushed upstairs to see his mother without looking in his father's direction and Jack felt as if he'd punched him in the stomach. He leaned against the wall and closed his eyes. There was a small touch on his shoulder. He opened his eyes and saw Colin looking at him sympathetically.

'He'll come round, Jack. Just give him time.'

Jack went into the kitchen without answering. He wondered if he ever would.

After Colin and Mary had left, Jack and Tom sat beside Lucy in her bed. Lucy had typed that she'd like Tom to draw a picture and now he was concentrating all his artistic efforts on creating the best picture in the world for her. He looked so vulnerable, Jack thought. The nape of his neck was far too exposed by a draconian haircut. His grandparents had obviously taken him to Colin's old-fashioned barbers. Jack had never seen his son's hair so short. It made him look even younger than twelve; far too young to have this much pain.

'I don't know where he gets his artistic talent from, Luc.'

'From Mum,' Tom said quickly, carrying on drawing. He

hadn't looked at his father once since he'd come home. Jack could remember a time when he'd been jealous of the closeness between Lucy and Tom; now he felt ashamed of such a shallow response in the face of such love.

'Yes, your mum's good at everything,' Jack said, smiling at Lucy. She started to type. Tom stopped drawing and watched her type.

u betcha!

'That's slang, Mum!' Tom sounded more like a parent than a twelve-year-old.

In Lucy's words, Jack caught a glimpse of the girl he had married; the forensic scientist with a great sense of humor; the girl who had started betting with him two weeks after they'd met about who could solve the crime they were working on first; she usually won. It had taken Jack only a couple of weeks to fall in love with her brilliance and her humor; amazingly, she had fallen in love with him too. He had never understood why, he was just thankful.

Tom went back to his drawing and Lucy pointed at the clock.

'It's 10 o'clock, Tom,' Jack said gently.

'So?' was his son's curt response.

'It's your bed-time.'

Tom glared at his father. 'You never want me to be with Mum!'

'That's not true. It's just late...don't you agree, Luc?'

Lucy blinked once. Her signal for yes.

'It's nearly the Christmas holidays! I can stay up as late as I want!' his son shouted at him.

'Stop shouting. You'll upset your mother.' Jack immediately wished he hadn't spoken as Tom's face creased with pain.

'I didn't mean to shout, Mum. Sorry.'

They held their breath as Lucy typed.

ok luv u now bed!

'I'll finish the drawing tomorrow, Mum. Love you too.' Tom

leaned over to kiss Lucy. 'Press your alarm if you need me in the night. Whatever time it is. Don't forget.'

She blinked at him once and he smiled at her. 'Night, night. Don't let the bed-bugs bite.' Her mantra to him when he was small.

'I'll come in and say goodnight later,' Jack said.

Tom picked up his drawing before saying: 'Don't bother.'

Jack sat there, stunned.

Lucy typed *luvs u no one else 2 kick u can take it*

'I'll try, Luc, but it's bloody hard.'

he needs u - now give me clues

Ten minutes later they were in Jack's study looking at his notes.

'That's as far as I've got. Paolo Cellini dies on the floor of his palatial apartment and everyone thinks he's had a heart attack, but I know he was killed by someone switching his heart tablets to these.' Jack brought out the two tablets that had rolled out from behind Cellini's bathroom radiator. 'Taste that, Luc.'

Jack put one of the tablets on Lucy's tongue so she could taste it. She typed *vitamin c*

'Yes, I know. I've been trying to work out who'd want him dead. I went to Cellini's funeral while you were in hospital. Mrs. M asked me go to, as she couldn't. It's very strange, Luc. An immensely wealthy young man makes a will stating exactly where he wants to be buried. In a run-down area of the East End. His girlfriend told me he was brought up there but I'd have thought a playboy would want to disguise his poor early life even after his death. His girlfriend was distraught at his funeral. She told me that they were going to be married.'

Lucy typed *u sure?*

'Course not. But she certainly thought so. Then I saw a blonde woman who seemed alarmed when a man smiled at her. He looked like a bouncer. I've discovered he's the manager at the Blue Notes nightclub where the girlfriend sings. He's in love with the singer.'

Lucy typed *whos the blonde*

'I don't know. Bianca, the girlfriend, said the photo reminded her of a school-friend but time changes people, doesn't it? She could look completely different now. '

Lucy typed *might not*

'So which clue would you follow?

Lucy typed *blonde & manager*

Of course, Jack knew this already, but Lucy needed to be involved. He sighed; he also knew he should show her the silk panties but he didn't want to; they would shine a floodlight onto something that was part of their history: sex. He opened his desk drawer and held them in front of her. 'I found them hidden in Cellini's bathroom. Look at the label. Ever heard of it?'

Lucy's eyes creased with pain before she looked at the label *La Soie* inside the panties. She typed the words: *no wish i had*

'Can you check the Internet for me tomorrow when I'm working? Find out all you can about Cellini's life. Perhaps there's a photo of the blonde woman on the net.' Jack showed Lucy the picture on his mobile. She made a strange sound when she saw her and typed

virginal

Jack stared at her, thinking about what Bianca had told him about her school-friend. *She was like a beautiful lily; half concealed but promising paradise, but...* If she was the same woman, it was the *but* that Jack was interested in.

CHAPTER 21

23rd July 2011

Mark looked in the lounge mirror as he put his bow-tie on, contemplating the long evening ahead. He didn't want to attend another charity dinner, but Angelica wanted him to go and she needed support. She'd been supporting children's charities for years and he knew how important they were to her. But he was tired; tired of concentrating on a hit-and-run driver no one seemed to be interested in finding; tired of looking at Angelica praying to a Black Madonna for a child; tired of only seeing his daughter occasionally. She used to stay with them every weekend, then every other weekend, and now not at all. Angelica always said she wanted her to stay and Mark knew she meant it, but his daughter Emily sensed that it made Angelica unhappy, so she told him it would be better if he took her out. The three of them used to have fun together when they were first married because Angelica thought they would soon have a child of their own, but for some reason it hadn't happened and Emily felt more and more uncomfortable staying with them. She had always been a sensitive child and she didn't want to make Angelica unhappy. So now, Mark picked her up from his ex-wife's house some weekends and took her out, but it was always difficult, constantly trying to think of places to take her. At first, Angelica came too, but for the last six months, she was always too busy with her charity work.

'Are you ready, Marky?'

Angelica walked into the lounge looking more beautiful than he had ever seen her; she was wearing a shimmering blue gown which made her blue eyes even more brilliant. Mark wondered for the thousandth time why she had married him when she could have had any man she wanted. He remembered the first time he had seen her at an art exhibition he and his wife had been invited to. He had never believed in love at first sight before he saw her; but he was lost from the moment she turned around and smiled at him. He and his wife had divorced six months later. He'd felt massively guilty about the effect on Emily, but there was absolutely nothing he could do about the feelings he had for this beautiful woman; he still felt the same after six years, in spite of her obsession with religion.

'Do you like the dress?' Angelica performed a flirtatious pirouette.

Of course he liked it; she was wearing it; she could wear the cheapest dress in the world and still look stunning. 'What do *you* think?' he said, smiling at her.

'I don't know. I want you to tell me.' She looked at him with that strange vulnerability she sometimes displayed as if she doubted her attractiveness.

'You look as beautiful as a swan.'

She frowned at him. 'That's a strange thing to say.'

'No, it's not. I love swans – they're majestic, slender-necked, heavy-bodied and have big feet. Just like you.'

She suddenly laughed and came to kiss him. 'I love you, Mr. Logan.'

'I can't imagine why, but the feeling is mutual, my love.'

An hour later, Mark was bored senseless by a succession of long meandering speeches telling everyone how wonderful they were for donating so much money to so many worthy causes. He knew he was drinking too much, but there wasn't much else to do. Unfortunately, Angelica was sitting opposite him, having an earnest conversation with an elderly lady. Mark liked Mrs. Montgomery, but Angelica had monopolized her for most of the evening and she was the only interesting person sitting at their table. The other people were so self-righteous about the importance of giving to those less fortunate than themselves that he wanted to strangle them. He smiled, thinking that might perhaps spoil the rest of the evening for them. There was an empty seat next to Angelica. The last guest who had been allocated to their table hadn't turned up. Mrs. Montgomery had told them that she thought that a great pity as he was a very interesting, intelligent young man who seemed to know a lot about everything. Mark was hoping he wouldn't show up; he couldn't stand another self-righteous prick at the table.

There was a sudden wave of interest at the other end of the room. Someone had just arrived and everyone seemed to know him. Angelica turned to see who it was and frowned.

'Oh no, he's not coming over here, is he?'

Mrs. Montgomery looked at her with surprise. 'Do you know Paolo?'

'I saw him at Sotheby's. I don't like him.'

'Really? I don't know why you don't like him he's—'

Before she could finish her sentence, Paolo was standing beside their table, smiling at everyone. 'I'm so sorry I'm late, but I had a business meeting that went on and on. Incredibly boring. Please forgive me. '

Mrs. Montgomery beamed at him. 'Of course, we do, Paolo. Do sit down.'

'Hello, Mrs. M. You must introduce me to everyone.'

'This is my neighbor, Paolo Cellini. He's a very astute art dealer.'

As she introduced him to everyone, Mark studied Angelica's

tight expression. She was the only one who wasn't smiling back at him. What had he done to upset her? He took an immediate dislike to the man as he talked to everyone, making them all seem important; he was far too charming; far too aware of the effect he had on people.

At first, Angelica ignored Paolo as he spoke authoritatively about Old Masters; the loss of the Correggio was too raw. But once he started talking about how the portrayal of the Madonna had changed over the centuries, she couldn't help but become interested.

'I'm sure that Mrs. Logan will know this as she bid for a Correggio at an art sale at Sotheby's recently.'

Angelica shot him a look. Was he taunting her? She was surprised to see him looking at her with respect before he turned his attention back to everyone at the table.

'Correggio was the foremost painter of the Parma school of the Italian Renaissance; he was responsible for some of the most tender, most natural images of the Madonna in the sixteenth century. The problem was, by the seventeenth century, she was all too frequently portrayed without any warmth; she looked cold and remote in paintings so people found it much more difficult to relate to her; it was hard to imagine her loving a child, then along comes Giovanni Battista Salvi who portrayed her as a tender, pure, loving Madonna and the Catholic Church loved him for it.'

'He was also known as Sassoferrato from the town he came from,' Angelica said.

Paolo turned to her and smiled. 'You know his paintings?'

'Of course, I do. Surely every Catholic does.'

'I've never heard of him, but then I'm not a Catholic,' Mrs. Montgomery said. 'Have you bought any of his paintings, Paolo?'

'A few, Mrs. M. You must come to see them one day.' He paused then looked at Angelica with such intensity that she found it difficult to breathe. 'Perhaps you will come too.'

'I'm sure Angelica is far too busy to visit your apartment, Paolo. Aren't you, my dear?' Mrs. Montgomery's eyes spoke a warning.

Angelica looked at her in surprise but understood the message. 'Yes, I'm afraid I am, Mr. Cellini.'

Mark watched them from the other side of the table; annoyed that Paolo Cellini had managed to dominate the conversation so completely that the self-righteous had forgotten all about self-righteousness and seemed to be enjoying listening to Cellini, instead of pontificating. Mark knew he was being petulant, but he hated the way people were hanging on his every word. There were more important things in the world than art, Mark wanted to shout at him, across the table, but no one was paying him any attention at all, especially Angelica. She had been engrossed in a conversation with the charmer for far too long. It was too noisy to hear what they were saying clearly. He poured himself another glass of wine. He'd forgotten how many he'd had. He looked across at Angelica; that bastard Cellini was staring at her with far too much interest.

'What are you talking about?' he shouted over to her, glaring at Cellini.

Angelica smiled at him. 'Old Masters.'

'What? At school?' Mark laughed.

Paolo stared at him coldly.

'Paolo was just saying that throughout history art has been perceived differently by so many people,' Angelica said, wanting Mark to join in their conversation.

'I have no idea what art is. Perhaps Mr. Cellini will enlighten me.' Mark leaned forward over the table, enjoying the annoyance that flashed across Cellini's face for a second.

'For me, art means what an artist means to portray; then what he actually *did* portray and how we respond to what he created.' Paolo spoke with authority.

People at the table, who knew nothing about art, nodded in total agreement.

'So what do you think Damien Hirst was trying to portray when he put a cow in formaldehyde?'

Angelica looked at Mark; startled by his belligerent tone. Paolo smiled at him as if the question was friendly.

'I imagine he thought he was trying to be original; no one had done it before.'

'There's a reason for that. It's fucking hideous!'

'Mark!' Angelica widened her eyes; she hated it when he became drunk.

'It's not something I admire,' Paolo said calmly, 'because I love classical painters and sculptors, but there are many forms of art. Some are difficult to interpret.'

'Isn't that because Charles Saatchi says so and you're just following the leader?'

Paolo stared at him impassively and didn't answer.

'Isn't that because Saatchi creates moulds to make him money?' Mark persisted. 'Then people like you come along and make more. Capitalism in a nutshell.'

'I think we ought to go home, Mark.' Angelica was worried about the sudden conflict at the table. She couldn't believe that Mark was jealous of a conversation she'd had with a stranger.

'No, please don't.' Paolo spoke quickly. 'Let's just change the conversation. After all, this is supposed to be an evening to celebrate children's charities.'

Everyone tapped the table in agreement, but Angelica started to get up. 'It's late and my husband has a busy day tomorrow. Please excuse us.'

The men stood up and Paolo immediately moved her chair back for her. 'Shall I get you a taxi?' The words and the meaning in his eyes meant two different things. Angelica shivered.

'No, thank you. Come on, Mark.'

'Night, night everyone. Wonderful evening!' Mark slurred as

he leaned against the table to help him to his feet.

Angelica put her arm through Mark's to steady him as they walked away. Paolo followed them and said. 'I'm asking Mrs. Montgomery to come to see Salvi's *Madonna and Child* next Tuesday at 5 p.m.'

She ignored him and carried on walking out of the room with Mark.

'Why the hell was that prick telling you that?' Mark said.

'I have no idea,' Angelica answered. 'He's a very strange man.'

Chapter 22

16th December 2012

Jack was at Mrs. Montgomery's apartment early the next day so that he could question Frank, the tapestry-obsessed concierge, before taking Mrs. M to the doctor. Frank was concentrating on creating the Battle of Hastings in embroidery.

'You've obviously got a lot of patience to be able to create that, Frank.'

Frank looked up at him in surprise. 'Hello, Jack. I suppose I have. I just thought I had a talent for it, but perseverance helps, I suppose.'

'You see everything that happens here, don't you? I'm sure you wouldn't neglect your duties.'

Frank looked aghast that someone might think he could. 'Of course not! I'm the forerunner of any battles that are fought here.'

Jack smiled at his overzealous job description, but who was he to say what people thought their job entailed? He seemed to spend more time talking to Mrs. M than being her chauffeur.

'Do you think anyone could get through the foyer without you noticing, Frank?'

'Not a chance,' he said without hesitation. 'And if they did, the CCTV cameras would pick them up.'

'What time did you come on duty the night Mr. Cellini died?'

'What's it matter what time I come on duty? He had a heart attack, Jack. It said so in the papers. Over a week ago now so why you still interested?' Frank looked up at Jack curiously.

'Something is puzzling me about that evening and I have to solve puzzles, that's all.'

'You sound like me brother Stan and he's got Asperger's. He were always lining up his pens like soldiers. You wouldn't credit some of the things he got up to, once—'

'So the day Mr. Cellini died you saw everyone who passed this desk?' Jack stopped him before he launched into a lengthy genetic profile of his entire family.

'Course I did. Once I comes on duty no one gets past me. Mind you, they could with the other bloke what calls himself a concierge. You know the one that looks as if he's too wet behind the ears to shave? Talks to his girlfriend on his mobile most of the time. I'd sack him if I was—'

'So from what time wouldn't they have got past you, Frank?' Jack smiled at the older man to stop him indulging in another diatribe.

Frank studied his embroidery as if the answer lay in his stitching. '10 o'clock. I started late that night. Minus 2 it was. Nearly froze me bollocks off.'

'You can even remember the temperature? Hope my memory is as good as yours when I'm your age.' Jack suddenly thought that perhaps he was overloading the flattery.

Frank beamed at him. 'Yeah – not all of us ancients have got Alzheimer's.'

'Could I have a look at the tapes? You know I'm an ex-DCI so there's no problem.' Jack kept his face impassive to disguise how important the tapes were to him.

'Sorry, Jack. But I wipe them after a week. If you'd asked me four days ago, you could have watched them. Not important, are they?' Frank looked up at Jack's impassive face.

'No, not really,' Jack said nonchalantly as he walked towards the lift, thinking *shit, four days ago I could have found out who the killer was!*

As he glided up in the luxuriant carpeted lift to the fifth floor, he tried to work out how Federico Batas and the unknown woman were linked. They came from different worlds. So how the hell did they meet? If he could discover that, he'd be closer to finding out who killed Cellini.

Alice, Mrs. M's helper, opened the door for him on his first knock as if she'd anticipated it.

'Hello, Mr. Bradley. I'm just off. Mrs. M is waiting for you in the lounge and the tea's all ready in the kitchen.'

'Thanks, Alice and it's Jack, not Mr. Bradley.'

She smiled at him before calling out. 'See you later, Mrs. M. Just off to get some food. Jack's just arrived.'

She closed the door behind her and Jack went into the lounge.

Mrs. M was reading Agatha Christie's *Death On The Nile* by the large window of her apartment, her glasses glinting in the winter sunshine.

'Morning, Mrs. M. So you're an Agatha Christie fan.'

She took off her glasses and smiled at him. 'Hello, Jack. Yes, I love the way she keeps me guessing who the murderer is and then solves it in such a clever way.'

'She's far too neat for an ex-DCI. We don't solve half the crimes that are committed.'

Mrs. M looked shocked. 'Good heavens! Do you mean there could be killers wandering our streets as we speak?'

'Fraid so – like some tea?' Jack said as he strolled into the kitchen.

'Yes, but make sure you don't put any arsenic in it!' she called out.

Jack smiled as he picked up the large tray Alice had arranged with the pot of Earl Grey Mrs. M loved and her shortbread biscuits.

'How's your wife, Jack?' Mrs. M said as Jack walked back in.

Jack put the tray on a table near her and watched her pouring out the tea.

'She wants to work,' Jack said, taking the cup she offered him. He sat down in a small armchair overlooking the window and looked out. It was good to see sunshine again.

Mrs. M looked startled. 'But I thought you said she had Muscular Dystrophy.'

'She has, but she's also a fighter. She wants to help solve Cellini's case. Did I tell you she was a forensic scientist before her illness? A brilliant one. She's working on the computer today, looking for information about Cellini and this beautiful blonde who went to his funeral.'

Mrs. M's eyes lit up. She put her tea down and asked. 'You mean there was a special one?'

'I think so. If you'd have seen her, you'd know what I mean. My wife said she looked virginal.'

'But how does your wife know? She was in hospital when you went to Paolo's funeral.'

'Modern technology, Mrs. M. I took her photo.'

Mrs. M put down her cup, shocked. 'You took a photograph at a funeral. It's not the done thing, Jack.'

Jack smiled. 'I don't normally, but there was something about her.' He got out his mobile, scrolled down to the woman's photo and leaned over to show her.

Mrs. M put her reading glasses back on. 'I'll never get used to all the gadgets we have now, Jack. In my day we used box cameras.' She looked down at the photograph and said with surprise. 'That's Angelica Logan. What was she doing at Paolo's funeral? She only met him once.'

Jack felt his heart racing. All the time the answer to the woman's identity was in this room. 'Who is she?'

'She's the wife of the editor of one of the most influential tabloids in London, Jack. Her husband's Mark Logan.'

Jack's stomach contracted at the sound of the name. It conjured up images he wanted to forget; memories of the night of the siege; the night when everything started to go wrong for him. The day after the siege, Alan had been delighted to tell him that the editor of *The Daily Reporter* was running a big story on how DCI Jack Bradley; one of the Met's top officers had mismanaged the siege and his name was going to be plastered all over the front cover in its next edition. The nicest thing Logan had called him was incompetent; the worst, Jack had tried to forget.

Mrs. M was giving him a sympathetic look. 'Are you all right, Jack?'

'I'm fine. '

'Angelica's husband certainly didn't like Paolo. I could tell that the first time they met at a charity dinner. He was far too interested in Angelica but she adores her husband. She's not the sort of person to have a liaison with a playboy.'

'How do you know?'

'Because we're on the same children's charities. She loves children. She told me, in confidence, of course, that she's desperate to have a child. A woman who's in love with her husband and is desperate for a child isn't going to have an affair with a charmer like Paolo.'

'She might, if her husband can't give her one.' Jack took a small sip of his tea and shuddered. He hated Earl Grey.

'Jack! That's so cynical. I didn't mark you down as a cynic.'

'It's not cynical, Mrs. M. It comes from long experience – from years of listening to people lie about their lives. People are incredibly clever at disguising their real lives.'

'You really think they could have been lovers? Oh, how wicked!

'Then why are your eyes shining, Mrs. M?' Jack teased her. He felt euphoric. Another piece of the puzzle had slotted into place.

'Do you know her address?'

'I'm afraid I don't. She's always too busy to call in. I don't know exactly what she does. She can't work for charities all the time, but perhaps she doesn't want to see an old bat like me.'

Jack smiled at her. 'You're the most interesting old bat I've ever met and I'm sure Angelica Logan thinks so too. Something else is keeping her busy and I intend finding out what that is.'

All he had to do was discover where Angelica Logan lived and tail her. And he knew exactly the right person to give him the answer: Jamila.

CHAPTER 23

17th December 2012

Jack was surprised by the exhaustion on Jamila's face highlighted in the light from the log fire. They were sitting in a corner of *The Red Lion*; the pub he and Lucy used to go to when they first started going out together. He'd been surprised that Jamila didn't seem to want to meet him when he'd rung her.

'So how are you?' Jack asked after he'd bought them two halves of beer.

Jamila sipped her beer. 'Tired. How's Lucy?'

The question threw Jack. 'The same. Her parents are staying with us over Christmas so her carer can have a long holiday. Good for Tom to have some company.'

'How are you coping?'

'Me? I'm fine. Better than you look at the moment. You're working too hard. What case are you on?'

Jamila sipped her glass of beer without speaking.

'Alan has told you not to talk to me about it, hasn't he?'

She looked at him and smiled. 'He's driving us all nuts, but I can't discuss the case, Jack. He hates the thought that you were a better DCI than he is. Why the hell did you have to resign?'

'You know why.'

'Oh come on. You know what short memories people have.

The super would soon have forgotten the publicity once some new story was uncovered. You should have stuck it out.'

Jack stared at the fire; knowing she was right, but hating to admit it.

'Are you still obsessed with that art dealer's death?'

Jack stared at her in astonishment. 'Is that what you call trying to find a killer? An obsession?'

'You told me you were obsessive when I first joined the Met. Once you've got your teeth into something, you don't let go. Mind you, it usually worked.' She smiled at him. 'What do you want to know?'

Jack smiled back. 'Am I that obvious?'

'Yeah,' Jamila said. 'If it'd been anyone else but you I'd have said no. I wanted an early night.'

Jack looked at his watch. 'It's only 7.30 p.m. You could be in bed by 8.30 if you hurry.'

Jamila smiled at him again. 'Well?'

'Could you get me an address? Remember Mark Logan, the editor of *The Daily Reporter*?'

'How could I forget? The guy who did a hatchet job on you in his paper and made you resign.'

'I need his address.'

Jamila looked worried. 'You're not thinking of doing anything you'll regret, are you?'

'No, I've already done that. His wife was at Cellini's funeral. She saw the manager of a jazz club there. They obviously know each other. She's frightened of him and I want to know why.'

'How's she know these guys?'

'I don't know, that's why I need the address. I'm going to tail her.'

'And then what?' Jamila queried.

'I don't know that either, but I'm not giving up until I've discovered the truth.'

Jamila sighed. 'I wish Alan was like that. If something doesn't fit in with one of his theories, he dismisses it. He only wants facts he tells us yet he keeps sending us out on wild goose chases so that we can't get any. I don't know how much longer I can stand working for him, Jack. We've got so many leads on this case but he keeps following the wrong ones.'

'What leads?'

'Tip-offs about where the drugs are coming in from.' She winced. 'Oh, shit.'

Jack smiled. 'Oh, come on – I'm not going to inform anyone, am I? Want some help?'

She looked around the pub as if Alan was about to step in at any moment.

'He never comes in here. Relax.'

'You're a mind-reader, Jack.'

He laughed. It was a good feeling.

'We had a tip-off about three weeks ago that a large haul of cocaine was being smuggled into the UK inside religious statues.'

'Religion is the opiate of the masses,' Jack said, smiling at her.

She frowned. 'Not in the mood for jokes. I've got a lot on my mind.'

'Do you know where they're coming in from?' Jack spoke seriously, matching Jamila's mood.

'South America, then it's shipped or air-lifted to countries all over Europe. That's the problem. We're having to check every consignment of religious statues arriving in every port and every airport. You know Brodie Clark, don't you?'

'Of course. The Head of the UKBA's border force. Worked with him last year on that drugs haul when all that cocaine was discovered on a yacht. Bloody great operation involving seven countries. It's not as big as that, is it?'

'We don't know...that's the problem. We've checked hundreds of cargo planes and ships arriving containing statues and the BA and SOCA found absolutely nothing. As if that's not enough, we're now facing a number of law suits from religious organizations for destroying some of the most expensive religious icons in the world. Alan is losing his hair over it and the super's ulcer is getting bigger. We can't keep smashing statues to get the drugs.'

Jack was puzzled. The dogs at Border Control were highly trained. They'd discovered tons of Class A drugs in the past. 'What about the sniffer dogs?'

'They can't seem to find anything, that's what no one can understand; even after we've had the tip-off that they're arriving. So we're opening random crates and smashing statues.'

'Perhaps they're not smuggling them in statues at all.'

'What?'

'The tip-off could be a plant, Jamila, to get you looking in the wrong places. I talked to Brodie last month when Border Control was tipped off that Class A drugs had been packed inside frozen animal carcasses. You know where they found the drugs, eventually? In innocent-looking boxes of Pringles; only each Pringle had been cut from cocaine. Labor intensive, but very ingenious.'

Jamila looked stunned. 'If you're right, Jack, we'll be massacred in the press. This is going to cost the tax-payer millions. Alan is going to have a fit.'

'Don't tell him yet. Check on the people who are giving you the info first.'

'We've used them many times before. They've always been reliable.'

'How much cocaine are we talking about?' Jack asked.

'About 25 million.'

Jack sipped his beer and raised his eyebrows.

Jamila groaned. 'I'll have to go back to the office to run more checks on them. I'll phone you with the address in the morning. Night, Jack.'

Jamila left, looking dejected, and Jack suddenly thought: religious icons + Paolo Cellini = drugs. His heart started racing.

When Jamila rang him in the morning to give him the address, he told her to take up kick boxing to get rid of her stress – it was better than kicking Alan. She'd laughed.

Today he was going to take Lucy out for a drive; her first for many months. Her parents were taking Tom to the pantomime and he'd planned a surprise for her; they were going to visit a house she'd always wanted to see. It was also, Jack discovered, only two houses away from the Logan's house.

He lifted Lucy's slight body into the car and put her wheelchair in the back and they drove across the Christmas-decorated city towards Hampstead. Jack glanced at her; she looked almost happy as the winter sun shone onto her face.

'Special day today, Luc,' he said when they reached Hampstead.

She typed *how?*

'Wait and see,' Jack answered as he turned into Keats Grove.

Lucy made an excited sound as she typed **keats lived here**

'Really?' Jack said disingenuously as he turned into the driveway of Wentworth Place and stopped the car.

u cant park here!

'I've arranged it, Luc. You've always wanted to see Keats' house and we never seemed to find the time, so here we are. I'll just get your wheelchair.' Jack got out, feeling good for the first time since her illness; at least they could enjoy one happy day together.

He didn't see the tears that ran down her face as she typed.

Jack wheeled the chair beside the passenger door and opened it. He saw Lucy crying and was upset. 'What's the matter?'

She tapped her fingers on her keyboard and Jack saw the word *happy*

Jack smiled at her. 'So am I. Come on, my lovely girl. You can see where Keats wrote some of your favourite poems. He lifted her out of the car and put her in the wheelchair. She looked at the beautiful two-hundred-year-old mulberry tree which covered one section of the beautiful garden around the house and almost smiled. A young woman came out and greeted them.

'You must be Mr. & Mrs. Bradley. We've put the ramp up for you on the ground floor, but I'm very sorry there's no lift for the basement or upper floor.' She looked at Lucy apologetically.

'Don't worry, I'll carry her, she's as light as a bird.'

The girl looked relieved. 'I hope you have a wonderful visit. Your husband told me Keats is your favourite poet.'

Lucy blinked at her once as Jack wheeled her into the house.

In Keats' parlour they listened to an audio tape of Keats' poem *An Ode To A Nightingale*; the poem Keats had written in only one morning. Jack watched Lucy's face as she listened and actually saw a glimmer of her old smile and his heart sang. He carried her down into the basement to see where the servants worked and up to second floor to Keats' small pink-painted bedroom and they looked out of the window at what he would have seen. After an hour, Jack's arms and back were cramped with tension and they decided to leave. As Jack wheeled her towards the car, Lucy typed: *thank u wonderful die happy now*

Jack blinked rapidly to stop his tears and said lightly. 'Didn't bring you here just for Keats, Luc. Remember the blonde woman I told you about? She lives just down the road. Thought we'd have a recce.'

Lucy typed *what a romantic!*

Jack laughed as he wheeled her down the drive of Keats' house and turned towards the Logan house. They stopped outside a large detached Victorian villa.

'This is it. How much do you think, Luc?'

Lucy typed *3 million*

'Should have been a newspaper editor not a DCI. Think I missed my vocation.'

Lucy typed again *no u didnt got 2 go back*

'One day, Luc. One day. We ought to go home. You must be

tired.'

As Jack was wheeling Lucy back to the car, a large Mercedes came out of the driveway of the Logan house and drove past them. There were two people inside it: Angelica Logan and Rico Batas; both of them looked grim.

'Bloody hell!' Jack said. 'The blonde and the Filipino manager coming out of the Logan house! What do think about that?'

Lucy typed *blackmail*

Jack stopped wheeling her and looked at her in surprise.

CHAPTER 24

12th August 2011

Angelica had never intended to go to Paolo's place. She had everything she wanted in life, except a child. Why should she go to a playboy's penthouse apartment to fuel his desire for dominance? But three weeks after meeting him at the charity dinner she was standing nervously outside his apartment ringing his doorbell. The door opened immediately and Paolo beamed at her.

'At last you've come!' The pleasure in his voice was genuine. It made Angelica feel very wanted. He was obviously overjoyed to see her. 'I didn't think you would.'

'Nor did I,' she whispered as she walked in.

He closed the door and guided her into the most exquisite exhibition of religious icons she had ever seen. She was transfixed; here was a cornucopia of paintings she could only dream about buying.

'You really like them, don't you?' Paolo smiled at her. 'You're not just going through the motions that people do who know nothing about art. It's wonderful to have someone appreciate them as much I do.'

An hour later, she was still studying the exquisite paintings and statues with a glass of Chablis in her hand. Paolo walked over to give her a top-up.

'I can't stay any longer, but thank you for showing them to me. It's given me great pleasure.'

'Not as much as it's given me,' Paolo said looking at her with the same intensity as he had at the dinner. 'But I've saved the best until the last. You haven't seen Salvi's *Madonna and Child* yet, remember?

Angelica glanced at her watch. Mark was working late tonight. She could see the painting and still be home before he got home to cook dinner.

'Where is it?'

'I don't display it. It's too valuable. It's in there.' He pointed into his bedroom.

She was appalled with herself; how stupid she'd been to go to a stranger's apartment.

He turned and saw the tension on her face. 'It's all right. I'm not going to seduce you. As a Catholic, I know you revere the Virgin Mary as much as I do. You are the first person I've showed it to. Please come and see it.' He made the sign of the cross in front of one of the paintings before walking into his bedroom. She stood in the doorway of the lounge looking at him. He moved over to a wall and pressed his fingers against it; a panel slid silently sideways to reveal a vaulted room. He pressed his splayed fingers against the vault door and it clinked. As he opened it a soft sensor light came on. Angelica was fascinated. She had heard about hidden rooms when she was a child and had always wanted one, but none of her collection was as valuable as his.

'Come,' he said simply and stood back so she could see. She walked over, barely glancing at the enormous bed that was center-stage and stood at the doorway of a security room; the room was filled with numerous statues and paintings, but the only painting she wanted to see was the one Paolo had spoken about. And there it was in front of her: Salvi's *The Madonna And*

Child. Angelica stared up at the beautiful face of the Madonna, seated in the foreground; her dark hair covered by a cream-colored cloth. A titian-blue cloak was draped over part of her body and underneath it was a rich red dress. Angelica's eyes moved down to the baby she was cradling so tenderly.

'She's everything a mother should be,' Paolo said. He was standing too close to her.

'And what's that?' she whispered.

'Tender, loving, forgiving.'

Angelica was disconcerted by his words; thinking of the anger and bitterness in her own mother. She had never been able to please her. 'Is your mother like that?' she asked him.

Paolo's face was suddenly full of sadness. 'My mother was like that. She died. And yours?'

'She's dead too,' she answered lightly. Why should she explain her complicated relationship with her mother to a man she hardly knew?

'Have you any children?' he asked her.

She winced at the rawness of the question and shook her head; unable to answer.

'That surprises me,' Paolo said.

She glanced at him in case he was mocking her, but his gaze was tender. She hadn't expected tenderness from such a man; every gossip columnist mentioned his debauched lifestyle.

'You possess the same translucence and tenderness I see in the Madonna in Salvi's painting. The only difference is his Madonna has brown hair and your hair outshines the sun. Can you see the resemblance between you both?'

Angelica was stunned. She had seen copies of this painting many times before, but had never noticed any resemblance at all. Did she look so virginal? So pure? Every time she looked into the Madonna's face, time simply stopped.

'I must go.' She walked away from the seduction of the room and his words.

'Have I said something to offend you?'

She shook her head. 'I'm sorry, I must go.'

'My remark was meant as a compliment. I don't go in for gratuitous flattery. I simply meant that you look as if you would love a child a great deal.'

Angelica turned away from him so he couldn't see the sudden tears that flooded her eyes; if only he knew how many times a day she prayed to the Madonna to give her a child.

Paolo turned her around gently. 'What have I said to upset you? Please tell me.'

He looked at her with such compassion that she whispered: 'What is beauty if the one thing you want more than anything in the world is denied to you?'

'And what is that?'

'A baby to love and cherish.'

'If only you didn't look so pure,' Paolo said, looking deep into her eyes.

She frowned at him; not understanding what he meant.

CHAPTER 25

16th November 2012

Giovanni Macari sat in his shabby house, waiting for his son's girlfriend to arrive. He hadn't known what to think when she had written to ask him if she could visit him. He had written many letters to Paolo since his mother's death, but he had never answered. They hadn't spoken since his mother Maria died ten years ago. He and Maria had been born in the same mountainous region in Italy and married when he was twenty-five and Maria was eighteen. She had had so much love and compassion to give that the loneliness of his loss was great, but he often thought that Paolo's arrival had prepared him for it.

A sudden knock on the door brought him out of the past, shuffling towards the door, thinking how vigorous he had been once. An attractive dark-haired young woman with sad eyes stood at his door, looking embarrassed. He couldn't think why.

'Come in and sit, mio caro. Thank you for coming,' he said as he closed the door. 'It is always a sadness when a father and son lose touch with each other.' What an odd English expression that was, Giovanni thought, but how could he tell her that he and Paolo had never had any touch to lose.

'Please sit down. How long have you and Paolo been seeing each other?'

Bianca smiled at him. 'Two years, Mr. Macari. We're going to be married.'

Giovanni raised his white eyebrows in surprise as he settled himself back in his favourite chair. 'I thought Paolo enjoyed his...freedom too much to settle down with one woman.'

'He's found the right woman to settle down with, but... sometimes he forgets.' She looked around the shabby room with its peeling paint and worn carpets, wondering why he was living in such a dilapidated house when his son was so wealthy.

'La mia casa non è buona. Mi scusi, I have lived here for over forty years. I even think in English, but Italian sometimes breaks through.'

'I understand Italian and your house is fine.'

'I'm too old to pretend and I know what you're thinking. It's an old wreck like me.'

'I don't understand why Paolo doesn't buy you a beautiful house. He has so much money he wouldn't have even notice.'

'I have always worked for my own money, Signorina Vella. I'm not going to change now. I was a tailor in Italy and when we came to England I went into business with my brother-in-law and we made money; a lot of money in the West End.'

Bianca looked at him in surprise. 'Then why do you live here?'

The old man sighed heavily. 'One night my brother-in-law disappeared with all the money. We never saw him again and I became bankrupt. It was a terrible shock for my wife, Maria. Her brother stealing from his own family. But you don't want to hear about my problems. Tell me how Paolo is. I don't hear from him.'

'He's always travelling around, Mr. Macari,' Bianca spoke quickly. 'I'm sure he would visit you if he wasn't travelling.'

'I would like to think so, but I haven't seen Paolo for ten years.'

'Ten years!' Bianca was stunned.

'I have brought out some things of Paolo's to show you.

Pictures when he was a boy. So beautiful with his golden hair. He was a gift from God, my wife said. They are on the table over there. Would you fetch them for me please?'

Bianca went over to a small rickety table, picked up the albums lying on it and sat down again. For five minutes she looked at grainy photos of the man she loved growing up and in each photo he looked like a confident golden cherub with two dark-haired parents. It was strange that he was so fair when his parents were both dark, Bianca thought, but she'd heard that sometimes hair color missed a generation; perhaps one of his grandparents had blonde hair. She closed the last album and saw that the old man was nearly asleep in his chair. She got up quietly and put the albums back on the table, then noticed a blue rattle with a silver band around it lying in front of a book. She couldn't resist picking it up. It made a tinkling sound. Mr. Macari opened his eyes.

'I'm sorry, you must be tired. Thank you for showing me the photos. Paolo was a very beautiful child, wasn't he?'

Giovanni nodded. 'Yes. Perhaps too beautiful.'

'Was this Paolo's?' Bianca asked, showing him the rattle before placing it back near the book.

'That's the only thing he had with him, the nuns told us when we adopted him.'

Bianca was shocked. 'Adopted? He was adopted?'

Giovanni looked at her in surprise. 'He didn't tell you? I thought he would if you were...but perhaps, he still didn't want to disobey his mother even though she's dead. She told him not to tell anyone about the adoption when we came to England. Paolo was her son and no one else's.'

'I don't understand.' Bianca looked at him in bewilderment.

The old man sighed as if the memory was too much for him. 'Maria and I had been married for twenty-five years but no bambinos came along and she was very sad. I said let's adopt one, but she said no. Then one day, some nuns from a nearby convent came to our little house in Oropa and told us a baby boy had been abandoned at their convent.'

Bianca was stunned. Not only was Paolo adopted but he had been abandoned! Why hadn't he told her?

'You look upset, my dear. It is not as barbaric as it sounds. Usually the abandoned babies are illegitimate. The mothers don't know what to do so the church found a way to help them. They built special rooms in the wall of some convents where girls could place their babies knowing that they would be well cared for by the nuns, then placed in orphanages.'

'But what if the nuns don't find them for a long time? They'd die.' Bianca couldn't believe what she was hearing.

The old man shook his head. 'No, there was a custom in Italy when Paolo was born that each convent that looked after abandoned babies had a small bell inside the special room. Once the babies were placed in a cradle, the mother rang the bell and the nuns would come. They would access the room from inside the convent so the girls could remain anonymous. It was a humane solution to a difficult problem.'

It was too much for Bianca to take in. Being abandoned must have affected Paolo. Was that why he was sometimes cruel?

'How old was he when you adopted him?'

'Eight months, but we had looked after him since he was about two months old the doctors thought. Of course, we didn't know his exact birth date.'

So Paolo doesn't even know when he was born, Bianca thought. That was so sad. She looked up and saw that the old man was looking at her with concern. She smiled at him to reassure him. What a lovely man he was, she thought. To be concerned about a stranger he had only just met.

'I wish Paolo had brought me to see you, Mr. Macari. I can't understand why he didn't.'

The old man stared out of a dirty window and closed his eyes again; too many painful memories were flooding in.

'I'm sorry.' Bianca said. 'It's none of my business. It's just that I'm sure you're a good father. You seem so kind.'

Mr. Macari opened his eyes and smiled at her. 'Grazie, mio caro... I must tell you something, but...it is very difficult for me. Paolo blamed me for his mother's death, that's why he changed his surname. He didn't want to be linked to me.'

Bianca looked at him, startled. So this was the reason Paolo hated his father; he was involved in his mother's death in some way. The old man's face creased with emotion as he stared at the worn carpet. She shouldn't have come here. This was too painful for him. But just as she was about to get up to leave, Giovanni started speaking with great difficulty.

'You see...we didn't go to the doctors early enough to stop her cancer spreading. The doctors...they told Paolo they could have saved her, but it wasn't my fault. Maria didn't tell me about the lump in her breast until it was too late and then she made me promise not to say anything to Paolo. She never wanted him to worry. He was her sun, moon and stars, Signorina. He grew up knowing he could do no wrong in his mother's eyes and of course, he worshipped her. What boy wouldn't with such adoration?'

So that's why Paolo feels that the world is his, Bianca thought. 'That must have been difficult for you, Mr. Macari.'

'Sì, lo era,' he whispered. 'Tell me about Paolo. I haven't seen him for such a long time. Are his tablets helping?'

'What tablets?' Bianca asked, puzzled.

He looked surprised again. 'He keeps many things from you, Signorina. We found out when Paolo was a baby that he had an arrhythmic heartbeat. He has lived on tablets to control his heart all his life. Perhaps that's why Maria was so protective of him. If you didn't know that they are obviously working.'

Bianca suddenly realized that she didn't know the man she loved at all.

'Has he changed?' Giovanni said, looking at her with a

desperate hopefulness.

How could tell this kindly man that his son was still the self-absorbed narcissist he had always been? So she invented a man who was becoming less narcissistic; who was beginning to see that he wasn't the center of the Universe; she painted a picture of a person they both wished Paolo was. 'Soon he'll realize how lucky he is to have you as his father, Mr. Macari.'

A slow smile spread across the old man's face on hearing her words. 'Lo pensi davvero?'

'I don't think so. I know. Paolo gives a lot of money to charity. He hides a kind heart.'

The old man nodded his head, but Bianca could see that he wasn't convinced. Suddenly, a small section of the ceiling crashed down onto the worn carpet in the corner of the room. They both jumped.

'You can't live in a house like this when Paolo has so much money, Mr. Macari!' Bianca shouted. 'I'll tell him that your house is falling down and he must buy you a new one!' She was almost crying with anger. But the moment she'd said the words she realized she couldn't. She'd found the old man's letters in one of Paolo's drawers in his apartment when she was looking for some clothes she'd left. How could she tell him that she'd read his personal mail when he was so secretive?

Mr. Macari smiled at her gently. 'I can see why Paolo likes you. You're a lioness. Just like his mother. But I don't want Paolo's money. I just want his love, but he gave it all to his mother.'

Bianca's eyes filled with tears; she wanted exactly the same love but never received it either. How odd to be united with a stranger through a lack of love.

'I can't understand why he won't see you. I wish I'd had a father as forgiving as you.'

'Grazie mille. That is one of the nicest things anyone has ever said to me, Signorina Vella. I'm glad Paolo is changing. One day,

I hope to see him again with you. Mi scusi devo dormire ora.'

Bianca saw the old man's eyes drooping and got up to kneel beside him. 'I'm getting a builder to repair the roof, Mr. Macari, and the bill will be sent to Paolo. No arguments. May I come again?'

'I would like that very much,' he said, patting her hand. 'Goodbye, mio caro.'

Bianca tip-toed out of the house as the old man went to sleep in his chair. If she could think of a way to make Paolo see what a lovely father he had, he might become the man they both wanted.

Chapter 26

18th December 2012

Tom was playing chess with his grandfather while Lucy watched every move they made; every time Tom made a mistake she tapped a finger on her lap-top. Her father smiled at her.

'My daughter isn't helping her son to cheat, is she?'

Lucy blinked at him twice and Tom laughed. 'Mum's just got a restless finger, Gramps.'

Jack looked up from his newspaper in surprise; he hadn't heard Tom laugh for such long time, he'd almost forgotten how infectious it was. He smiled at his son, willing him to look at him; of course, he didn't. He was trying to win the game to show his mother how clever he was; always wanting to impress her. He'd always known that his mother was more brilliant than his father, even as a small boy. Jack turned his attention back to the newspaper; it was so much easier to focus on other people. He didn't know why he still bought *The Daily Reporter* after the mauling he'd received last year; *perhaps I'm a masochist*, Jack thought as he turned the page and saw another large spread on the hit and run. All the other newspapers had turned their attention onto the problems in the Middle East. Jack knew why Mark Logan was still writing about it; he had the same interest in the family as Jack did; they both wanted to help a small Albanian boy who had watched his mother burning to death in front of him. He suddenly threw the paper away from him; this wasn't helping him forget anything.

'Checkmate, Gramps!' Tom scooped up his grandfather's queen and laughed at the astonished look on his face.

'Well, I certainly didn't see that coming. You're almost playing as well as your mother did.'

They smiled at Lucy; for a moment forgetting that she couldn't smile back.

Jack looked at the clock. 'Well done, Tom. You're getting very good. Think it's time for bed.'

Tom looked at him and started putting the chess pieces away slowly.

'You heard your father, Tom,' Colin said. 'I'll do that. Don't forget to give your grandmother a kiss before you go up.'

Tom immediately got up to kiss his mother and recited his usual mantra to her, then smiled at his grandfather. 'Night, Gramps.'

Jack tightened his stomach muscles, knowing what was coming. 'Night, Tom.'

'Night,' he answered curtly as he brushed past his father without looking at him. He pushed open the kitchen door to say goodnight to his grandmother who was clearing up.

'He'll come round, Jack. I'm sure he will.' For the first time, Colin looked at him with sympathy.

Lucy's eyes swiveled towards Jack and she started typing.

He immediately felt sick, thinking what she was going to type, but got up and stood beside her and looked down at her lap-top and saw the words

need to talk

Five minutes later, Jack sat at his desk in the study watching Lucy laboriously typing; his heart thumping. He wanted to kneel in front of her and lay his head in her lap; he wanted her to stroke his hair as she used to when he was tired; he wanted her to stop typing.

She suddenly stopped and looked at him. He got up slowly and leant beside her and read

want u 2 do something important

Jack closed his eyes; he didn't want to read any more. A sound like a woodpecker filled the room. Lucy was tapping on her keyboard. He opened his eyes and continued reading

find out who killed Cellini

Jack smiled at her. She wasn't asking him to kill her! 'I'm working on it, Luc. You know that.'

She looked down at her lap-top; she had written a lot more.

find out why manager blackmailing the blonde/ find out if cellini involved with drugs

Jack stared at her. 'We don't know if the manager was black-mailing her. This isn't like you. You work with facts – I'm the one who works with hunches. What could he have on Angelica Logan?' He had a sudden thought. 'Unless he saw her with Cellini and put two and two together to make 46.'

She typed *think they had affair?*

'She was at his funeral, remember. Suggests an intimacy, doesn't it? But if they were, they'd have met discreetly at Cellini's apartment, surely, so how the hell would the manager have seen them together?'

Her fingers were tapping the keys again. 'You'll wear yourself out, Luc. Stop typing.'

another link somewhere got to find it for me and Tom

'For Tom? Jack looked at her in surprise as she typed another sentence.

wants 2 b proud of u

'I know he's embarrassed that I'm a chauffeur.'

get back 2 yr real job and solve case

Jack looked at her, knowing that she was right, but he couldn't go back *until* he'd solved the case and he didn't have enough evidence to prove anything. 'I'm going to tail Angelica

Logan tonight, Luc. Don't wait up for me.'

as if i would!

Jack smiled at her.

He'd been sitting, frozen outside the unlit Logan house for nearly two hours; no one had gone in or out during that time. He wondered what the hell he was doing, sitting in a freezing car in the dark, miles from home on the off-chance that he would see something that would help him solve Cellini's murder. He didn't know much about statistics but the odds were stacked sky high against him finding out anything tonight. He looked at his watch in the streetlight and thought he should push off home, even though he had no work in the morning. Mrs. M had given him time off for Christmas with full pay so long as he came to see her regularly with an update on what he had found. Jack smiled in the darkness. Mrs. M should have become a detective herself, instead of being an actress.

Just as he was about to start his car, the road was suddenly illuminated by a car's headlights. Jack ducked down as the lights swept over his car, then turned into the Logan drive and were extinguished.

Within seconds, Jack was out of his car and creeping up the Logan's S-shaped driveway, not noticing the moonlight illuminating the frosted scrubs and plants. He moved into the shadow of a beech tree and saw a black Lexus RX standing in front of the house with the car's interior light on. There was only one occupant in it. As Jack saw who it was, the breath punched out of his lungs. Stella! What the hell was a prostitute doing sitting outside the Logan house? He watched her, confused by her actions: her hands scrubbed her face with something Jack couldn't see. A pause, then suddenly her hand was on her hair –it came off! Jack drew in breath, realizing what was happening. Stella suddenly disappeared deep in the car and Jack stood on tiptoe in a vain attempt to see what she was doing. A dog barked in the distance and he jumped. The click of a car door. It opened and there in the moonlight stood a different woman: an elegant woman, wearing a dark coat. She walked towards the front door and a light came on. A stone slipped under Jack's foot and he held his breath as her head tilted towards him; ash-blonde hair shimmering like shot silk, translucent skin lit by an inner light. And from the shadows, Jack experienced the awe he felt when looking at a da Vinci Madonna: Stella had metamorphosed into the beautiful blonde at Saul's funeral.

CHAPTER 27

13th September 2011

Every night Angelica's sleep was punctured by Paolo's last words to her: *if only you didn't look so pure; if only you didn't look so pure...* The words echoed in her head as she tossed and turned in bed. After four weeks, the desire to see him was too strong; she found herself standing again outside his apartment waiting for him to open the door. Again, he opened it immediately as if he had been waiting for her knock for four weeks.

'Angelica – bella come un angelo,' was all he said as she walked past him into his lounge and sat down.

He sat down beside her and smiled at her. 'I have never waited so long for a woman before.'

'But I'm not just any woman.'

'I know that; that's why I waited.' He stared at her with the same intensity as he had on the first night they had met.

'What did you mean when I came last time?'

Paolo could have pretended he didn't understand her question, but he had been waiting for her to ask him for four weeks; he couldn't wait any longer.

'If you didn't look so pure, I would carry you into my bedroom and we would have enjoyed each other's bodies for hours and hours.' He lifted a finger to her face and traced its perfect outline. 'But I can't. I can't make love with a Madonna.'

Angelica felt her heart racing; she had never wanted a man so much before, but she didn't want to make love, she wanted sex and every part of her was determined to have this beautiful man.

'Where's your bathroom?' she asked.

Paolo looked at her in surprise. 'Through there.' He pointed to the bedroom she had entered earlier; the room with a secret vault in it.

'I'll be some time. I don't like to hurry.' Angelica walked towards it, knowing that his eyes were following her every movement.

Paolo's bathroom was as elegant as the rest of his apartment. Normally, Angelica would have feasted her eyes on the blue Italian tiles covering the walls and the colorful antique Oushak rug half-covering the marbled floor, but tonight, she was too aroused to notice the elegance; she wanted sex and she knew how to make Paolo as aroused as she was. She opened her bag and brought out her outfit and laid it out on the large chaise longue which stood near the bath. She took off her elegant dress and silk underwear and stood naked in front of the ornate Italian mirror over the enormous sink. The under-floor heating was perfect for nakedness. She took her theatrical make-up kit out of her bag and set to work on her transformation; anyone could make themselves look like a tart; but there was an art to looking like a high-class hooker and Angelica had perfected it. She applied dark foundation to her face which transformed her perfect porcelain skin to one of a dusky tone which suited her outfit. Then she concentrated on her eyes, outlining them with kohl to make them dramatic and applied black mascara to her blonde eyelashes. The finishing touch was the application of red glossy lipstick which always made her lips look wet and inviting. She looked at herself in the mirror and smiled; she was almost ready. She reached over for her tight red basque and put it on. Next she slid on her black fishnet stockings and attached them to the basque. Then she reached into her bag for her brassy blonde wig; her hair was too pure for the outfit. Only her red five-inch high-heeled shoes to put on and she was ready. The transformation had taken her a quarter of an hour. But Paolo was very special, Stella thought as she tottered out, longing to see his reaction.

Paolo was lying on the settee listening to Bach when she walked in. He shot upright in amazement. 'Come è possibile? Angelica?'

'Who's Angelica, love? I'm Stella. Yours for the night. Cut the music. It's all wrong for what we're gonna do.'

Paolo was lying naked on the bed with his hands and legs tied to the bed posts. His heart was racing and a light sheen of sweat covered the whole of his body as Stella massaged him; she always finished in his groin and his penis was so engorged with blood that he thought it might explode; he was quivering with sexual excitement and still she was making him wait; he didn't know whether it was pleasure or pain. It was the most exciting massage he'd ever had in his life, but he didn't know how much longer he could wait before coming.

'Please, please...' he kept whispering. Suddenly she started sliding her naked body up and down his body rhythmically.

Stella kept whispering. 'Hold on a little longer.'

He could hear someone moaning from a long way away and suddenly realized it was him. Then just as he thought his heart couldn't take any more she thrust her vagina down hard onto his penis. He screamed as he climaxed. He couldn't wait any longer.

She handed him some tissues like a pro and said, 'You'll get better at waiting, love. I promise.' And he had. They'd had sex three times with him tied up and each time she managed to delay his climax longer and longer as he rode wave after wave of ecstasy. Then he tied her up and licked her until she was screaming for him to enter her but he wouldn't. He kept her waiting and waiting as she writhed around the bed, until at last he thrust himself deep inside her and they climaxed noisily together; it was the most exciting sex Paolo had ever had and he'd had a lot. Eventually, after two hours, he was too exhausted to continue and fell into a deep sleep.

When he woke, she was gone. He stretched out on the bed and smiled; at last he had found his perfect partner.

Chapter 28

6th December 2012

Rico stood in a dark alleyway, hunched up in his heavy overcoat stamping his feet against the cold. He must have been insane becoming involved with drugs. He'd lived in fear from the moment Cellini had told him how much money he could make it if he helped him with one special assignment. The one assignment had become many. He should have told him to fuck off. But how could he? Cellini was his boss; he had numerous methods designed to make people's lives very difficult if they didn't agree with him. His religious parents would die of shame if they discovered what he was mixed up with and for the first time since he had left the Philippines, Rico was glad that they were a long way ago. They'd never know where his money came from and now his parents and sisters had clothes to wear and food to eat. If he had to rely on what Cellini paid him at the club, he'd have nothing left to send them each month. He felt tremendous guilt about what he was doing, but what man wouldn't help his family if they were hungry? So far, it hadn't been dangerous, but Rico knew it could become violent at any moment. He didn't like violence, although everyone told him he looked as if he was born to commit it. If only he could find a way to send money to his family without being involved with drugs, but it was impossible.

He pulled his collar up around his ears as an icy wind whipped through the alleyway and glanced at his watch; the luminous dials shone into the dark. 11 p.m. The man was late. Rico swore softly. Suddenly he saw his small squat shape hurrying towards him. He didn't even know his name.

'It's arrived. Pick it up from the gallery tomorrow morning Capote says and bring the stuff to the warehouse tomorrow night at 10 p.m.' He spoke fast as if words were in short supply.

'I work nights, remember? I can't leave the club early again. I don't finish work until 3 a.m.'

'Like I said. Capote expects you at 10 p.m. at the warehouse. And he don't like waiting. Remember that.' With that curt warning, the squat man weaved away without another word.

Rico wanted to run after him and scream at him. *Why should I take all the risks you fucking messenger boy?* But he did nothing; he stood watching the man's squat figure disappear around the corner. Rico hurried up the alley, anger spreading around his body at the hopelessness of his life. Then just as he reached the end of it he saw a large black car speeding down the crowded road. Rico watched in horror as a small boy ran from behind a coach across the road in front of the car. He wanted to shout a warning, but couldn't open his mouth. Everyone else seemed too busy to notice what was happening. Then just as Rico found the power of speech, the car smashed into the boy's body. Rico watched in slow motion as the car-driver's mouth opened in a silent scream. He waited for her to get out of her car and go to the boy, but she didn't move. At the back of his mind, Rico registered the first three letters of the registration – ACC – before time suddenly speeded up and her car shot off down the road before anyone else seemed aware of what had happened. Rico was shaken; he wanted to run over to help the boy, but how could he become involved? He couldn't be a witness. As a crowd of shocked passers-by suddenly gathered around the boy's body,

Rico hurried away from the horrific scene he had just witnessed, but he knew, even as he hurried away from it, he would never escape it; the memory would be replayed over and over in his head for years to come. He couldn't have done anything to protect the boy, but there was *something* he could do: find the bitch who'd hit him and blackmail her. Rico suddenly smiled; he had found a way out.

CHAPTER 29

19th December 2012

The next morning after Lucy's parents had taken Tom shopping to buy Christmas presents, Jack had told Lucy the incredible news about Angelica Logan. They had spent the morning on the computer in the study writing down all the information they had found, but even with two sharp brains on the case, neither of them could find a definite link between Cellini's affair and his death.

'Why would you want someone dead if you were having an affair with them, Luc?'

He watched her typing for some time then read

perhaps he was tired of her and blackmailing her too

'But why would he be tired of a beautiful woman who could transform herself into a sexy hooker? That's every man's fantasy,' Jack said without thinking; then cursed himself as her eyes filled with tears.

He was on his knees in front of her kissing her eyes. 'Not me, Luc. You're everything I've ever wanted in a woman.'

not now

Jack hugged her hard; why was life so appalling for her and so easy for other people? He couldn't make any sense of the world at all. His Lucy had been bright and bubbly and kind, so why her? Why his lovely girl? Jack wanted to scream.

She tapped on her lap-top. Jack leant back to see what she was typing.

self pity sorry what if he had something she wanted and wouldn't give it 2 her

'Christ, Luc. That's a bit of a long shot. It could be anything,' Jack said, then suddenly he had an image of Angelica Logan standing under an elder tree fingering a rosary. 'You could be right. They're both Catholics. What if Paolo Cellini had some religious icon Angelica Logan desperately wanted.'

enough 2 kill 4?

'I don't know. That's what I've got to find out.'

go 4 it jack!

'I will, Luc. I promise. When your parents come back with Tom, I'll go to see Mrs. M and try to get into Cellini's apartment.'

An hour later, Jack was driving through the heavy Christmas traffic towards Mrs. M's apartment trying to think what religious icon was so valuable that it might make a beautiful Catholic like Angelica Logan desperate enough to kill a lover. The problem was, although Jack loved art, his knowledge of religious icons wasn't specialized enough. Trying to find the answer would be like trying to find an unknown religious icon in a Catholic Cathedral. And even if he did find it, the only proof that would give him was Angelica Logan was a thief, not that she was a killer. It seemed hopeless.

Mrs. M sat on her large settee, stunned by Jack's news.

'Well, this is turning out to be a Christmas I'll never forgot. Paolo was having an affair with one of the most virginal women I've ever met and now you're telling me you think she killed him by changing his medication. You really think Angelica Logan capable of murder just to get a religious icon, Jack? It's unbelievable. She's such a lovely woman.'

'I don't know what she's capable of, Mrs. M. I've never met

her, but I've met a few charming killers in the past. History is littered with people being amazed by what people are capable of. And I don't know how important the religious icon was to her.'

'I'm having another Whisky Mac, Jack. Do you want one?'

'A small one, Mrs. M. Still got to drive home. I'll get them.' Jack got up and poured them some drinks while Mrs. M stared into the distance.

'I can't imagine anyone killing for a statue,' she said at last.

Jack turned to her, stunned. 'You must be clairvoyant, Mrs. M.'

'I've been called many things by many men, Jack, but never clairvoyant. What have I said?'

Jack gave her a large Whisky Mac and sat down. He couldn't talk to her about the drug smuggling that Jamila was working on. She was bound to mention it in passing with someone she met. 'You triggered an association of ideas in my head. They might be useful.'

'Don't clam up on me, Jack. I need a little excitement in my life.'

Jack smiled at her. 'I think you've had a life-time of excitement. You need to relax now.'

'Rubbish! I'll relax when I'm in my coffin and not before. You think that Paolo had a statue in his apartment that was vitally important to Angelica?'

'Yes. Have you still got the key to Cellini's apartment, Mrs. M?'

'Isn't that breaking and entering, Jack?'

Jack smiled at her. 'Not with a key it isn't.'

Mrs. M reached for her stick and got up. 'Come on, what are we waiting for?'

Five minutes later they were roaming around Cellini's apartment looking at all his religious icons.

They wandered around for some time. 'Do you know what I find odd, Jack?' Mrs. M said, as she studied the large triptych that Jack hated covering one wall. 'There are no images of Jesus at all. He obviously wasn't interested in him.'

'Do you remember what Paolo said the night a crate was delivered to him?'

'Well, it's fading fast but something about having bought something that God would have wanted if he had the money, then something in Italian.'

'Can you remember what? It could be important.'

Mrs. M sat down on one of Paolo's settees and closed her eyes, then put a finger over her mouth in a gesture to silence Jack as she thought.

At last she said. 'It was something like *La Regina Nera*. *Regina* is queen, isn't it?'

'And *Nera* means black. *The Black Queen*. You're brilliant, Mrs. M. Thank God for your memory.'

Mrs. M frowned at him. 'You mean you're looking for a chess piece?'

Jack stared at Mrs. M for such a long time that she said: 'Have I got something on my nose, Jack?'

'No, I'm thinking. Paolo collected religious icons so I think that *The Black Queen* must be another way of saying *The Black Madonna*.' Suddenly Jack's eyes shone with excitement. 'There's no Black Madonna here so if I can find it in Angelica Logan's house, I think we have the motive for killing Paolo Cellini. There's another reason why I need to find the statue but I can't tell you yet. It's linked to a big operation the Met are working on.'

'I won't tell a soul, Jack you can trust me.'

Jack smiled at her and shook his head. 'I can't, but there's something I'd like you to do, Mrs. M. It's important.' She looked excited until he continued: I'd like you to come with me to Angelica Logan's house and introduce me.'

The light died from Mrs. Montgomery's eyes. 'Oh dear... "Stir not murky waters if you know not the depth or the creatures that dwell beneath the surface."'

CHAPTER 30

8th December 2012

Angelica knelt before the Black Madonna knowing what she was asking her was impossible; she wanted forgiveness for all her sins and she had committed so many. Tears ran down her face. But as she looked up at the Madonna's face, she saw that she wanted to forgive her.

'Forgive me my sins, Holy Mary; forgive me the sins of my youth and the sins of my age, the sins of my soul and the sins of my body, my secret and my whispering sins, the sins I have done to please myself and the sins I have done to please others. Forgive those sins which I know, and the sins which I know not; forgive them, Holy Mary, forgive them all of Thy great goodness. Amen.'

Angelica had repeated the prayer many times before the front doorbell rang. She carried on praying; she couldn't be disturbed when she prayed. Someone started banging on the door; she continued praying. It went silent. Then suddenly there was a loud banging on the French doors in the dining room. She couldn't ignore it. She took out her mobile as she crept out of the prayer-room and peeped through the open doorway into the dining room; a small tough-looking Filipino man was standing in the garden holding up a large piece of paper to the glass.

Angelica was terrified; the man looked frightening, but she wanted to know what was written on the piece of paper he was holding. She held her mobile to her ear as she crept forward so that she could phone Mark at any minute. When the man saw her, he shook his head and gestured towards the piece of paper and mouthed important to her. Although her heart was racing in fear, she moved towards the French windows, thankful that they were triple-glazed and alarmed. He couldn't touch her in here. Then she read what he had written and groaned loudly. I SAW YOU HIT THE BOY. I WANT MONEY.

He gestured for her to open the French doors. Angelica gestured towards the front door; she wasn't going to let him in here; it was too close to her prayer-room and her shrine to the Holy Mother. She kept chanting her Hail Marys as she dragged herself towards the front door, thinking she might faint before she could open it. How could she cope with this situation? She opened the door with the heavy chain across it. There he stood, smiling coldly at her; she shuddered.

'Good afternoon, Mrs. Logan.' He studied her. 'A very clever disguise. The hooker and the housewife. Open the door please.'

Angelica undid the chain with shaking fingers. How did he know? Her mouth felt full of chalk; she couldn't swallow.

'You want to know how I found you?' The man laughed. The sound was appalling. 'You shouldn't have a customized car plate if you want to be anonymous, Mrs. Logan. I saw your car parked outside Mr. Cellini's art gallery one day and asked the manager who you were. At first, I thought the hooker must have stolen it, but then I realized Mr. Cellini liked games. I like games too, especially if I can't lose. I want £10,000 to keep quiet and I want it now.'

Angelica stared at him in horror and whispered. 'I don't keep large sums of money in the house.'

'How much have you got?' Rico said, giving her a friendly smile. 'I'll wait here until you get it.'

Angelica had to sit down on one of the hall chairs before she collapsed. 'Only about £50.'

'Then we'll go to your bank and you'll withdraw £10,000. If not, I'll go to the police. Isn't your husband's newspaper running a big campaign to catch the hit-and-run driver? Imagine his surprise when he realizes that he's been after his wife all along and she's having an affair with a playboy. You can imagine the headlines in all the papers, can't you?' Rico started to laugh as if he had made a joke.

Angelica held on the chair as the hall swayed around her. This couldn't be happening. Things like this didn't happen to people like her.

'Don't pretend you're ill, Mrs. Logan. It'll only annoy me. Now get your coat on. We're going for a drive.'

Angelica drove down Hampstead High Street on automatic pilot. She had enough money in the bank, but she knew he'd come back for more and there was nothing she could do about it. How could she stop Mark finding out? She stopped the car near the bank, put some money in the meter and walked on trembling legs into the bank.

Rico waited for her in the car; knowing he had a meal ticket for life. It was wonderful. Soon he wouldn't have to hide in an old basement anymore in case they found him. He could leave the country and disappear. No one knew where his family lived in the Philippines, but he still wasn't going home until he was certain the gang couldn't find him. He and Bianca could live together on an island somewhere remote and neither of them would ever have to work again if they didn't want to. He felt relaxed for the first time since he'd been involved with Cellini. It was a good feeling. Five minutes later Angelica Logan walked back towards him; she was certainly a beautiful woman, he thought, but too thin and icy for him; he liked warm women with meat on their bones. She got in the car and gave him a large envelope with a trembling hand.

'I won't check it, Mrs. Logan. I trust you. Now I'd be grateful if you could drive me back. So much nicer than going on a crowded tube. I hope that's okay with you.'

Angelica started the car without saying a word.

Rico sat back in the luxurious car and thought how incredible life was; two days ago he was in deep shit, now he had a good income for the rest of his life and he didn't have to work for it; he hadn't felt this happy for a long time.

CHAPTER 31

19th December 2012

Jack had been at the Blue Notes club for an hour, listening to Bianca sing; she was good. The atmosphere at the club had completely changed from his last visit; it was vibrant. Bianca seemed to be coping with Cellini's death much better, he thought, as she finished her number and smiled at the audience. Everyone clapped enthusiastically. He looked around for the manager, but there was no sign of him.

Suddenly, she was sitting at his table with a large drink in her hand, looking at him questioningly. 'So – what did you find out?'

'Stella is a Mara-Hari figure: a hooker and a woman called Angelica Logan.'

Bianca's glass smashed onto the floor. She didn't speak for a few moments. The mess was cleaned up within seconds. Jack wished that the Met was that efficient; desks had been littered with rubbish for days when he worked there. Pierre, the barman brought her another whisky.

Bianca smiled at him. 'Thanks, Pierre.'

She suddenly looked at Jack and started laughing. 'Jesus! Why didn't I see it at school?'

Jack frowned at her. 'What?'

'No one could believe that she was a nymphomaniac because

she looked like the Madonna.'

So that's why she liked transforming herself to have sex, Jack thought. 'I think she switched Paolo Cellini's heart tablets.'

Bianca's eyes opened wide and she went very still. 'Are you sure?'

'No, but I'm trying to prove it. Where's the manager?'

Bianca looked at him, puzzled by the change in conversation. 'He's ill. Not been in for days. Why?'

'I just wanted to ask him what he was doing in Angelica Logan's car a couple of days ago.'

Bianca's jaw dropped. 'Rico wouldn't go with that bitch!'

'I don't think he was having sex with her, I think he was blackmailing her about her affair with Cellini.'

Bianca suddenly smiled at him. 'Good. I hope he drains her for every million she's got.'

'Blackmail's illegal, Bianca.'

'So is murder. She deserves to suffer. She almost destroyed my life, Jack. I was expelled from the convent because she lied about me. My parents never recovered from the shame and died believing her lies. You know how bad that was?'

Jack suddenly understood why she had likened Angelica Logan to deadly nightshade. 'But you turned your life around. You're a great singer. What has she got compared to you now?'

Bianca smiled at him. 'So perhaps there is justice, after all, Jack.'

Jack looked away from her, thinking of Lucy. 'Not for everyone, there isn't.'

She leaned over and touched his hand. 'Sorry. That was a stupid thing to say.'

'How important do you think a statue of the Black Madonna would be to Angelica Logan?'

Bianca looked at him, startled. 'Very. We had a Black Madonna in our convent chapel. *La Regina Nera del Cielo.* The Black Queen of Heaven. The nuns thought Angelica was the most pious girl in the school. She was always praying to her.'

Jack smiled; another small piece of puzzle was slotting into place. 'Thanks, Bianca. That's very helpful. Sorry I can't stay for your second half. Another time.' He got up to leave.

'Don't forget, Jack. I'll be waiting.' She smiled up at him.

CHAPTER 32

20th December 2012

Jack was driving Lucy and Mrs. M down Hampstead High Street which was garlanded with Christmas lights. Lucy wanted to go so that she could see how good Angelica Logan was at lying. There was silence in the car, then Mrs. M burst into embarrassed conversation, but the moment Jack mentioned how much Lucy loved the theater, Mrs. M was in her element, regaling stories from her heady actress days. Jack glanced at Lucy; he could have sworn that he had seen her smile when Mrs. M told them about her first boyfriend who opened the wrong door in a fringe production and had brought the entire set down onto the actors. The worst thing about it, Mrs. M said, it was supposed to be a tragedy. Jack laughed. The newspapers wrote that it was the most amusing tragedy ever written. Lucy typed questions to her about all the actors she'd worked for and soon the car was buzzing with energy. They were all surprised when Jack turned into the Logan drive and stopped.

'Oh dear, I don't think I'm up to this, Jack.'

Jack turned around to her in surprise. This was the first time he had ever heard her sound nervous. 'Rubbish, Mrs. M, you've just been entertaining us with all those acting stories – how difficult is it to act the part of a woman who's suddenly been taken ill? Don't forget we have Lucy as back-up.' Jack smiled at his wife. 'Sorry, Luc. You know what I mean. I'll get Lucy's wheelchair and off we go.'

'She might not be in, Mrs. Bradley,' Mrs. M said, hopefully as Jack opened the boot.

Lucy typed *police watching house she's there*

'This sounds like a big operation,' Mrs. M said in excitement.

it is Lucy typed just before Jack opened the door and put her into her chair. 'Don't forget to call her Lucy, Mrs. M.'

'And don't forget I'm Margaret, Jack, not Mrs. M.' He smiled at her as they approached the front door.

They listened to the melodic chimes resonating through the house accompanied by the sound of Mrs. M's deep breathing to steady her nerves.

'Lean against me, Mrs.-Margaret,' Jack said quickly as the door opened and a very pale Angelica Logan looked at the trio in surprise.

'I'm so sorry to bother you, Angelica, but...' she groaned as if she couldn't continue.

'She needs water for her medication.' Jack looked at Angelica's worried face; she obviously didn't want them in her house, but she didn't know how to refuse them. She glanced down at Lucy and tried to disguise her shock.

'Of course. Come in. Do you need help?' she said to Lucy.

Lucy blinked at her twice. 'The wheelchair is motorized,' Jack said as he helped Mrs. M over the threshold. She was now so much in role that she was groaning loudly as if near death. Jack raised his eyebrows at her and she moderated her agony. Lucy followed them into the hallway, noticing every expensive item of furniture there; every antique chair and carpet.

'Can you manage to walk into the lounge, Margaret, while I get the water?' Angelica said as she hurried into the kitchen.

Mrs. M staggered into the lounge and collapsed into the nearest chair as Angelica hurried back with a glass of water.

Looking like a fish out of water, she gesticulated to Jack to get her tablets out of her bag. The room was full of tension as they watched him frantically get the tablets and give some to her. She swallowed them, gulped back the water gratefully, then closed her eyes to recover. Jack suppressed a smile; she must have been a good actress.

'We're sorry to disturb you, Mrs. Logan, but Margaret told me that you lived nearby before she felt ill.' He desperately hoped she wouldn't remember that she'd never given Mrs. M her address.

Mrs. M opened her eyes and smiled at Angelica. 'Thank you, my dear. I feel much better now. My heart isn't as strong as it was.'

They all studied Angelica's face to gauge her reaction to her words but her face was impassive. Jack suddenly realized that Angelica Logan was as good an actress as Mrs. M.

'I'm glad you're feeling better, Margaret. I'm awfully sorry but I'm going out in a minute so I'll have to ask you to leave.' She looked at them apologetically.

Jack thought fast. 'I wonder if my wife could use your toilet facilities before we go. It's always a difficulty when we go out.' He smiled at her.

Angelica was taken aback; it was impossible to refuse such a request.

'Of course, I'll show you where it is.' She stood up to lead the way out. Lucy glided towards her in her wheelchair, glancing at Jack as she did. 'I need to help her, Mrs. Logan.'

They went out into the hall and followed Angelica down it. There were numerous doors leading off the hall. Angelica opened one of them and showed them into an enormous room with a toilet, bidet, large sink and a luxurious shower at the far end; it was four times the size of their downstairs toilet at home.

'We're sorry to stop you going out, Mrs. Logan, but it's always difficult for my wife when we go out. It always takes some time,

I'm afraid.'

'Oh, don't worry. I'll go back and have a chat with Margaret.'

Jack took Lucy's catheter from the side of the chair and flushed its contents down the toilet. Such intimacies no longer embarrassed either of them; Jack had been doing such things for two years.

'I'm going to have a quick recce, Luc.'

She blinked at him as he opened the door and crept out. Jack's heart thumped hard against his rib cage as he looked around the hall; Angelica Logan could come into it at any moment and ask him what the hell he was doing. He opened a door and saw a large dining-room with two large French doors leading into the garden; there was nothing to interest him here. He closed the door quickly and opened the one next to it and gasped. In front of him was a Catholic prayer-room. A large dais stood in the center of the room and sitting on it was a two-foot-high Black Madonna with golden robes. Jack looked at the statue intently; the figure was pregnant.

So this was the statute that must have been delivered to Paolo Cellini the night he died. Here was the motive he'd been looking for; a statue that might be full of drugs. Jack put a hand up to his chest to steady his racing heart, closed the door quickly and hurried back into the toilet where Lucy was waiting for him.

'It's there, Luc. It's there. Let's get out.' Jack felt like shouting.

They went back into the lounge where Mrs. M was regaling Angelica Logan with the same anecdotes she had told to Jack and Lucy in the car; but Angelica's eyes were darting around the room nervously. She jumped up when she saw them and said, 'I'm sorry, you must go – I'm incredibly late.'

Mrs. M and Jack thanked her profusely as she ushered them out of the house. Jack got Lucy into the car without saying a word until he was out of the drive and around the corner.

'The Black Madonna's in her house!'

Mrs. M gasped. 'My God – does that mean Angelica killed

Paolo to get it?'

'I rather think it does, Mrs. M.'

'It's unbelievable,' she answered.

Jack glanced at Lucy who was typing and read: *almost cracked it jack*

'What do you mean – almost! It's a bloody coup, Luc!' The adrenaline surged through his body; he felt he could fly, then he realized that she was right, before he could go to the Met with his discoveries he had to get some more evidence so that his son could be proud of him again.

CHAPTER 33

20th December 2012

Angelica had carried on with her charity work as if nothing had happened; as if the bottom of her world hadn't disappeared underneath her. She was good at acting; she'd been doing it all her life. Mark didn't notice anything wrong, except to say that she was looking a little pale and perhaps they should go on holiday. How could she go on holiday with this appalling man blackmailing her? Each night her dreams were full of Mark's horror on discovering that the woman whom he thought perfect was as flawed as a large carbon spot deep within a diamond. His perfect wife was not only a whore, but a child-killer. Mark had told her that the Albanian boy had died and when she had cried, he'd said that she was the most compassionate, beautiful woman he had ever met.

She was kneeling in front of her Madonna who could, perhaps, save her from the eternal fires of everlasting damnation. The front-door bell broke into her prayers repeatedly. 'Please Holy Mary, don't let it be him.' She prayed fervently, but the ringing persisted and she knew that it was. She got up from her knees, trying to control her shaking and walked to the door. The ringing would continue if she didn't answer it. She opened it slowly, trying to delay the moment when she would have to see him again.

'Good evening, Mrs. Logan. I was just passing and I thought I'd drop in.' He walked into the hall without waiting for an invitation.

Angelica closed the door. 'I gave you £10,000 a couple of weeks ago. You can't expect any more.'

He looked at her in mock surprise. 'I'm afraid that's exactly what I expect, Mrs. Logan. I'm sure your husband will have told you that the boy you hit has died; that makes it rather more difficult for you now, doesn't it? Your husband wrote in his newspaper that he was determined to get a conviction for manslaughter once he discovered who was responsible. Do you want me to tell him?'

Angelica suddenly felt incredibly cold. This man had the power to destroy her life and he was enjoying the power. 'I didn't see the boy. Please believe me. I love children. It's haunted me every night since it happened.'

'You were driving too fast, Mrs. Logan and if you love children as much as you say, why didn't you stop? Only a monster drives off after hitting a child. Where I come from, children are cherished, not killed.'

'I didn't mean to kill him!' Angelica could hear herself shouting. She never shouted but she couldn't seem to stop. 'I didn't see him! I didn't see him! I didn't see him!'

Rico hit her across her face and she slumped onto the carpet. 'Don't shout at me, Mrs. Logan. I don't like it. I'm trying to be reasonable. Now here's a solution to the problem that would benefit us both.' He looked down at her, slumped on the carpet. He hated weak women. His Bianca would have hit him back, but then, he would never have hit her. 'You give me a million pounds and I disappear from your life forever.'

She looked up at him in astonishment and wiped a small line of blood off her chin. 'A million pounds! Where am I going to find a million pounds?'

Rico's body tightened. He really hated rich people who pretended they weren't. He started towards her prayer-room. Angelica jumped up as if she had been struck by lightning. 'That's private! Don't go in there!'

What more invitation could I want? Rico thought as he walked into the room and stopped dead. Standing on a small dais was the statue he had been looking for since Cellini died – the Black Madonna.

'Where did you get the Madonna from?' he shouted as hurried towards the statue and lifted her off the dais, desecrating Angelica's room. She was appalled.

'How dare you go in there!' She ran in after him. 'This is my private space!'

Rico turned to look at her; his face like granite. 'I don't take orders from women like you. Where did you get it?' He shouted in her face and Angelica was a jelly; she couldn't speak. 'You stole it from Cellini's apartment, didn't you? What a bitch! Not satisfied with being a whore and a murderess, you're also a thief!' Rico suddenly smashed the statue onto the parquet floor, expecting to see bags of cocaine inside it; there was nothing. He was stunned.

Angelica's screams bounced off the walls. He had destroyed the one person who could have saved her. She ran over to her shrine and picked up one of her antique silver candlesticks and smashed it down on his head. He collapsed onto her Persian rug, blood pouring from the wound in his head.

'Are you insane?' she screamed at him. 'You've killed my Madonna! You've killed my Madonna!' She collapsed onto the rug, sobbing as she gathered up pieces of her precious statue; she knew now that there would no redemption for her; she was damned for all eternity. She sat holding pieces of the Madonna for a long time while the man's blood spread over the rug. She suddenly looked up at the clock. Mark would be coming home in an hour, she must tidy up. She stood up, thinking what to do.

Dispose of the body, but how? She looked down at it for some time; then the solution came to her. She knelt down and rolled the rug around the body. She had to get it out of the house but she wasn't strong and although the man wasn't tall, he was stocky; she'd need all her strength and courage. Just as she bent down to lift the end of the rug, she heard the front door open and Mark called out 'Angel.' For a second, she froze, then ran across the room, opened the door and closed it before he could come in.

'Your face looks flushed, what have you been up to?' Mark said as she rushed into the hall. He came up to kiss her.

'A few exercises. Thought I should keep fit.'

He pushed a strand of hair behind her ears. 'In your prayer-room? Funny place to do exercises.'

Angelica held herself together tightly so she wouldn't start screaming. 'Lots of floor space. You're home early.' Was her voice normal?

'Forgot my memory stick. Really sorry, darling, but I've got to go back into work. We've had a tip-off about a huge amount of cocaine being shipped into the UK. It's a big story. I might be working on it for hours. Hate to come back and leave you so quickly. Will you forgive me?'

Angelica kissed him lightly. Perhaps the Madonna *was* still helping her. 'Of course I will. Your work's important.' It took every ounce of her strength for her to be able to smile at him normally. 'Go on. I'll wait up for you.'

Mark stared at her in amazement. 'I can't believe I'm so lucky. Night, darling. I'll be home as soon as I can.'

Then he was out of the door and Angelica slid down one of the walls; the effort of standing was suddenly too much. She didn't want to go back into her prayer-room; she wanted to sit here and have her life back again, but she couldn't. She stood up and stumbled back into the desecrated room. The rolled rug looked innocuous lying on the floor; the blood stains were invisible from the outside. She went to get some gloves from one of the kitchen drawers, then walked back into the prayer-room and started pulling the rug with the body on it towards the door. It was a lead weight. Half-an-hour later, she had only pulled it halfway across the room. She sat on a chair and breathed deeply. She had to find the strength to get the body into the car. She had to! Her Lexus was parked outside the kitchen; she started dragging the body again. It took her another half-an-hour to reach the kitchen door. She sat down at the kitchen table to rest and thought how she could lift him into the car. The boot was high. It was impossible! Then she remembered Mark's hydraulic loading ramp in the garage and ran to get it. It scraped noisily along the concrete garage door as she pulled it. Thank God their garden was large enough to muffle the noise so the neighbors couldn't hear. At last, she managed to drag it into place below the car boot; then stopped, panting with the exertion. She staggered back into the kitchen and dragged the body towards the ramp. It felt heavier now. Then she realized with horror that she'd forgotten to check the man's pockets to see if he was carrying anything that would incriminate her. Groaning, she unrolled the carpet and shuddered as she saw the man's bloody face again. She knelt down beside the body, taking small breaths to stop herself from fainting as the smell of blood reached her nose. Her hand shook as she searched into his left pocket. It was empty. She was so close to the body she could smell its sweat. It was rancid. She clamped her hand across her face to stop herself from gagging. How would she find the strength to continue without the Madonna's help? She stood up shakily, glanced at the kitchen clock and groaned again. She had taken over an hour. Mark could come back at any moment and discover her leaning over a bloody corpse and her marriage would die. She moved over to the other side of the body. She couldn't possibly lean over it to reach the other pocket for how could she look into the eyes of a man she had just killed? She closed her eyes and felt around the outside of his pocket with trembling fingers until she found the top and slipped her hand inside it; all the time willing her body to obey her. Her fingers touched a bundle of papers. She took them out and opened her eyes. In front of her was a small crumpled photo of a dark-haired woman, a receipt from a dry-cleaners and a parking ticket. Small traces of a small life, she thought. She stood up and willed herself to walk in a straight line towards the study and put the evidence into the paper-shredding machine. It gobbled it up greedily. She returned to the kitchen, feeling much stronger; the man was now anonymous. She rolled him up again and lifted the end of rug and dragged it out of the kitchen towards the Lexus. It took her another half-an-hour, but at last she got it onto the ramp and pressed the button; the ramp silently lifted the body up to the boot. She released the button and it stopped, level with the boot. The body rolled into the boot as she pushed against it hard. Suddenly, an arm fell out and Angelica leant against the car, feeling sick. She breathed deeply to stop the nausea. *I've done it*, she kept telling herself! *I've done it!*

Quarry Road was unmade so Angelica was thankful she was driving her Lexus as the car bumped over the pot-holes. Her headlights picked out all the posters of the new lake and gardens they were building on the site. She wasn't interested in either, except in the knowledge that after Christmas the quarry was going to be flooded and then no one would ever find the body. And even if they did find it before the flooding, nothing would connect it to her. But first she had to get it out of the car, unseen. Fortunately, all work had stopped for Christmas, so the road was completely empty. She moved two of the barricades around the site and drove as near to the edge of the quarry as she dared and cut the engine. Thank God Mark had bought a ramp last year when he wanted to transport his motorbike. She got out of the car with a torch in her hand, but dropped it in alarm as a sudden flash of lightning streaked across the sky. She picked it up, then realized it was impossible to hold the torch and move the body at the same time. She couldn't put the headlights on in case someone came up the road. She jerked as she heard a sudden rumble in the distance. *Holy Mary Mother of God, don't let a lorry come down here please,* Angelica prayed, before realizing that the rumble was thunder. She opened the boot quickly, angled the torch inside it and got the ramp out. It only took a moment to get it level to the base of the boot, but it seemed an eternity to her. She steeled herself to reach into the boot to pull out the carpet, praying that another part of the body wouldn't be exposed; it wasn't. She tied some cord she had brought around the rug so it would stay in position; then wheeled the ramp over to the edge of the quarry. It was difficult seeing what she was doing as the torch light was directed into the boot, but there was a full moon so she could see the outline of the quarry disappearing into nothingness. She tilted the ramp until the body started sliding down it, then suddenly it was gone and she was sitting on the ground, shaking. Now Mark would never discover what she had done. She was safe.

Chapter 34

22nd December 2012

Everyone was eating breakfast in the kitchen, except Tom who was, as usual, drawing another picture for Lucy. Jack felt happier than he had for a long time as he looked at Tom who was unaware that his parents and grandparents were watching him with so much love; he was completely focused on his drawing. He had a natural talent, Jack thought.

He smiled at Lucy as Mary fed her, Jack knew Lucy hated being dependent on them, but there was nothing they could do about that. Lucy's parents were still in denial about their daughter's illness. They often spoke about them all having holidays together when Tom was older. He could never tell them of Lucy's wishes because they would never have believed him.

As usual, when Jack's thoughts turned pessimistic, he sought external stimuli; he reached for a newspaper and suddenly found he couldn't breathe.

Yesterday afternoon a body was discovered in the Overlands Quarry half-covered by an expensive Persian rug. Mr Dick Pearson, a foreman at the site, had gone back to get some equipment that had been inadvertently left there. When he glanced down the quarry, he saw a rug caught on one of the ledges that had been cut into the sides of the quarry for access purposes. He was extremely shocked to see a leg hanging outside of it and rang 999 immediately. Within ten minutes the police and ambulance services had arrived on the scene. The man, who comes from the Philippines, was winched up the quarry and taken to hospital where it was discovered that he was still alive, but in a critical condition. Unfortunately, there was nothing in his pockets to identity him. The police are now searching the area for evidence. A police spokesman said that they have found a number of tire marks around one section of the quarry which have been photographed and will be analyzed by a team of forensic experts. If anyone knows of a missing Filipino man or has some information concerning this incident please call 101.

Jack looked across at Lucy; no one apart from her could tell that he was excited about something; years of keeping his face impassive in front of criminals, judges and juries had made him a master of disguise. Lucy typed something to her mother, then pressed a button on her motorized wheelchair and moved beside him. He held up the article for her to read; her eyes blinked fast; her signal that she was excited.

'I think it's the manager of the club, Luc.'

lets go into study she typed.

'We've just got to check something on the computer, folks. Back soon,' Jack said casually.

Mary and Colin smiled at him. Since they'd been staying with them, they had come to realize how close their daughter and son-in-law were and their animosity had disappeared.

The moment Jack and Lucy were in the study, Jack logged onto the computer and studied everything he'd written down about the case.

'My God, Luc. It's incredible. The mind boggles.'

need to tell the met

'Oh, no. Alan will take the case over and it's all ours. I'll ask Jamila to come here and we can talk to her.'

When Jack had phoned Jamila and told her that he'd discovered a link to Cellini's death, the missing drugs and Angelica Logan, she was in their house within an hour with some photos from the quarry crime-scene.

After she'd made polite conversation with Lucy's parents and praised Tom's drawings, Jack told them that they had something to discuss with Jamila in the study. Jack saw Tom looking at him curiously; he knew Jamila would never have come to the house during the day unless it was urgent. *It's the first time he's been interested in what I'm doing since I left the Met*, Jack thought.

'You need to get a search warrant and impound the stolen statue, Jamila. I think it's full of drugs,' Jack told her once he'd shut the study door.

Jamila shook her head in disbelief. 'I can't get my head round all this, Jack. You're telling me that Logan's wife – *the perfect wife* – was not only a hooker and a thief, but a woman who tried to kill two men and was mixed up with drugs! It's like the plot from a bad Dan Brown novel!'

'Wouldn't know,' Jack said. 'Never read any. I don't know if she was involved with the drugs, but she's certainly implicated in everything else. Can you show us the photos from the quarry?'

Jamila took out a number of photos from the small case she always carried with her and gave them to Jack. He sat down next to Lucy and they studied the tire marks around the quarry.

bet they come from Lexus RX Lucy typed.

'How do you know?' Jamila asked her in surprise.

look like them & logan has one

'I wish you could do the analysis for us, Lucy.' Jamila suddenly looked embarrassed as she realized what she'd asked.

'She could, if you bring a copy of the photos here,' Jack said.

Jamila looked at Lucy typing as Jack moved onto the other photos.

haven't got right software get dan simmons onto it

'Okay, Lucy.' Jamila smiled at her.

Jack was studying the photos of Federico Batas' unconscious

body; half rolled up in a Persian rug and gasped.

'My God – the last time I saw that rug it was lying on the floor of Angelica Logan's prayer-room,' he said excitedly. 'We've got two pieces of vital evidence here! Get that search warrant, Jamila.'

Jamila's face flushed as she looked at him. 'I can't do it without Alan's authorization, Jack. He *is* my boss.'

Jack and Lucy stared at each other; both knowing what the other was thinking.

'And you know what Alan will do, don't you?'

Jamila was worried. She was putting her career on the line for Jack; she had always followed the correct procedures at the Met, even when Jack deviated from them, but he'd been her boss then so it had been his responsibility if something went wrong. But he wasn't now; the responsibility was all hers if she didn't inform Alan. She didn't know what to do.

'Please, Jamila.' Jack was surprised to hear himself almost pleading with her. 'Once you've got a tire match to her car and the statue, we'll have enough evidence to go to the chief super. If you go to Alan now, you'll be off the case and all the credit will be his. Is that what you want?'

Jack and Lucy stared at her.

Chapter 35

22nd December 2012

Mark sat in his office reading Hal's headlines. BLUDGEONED BODY FOUND IN QUARRY. The headline was emotive; in fact, the whole article was emotive; it was designed to make people worry about the violence in the UK and the incompetence of the Metropolitan Police. *Two weeks ago, a young Albanian boy was left in a pool of blood to die in the street,* he'd written, *now another anonymous monster has bludgeoned a Filipino man half to death before throwing him into a quarry. And what have the police discovered? Nothing about the hit-and-run driver who is still free to kill other innocent people and the only pathetic evidence they have discovered about The Man In The Quarry Case are a few tire tracks. This level of incompetence equals the incompetence shown by the Met last year,* he continued, *when the mother of the hit-and-run victim burned to death in a bungled raid.*

There was a sharp knock on the door, but before Mark could say enter, Hal stood there beaming at him. 'What do you think of my article? Punchy enough?'

'It's punchy all right,' Mark murmured, wondering why he'd settled for being the editor of a tabloid, instead of a broadsheet.

'You've got to go with the mood of the public, Mark. People are angry about two crimes being committed just before

Christmas, especially as a twelve-year-boy died.'

Mark thought how ironic Hal was repeating something he'd told him the previous week when people had lost interest in the hit-and-run. Now suddenly, because of another crime, everyone was angry about violence. The fickleness of readers, Mark thought.

'They must have found out more about the quarry incident than just tire tracks,' Mark said.

'Not when we went to press last night. Want me to dig up some dirt?'

'Facts would be fine, Hal. Try to stick to the facts. Go to the hospital and be charming with the nurses and ask about the Filipino's condition. One of them might mention something that would give us a lead. But be discreet, you won't be popular with the police and they'll be at the hospital.'

'You can rely on me, Mark,' Hal smiled at him. 'I've got a way with women.'

Mark looked up at him and suddenly realized that he wasn't going to send him. Hal could write good stories, but it really wasn't anything to do with Hal and he certainly didn't have "a way with women". 'I think I'll go myself. You can work with Peter on the future of eugenics. Scientists are predicting that within five years people will be paying to have access to a prospective long-term partner's genetic code. Think of the implications, Hal. It's going to be a big story.'

Hal looked excited as he plodded out of the room. He hadn't even noticed that Mark had pulled him off a story he was only just getting his teeth into.

Mark parked his car in Whitechapel Street and got out, wondering why he hadn't sent Hal; he wasn't subtle, but he was a good reporter. The fact was, he couldn't concentrate at the office and needed to get out. As he turned into East Mount Street he thought about Angelica; there was something wrong with her, but he didn't know what. Perhaps it was all linked with her not becoming pregnant. They'd have to go to the doctor again soon and find out what the problem was, Mark thought as he walked in the A & E department of the Royal London Hospital.

A woman at reception told him where the trauma center was. When Mark got there, he saw a policeman standing outside a windowed room; he knew he'd tell him to leave once he found out who he was. Mark strolled down the corridor as if looking for someone and saw a nurse checking Batas' drip and an exhausted-looking dark-haired woman sitting beside him. Mark strolled on towards a vending machine and decided to wait until the nurse came out. He waited a long time, then saw another nurse approaching the room and walk in. Soon the first nurse came out and walked towards him. Now was his chance. 'I wonder if you've got any change for the machine,' he said disingenuously, giving her a broad smile.

She searched in her pockets and looked at him apologetically. 'Sorry, excuse me.' She hurried off down the corridor.

Mark swore silently; he was obviously losing his touch. He wondered if there'd be any point in waiting. Most probably all the nurses would be too busy to talk to him. Then just as he was about to leave the dark-haired woman came out of the room and headed for the vending machine. Mark searched his pockets for money as she approached him.

'You go first,' he said, smiling at her. She didn't look at him; there were dark shadows smudging her eyes. For the first time Mark felt his presence was a terrible intrusion on people's private grief.

'I'm sorry about your boyfriend.'

She shot him a look. 'What?'

'I couldn't help noticing you coming out of that man's room; the one who was dumped in the quarry. You must be so angry.'

Her eyes flashed at him. 'Angry! I could kill her!'

Mark felt a shock jolt his body. 'You don't think a woman

would do such an appalling thing.'

'This woman is capable of anything!' she shouted, her hands shaking so much that she couldn't get her coins into the machine.

'Let me,' Mark said, taking the money off her and putting it into the slot.

She punched a button for coffee.

'How do you know?'

'Because I went to a convent school in Italy with her, that's why!' she shouted again. 'She's a whore who looks like the Virgin Mary! Now leave me alone!' Her eyes flooded with tears as she ran off down the corridor without her coffee.

Mark leaned against the vending machine and couldn't move.

He was an automaton as he drove home; he couldn't see the scenery or feel any sensation; he felt as if he had closed down. He hardly remembered getting out of the car and walking into the house. He put his keys down somewhere and wondered if the house was the same as it always was. He didn't know. He went into Angelica's prayer-room and was stunned to see that the Black Madonna had gone, along with the beautiful Persian rug she had bought at Sotheby's.

'Angelica!' he called, feeling a heavy weight pressing down on his chest. 'Where are you?' The house was silent; he felt suddenly afraid and ran from room to room, looking for her. She was sitting on the bed in their bedroom completely still, staring at the wall. Every fear Mark had ever had was confirmed by her expression; she looked as if she wasn't there.

'Angel. What's the matter?' She didn't respond to his voice or even seem to notice he was there, as if she had suddenly gone deaf and blind. He leaned down in front of her and marveled at her face for the millionth time; it was impossible for her to have done anything wrong. 'What's the matter? Speak to me.' He touched her face gently and she suddenly came to life.

'I'm lost, Marky. Completely lost. There's no hope for me now she's gone. I'm going to suffer the torments of everlasting damnation.'

Mark felt his eyes stinging. 'What are you talking about?'

She suddenly looked bewildered by his lack of understanding. 'She was the only one who could save me and she's gone.'

Mark wanted to shake her. She was talking about a meaningless idol. 'You don't need a statue, Angel. You'll be all right with me. You don't need it.'

She looked at him as if she had just seen him for the first time. 'No, I won't. He smashed my Madonna into pieces along with my soul.'

Mark tried to control his sob in his voice, 'Angel, we've got to get you to a doctor.'

'Oh, Marky. How can a doctor redeem me after all the things I've done. You don't know me at all.'

Mark's leg muscles suddenly gave way and he collapsed onto the carpet. It couldn't be true. It couldn't be true.

'He was only a baby, you see. I was a wicked child. My mother told me I was wicked even before he was born.'

'I don't understand what you're talking about.' He felt as if his world was disintegrating.

Angelica smiled at him. 'Didn't I tell you I had a brother once upon a time? A tiny brother, but the moment I saw him, I knew I would lose my parents' love so... I had to give him away.'

'What?' Mark stared at her in horror.

'I was eight years old and the four of us were on holiday.'

Angelica stared up through the shade of the large olive tree they were resting under. A gigantic knot in the gnarled olive trunk looked like the face of an old man. She watched large red-headed ants worrying around his face. The sun flickered through the leaves; it was too hot to be out. They should be back in the cool of their house, she thought. She liked her room. It was white. Her parents were asleep near her baby brother's Moses basket; he was

LINDA M. JAMES

never far from them now. Once it had been her who was close to them. She stood up quietly and watched them sleeping; her parents were so beautiful; her father so tanned and dark; her mother so blonde and fair. They were lying on a rug and her mother's head rested on her father's lap. Everyone said Angelica would grow up to be as beautiful as her mother, but she didn't think she would because her mother didn't think she would. She looked at the small shape in the basket; so precious to her parents and so hateful to her. Why should her life be ruined by such a tiny creature?

She picked up the basket and walked away from her parents. She had been waiting for this moment for a long time. She hurried through the olive grove with her baby brother and felt happy for the first time since he'd been born; soon she would be the most important person in her parents' lives again.

It was an exhausting walk to the convent and she was very tired by the time she arrived, but the Madonna was waiting for her. She was standing on an altar above a small hatch in the convent wall and staring down at her with love. Angelica knew that the church helped people with problems. She took off her brother's clothes gently so as not to wake him and opened a small hatch in the convent wall. There was a room behind it with a baby's crib waiting for him. Angelica placed her baby brother tenderly in a crib. She had a surprise for him; she wasn't going to leave him with nothing. She had saved up her pocket money to buy him a new present; a beautiful blue rattle with a silver band around it which she had hidden since she had bought it. It was her parting gift to him. She rang the bell, closed the small hatch quickly and raced back with her brother's cradle and clothes through the olive grove to her parents. What if they'd woken up – what would she tell them? Her heart pounded as she saw the large gnarled olive tree where they'd all had lunch and rested. But the terror subsided as she saw her parents lying in the same positions, fast asleep. Angelica smiled, knowing the Madonna

181

had helped her. Placing the cradle exactly where it had been, she lay down near her mother, utterly exhausted. At last, she was where she belonged. She fell into a deep sleep.

CHAPTER 36

23rd December 2012

It was dark by the time Jamila could get a warrant to search the Logan house. She had taken two PCs with her. They were all taken aback by Mark Logan's violent response when he saw the warrant. His wife was ill in bed, he screamed at them. How dare they enter his house with some cock-and-bull story about a Black Madonna and a Persian rug! They'd never owned either. He wrote down their names before they searched the house, accompanied by Logan telling each one of them exactly how he was going to run a big campaign in his newspaper on police harassment and cite their names. Is that what they wanted after all the bad press they'd had recently? The publicity certainly wouldn't help any of their careers, would it? They were intimidated by his threats, but Jamila knew that Jack wouldn't have put her in this position unless he was sure of a conviction. She had to prove him right and put pressure on Mark Logan. Mark Logan was glaring at Jamila as they all stood in the hallway.

'You want to know how we discovered that you own the items we're looking for, sir. One of my colleagues saw them in the prayer-room over there a couple of days ago,' Jamila continued.

'That's not possible,' Mark snapped. 'We don't know any

policemen. Did he break in?'

'No, sir, your wife invited him. One of your wife's friends was taken ill near your house and they came in to get her a glass of water. The door to the prayer-room was open. My colleague saw both items clearly. And before you repeat that you've never owned such items, sir, remember we can check. The purchase of an expensive Persian rug would be easy to trace, especially as your wife's friend told us that Mrs. Logan often buys expensive items from Sotheby's. We also know that your wife has been having an affair with Paolo Cellini for a year and the man found in the quarry was blackmailing her, sir.' Jamila thought Jack would have been proud of her. Mark Logan looked as if she'd struck him across the face with a heavy weapon, but Jamila remained objective; she was only doing her job. 'We're collating all the evidence at the moment, sir, so please don't go anywhere.'

Suddenly, all the composure on Mark Logan's face dissipated; he collapsed onto a chair, looking utterly bereft and covered his face with his hands. At that moment, Jamila felt sorry for him; he obviously didn't know anything about his wife's real life at all.

But as they were driving back to the Met, she realized that without the statue they were still no further forward in cracking the drug smuggling. She couldn't understand how they could get through all the checks they were doing at the docks and airports. She dreaded seeing Alan; he wanted a result.

CHAPTER 37

23rd December 2012

Every day, Bianca felt as if she was in shock; the man she loved was dead and her best friend soon could be; she had been going to the hospital every day since she'd heard Rico had been found in a quarry, half dead. Every day, she wondered why her life was so traumatic. She sat beside Rico for hours waiting for him to open his eyes. The doctors had told her to talk to him, but she knew what he liked most; her singing, so every day the staff at the hospital had had a free jazz concert as Bianca had poured out her heart and soul to make him recover. She'd been doing it for days and he hadn't responded at all; she was obviously singing to a man who couldn't hear her. She had just finished singing one of his favourite numbers: Magic Sam's *All Your Love*. She'd had an appreciative audience outside the window, but not inside; there was still no response from Rico.

She leaned her head against his in despair. 'Hey, Rico, come on, this is your favourite song. *Oh your love, pretty baby, I have in store for you, you know I love you baby, I hope you love me too.*' Bianca whispered the lyrics into his ear. Suddenly she felt his arm twitch and she shot up; his eyelids flickered! 'That's it, Rico. Come on, come back to me!' He slowly opened his eyes and looked at her. Bianca sobbed. 'I thought you were going to leave me alone,

Rico.'

'No way,' he croaked through parched lips.

Bianca pressed the alarm button and suddenly the room was swarming with medical staff. 'He's come back to me,' she kept saying over and over again.

An hour later, Jack was striding down the corridor towards Batas' room. He stopped as he saw all the hospital staff going in and out of the room; something had happened. A nurse was hurrying up the corridor towards him.

'Is he okay?'

She kept walking but turned back to look at him; Jack knew she was trying to work out if he was from the press. 'I can't speak about patients to strangers. Excuse me.' She hurried on. Jack followed her.

'I'm a family friend. I know Rico.' Jack was beginning to find lies easy to find.

The nurse stopped walking and looked at him skeptically. 'Then you'll know his girlfriend.'

'Bianca,' he said, without missing a beat. 'Is she okay? I've been worried about her.'

The nurse smiled at him. He'd obviously passed the test. 'Mr. Batas is a lucky man. She's been singing to him every day and he regained consciousness earlier today. You can speak with her, but you won't be allowed in to see him yet. No one is except her.'

'Thanks,' Jack said before hurrying back to Batas' room. He stood outside the window, watching two doctors running some tests on him while Bianca sat beside him, holding his hand. Jack didn't know if Batas qualified as being lucky after being smashed on the head and thrown into a quarry, but perhaps he was; he was still alive and Bianca was obviously a good friend. Jack suddenly realized what was missing: a policeman outside his room. He was just about to ring Jamila to tell her when Bianca looked up and smiled at him. She struggled to get on her feet and walked towards him.

'What are you doing here, Jack?' Bianca's eyes were heavy from lack of sleep.

'Hoping your friend would give me some information that would help us convict Angelica Logan. How about this? She was the driver who killed that kid two weeks ago.'

She gave him a small smile. 'I'll get it for you when Rico's feeling better. I want the bitch locked up for life for what she did to Rico. Will you do something for me, Jack?'

'Anything I can, but you should go home and sleep. You look shattered.'

'I am. I want you to keep the press off his back. They'll be swarming over him like maggots once they discover he's regained consciousness. There used to be a policeman outside his room, but he left before Rico became conscious. I think they thought he was going to die.'

'I'll ring a colleague then I'm driving you home.'

Bianca was swaying with exhaustion. Jack rushed to get her a seat from further up the corridor and pushed her onto to it.

'Rico was mixed up with something nasty. You've got to help us, Jack. The last time I saw him he was terrified.'

Jack's nerves tingled. 'Why?'

'Some guys wanted a statue and Rico couldn't find it. Told me I'd find him with his throat cut in an alleyway if he didn't. I didn't believe him then.' She leaned her head against the hospital wall and closed her eyes.

Jack's heart was racing. Rico was involved with the drug smuggling. While Bianca rested, Jack phoned Jamila and told her that Batas was conscious and needed protection. He wanted to tell her about what Bianca had told him but he needed to check Cellini's apartment first.

He touched Bianca's shoulder and she opened her eyes. 'I'm taking you home, Bianca. You'd better tell the staff.'

Bianca slept all the way to her flat as Jack drove through the dark streets; his brain in overload. The Black Madonna was as popular as the Mona Lisa, he thought. So where the hell was it? Jack desperately wanted to question Bianca about what Batas had told her, but he knew she needed sleep far more than questions. He took her up to her flat, left her to collapse into bed and sat in his car to think. He reached into his pocket for his mobile and touched some bubble wrap. What was bubble wrap doing in his pocket? He suddenly had an image of him picking it up from Cellini's bedroom floor. A light went on in his head. He started the car and headed for Palladian Mansions.

Jack was surprised to see Carla, Cellini's maid open Mrs. M's door.

She smiled at him. 'Signora Monty give me job, Signore,' she said in broken English. 'She nice lady.'

She took Jack's coat and he called out to Mrs. M as he walked towards the lounge.

Mrs. M had her feet up, watching T.V. with a half-empty bottle of Scotch whisky and a bottle of green ginger wine on a table near her when Jack walked in. She turned to him in delight. 'Jack, have a Whisky Mac! Have two or three!'

Jack smiled at this effusive welcome. Mrs. M was drunk. 'Just a small whisky for me. ' He sat down near her while she poured him a drink with a less than steady hand.

'Now spill the beans.' Her eyes shone with excitement. 'What new developments have you discovered?'

So Jack wove a story highlighting the drama of Rico's near-death experience and his recent return of consciousness which would lead to Angelica Logan's future conviction. He left out any mention of the drugs. At first, Mrs. M was riveted; then she frowned.

'But if he testifies, Jack, he'll have to admit he was black-mailing her. How many years will he get?'

'The maximum sentence is fourteen.'

'Fourteen years!' Her eyes flashed. 'That's outrageous!

Dickens was right. The law *is* an ass! Some murderers get out in less! You should start a campaign to change the law, Jack. I'll start a petition after Christmas to help you.'

Jack laughed at the thought of him going to the chief super saying he was going to change the law with the help of an eccentric old lady. 'It's not likely he'll get the maximum sentence after what Angelica Logan did to him, Mrs. M.'

'But that's not the point, Jack. The point is...' Mrs. M waved a whisky glass in his general direction and frowned. 'What *is* the point, Jack?'

Jack smiled. 'The point is I need to find the crate that the men delivered the night Cellini died. I've missed something.'

'How's finding a crate going to help you?'

'"Assume nothing. Believe nothing. Check everything." My wife's mantra when she was a forensic scientist, Mrs. M.'

'Sounds very clever, Jack – whatever it means.' Mrs. M's eyes suddenly drooped and her glass dropped from her hand before Jack could reach it. He picked up the glass from the carpet and went to look for the maid as Mrs. M started to snore.

Carla was tidying up the already tidy kitchen and listening to some sentimental song on the radio. She didn't hear him come in.

'Carla,' Jack said.

Her body jerked as if she'd been electrocuted. 'Santa Maria Madre di Dio!' she gasped. 'You scare me, Signore! My nerves...she...' She stopped; obviously not having enough English to explain her fragile nervous system to Jack.

'Sorry, I just wanted to ask you if you know where the crate was.'

Carla looked at him with incomprehension and Jack realized that Cellini must have communicated with her solely in Italian. He wondered how Mrs. M coped.

Jack got out the notebook he always carried around with him and drew a picture of a crate while she watched him. When he finished, he mimed looking around the room for it and she suddenly clapped her hands.

'I show, Signore.'

Jack went back into the lounge to check that Mrs. M was okay before Carla and he walked out of her apartment. Jack locked Mrs. M's door securely and they went into the lift. Six floors later, they were in the basement and Jack was walking around an enormous room, divided up into lockable storage rooms. Carla marched past him and opened Cellini's storage room and showed the empty crate to Jack. She made a wide expansive gesture with her hands as if to say: what's the point of looking at an empty crate? 'Nulla qui!' she said, obviously thinking him mad.

Jack searched his brain for his O-level Italian, trying to dredge up a few words. He didn't want her staying any longer. 'Grazie, Carla. Si può tornare alla Signora Montgomery ora,' Jack replied hesitantly, but thinking his pronunciation was pretty good for someone who hadn't spoken Italian for ten years. She frowned at him with incomprehension and he realized that perhaps it wasn't good at all.

'Che cosa hai detto?' she asked him.

Jack repeated his phrase, but changed his pronunciation; this time, she smiled at him.

'I understand, Signore! I go see Signora Monty.'

They beamed at each other with mutual linguistic appreciation; then she left him alone in the lonely room.

Jack closed the storage-room door and walked around the crate, studying it from all angles. What if he'd been right when he'd told Jamila that the drugs might not be hidden in the statues? He studied the inside of the crate; then studied the outside. His heart suddenly leapt. Why were the dimensions between the outer and inner walls so thick? Taking his Swiss Army knife out of his pocket, he carefully leveled out one of the boards; then suddenly sneezed. It must be his hay-fever again. He lifted out the board carefully; years of training had taught him that searching for evidence must be performed with the minimum amount of damage. Blood suddenly flooded into Jack's face as he saw what was nestled neatly underneath the board: hundreds of small bags of white powder. Jesus Christ! The crate was over a metre high and wide; the haul would be worth millions! He whipped out his mobile and rang Jamila and told her to drop everything she was doing to meet him at once.

The adrenaline surged through his body as he phoned Colin to tell him he'd be late home; he was working on something important. He heard Colin tell the others and suddenly Tom was on the phone. 'You're working under-cover, aren't you, Dad? Is it big?'

'Yes, it is. I can't talk about it until we've found all the people responsible. Don't tell anyone, Tom. I'm relying on you. It's very important.' He finished the call, feeling euphoric; it was the first time Tom had wanted to speak to him since he'd left the Met.

Jack paced up and down the basement as he waited for Jamila. Catching a drug-smuggling gang was always dangerous because of the vast amounts of money involved, but there must be a way to do it. Jamila arrived before he had thought of a solution; he didn't know how she'd managed to get there so quickly, but he didn't care. He took her to the locked room and showed her the drugs.

She gasped with shock. 'There's so much, Jack. I can't understand why the sniffer dogs didn't smell it all.'

Jack leant against the crate. 'Did anyone report some of the dogs sneezing?'

Jamila looked at him in astonishment. 'What's that got to do with anything?'

'But have they, Jamila?'

Jamila tried to remember all the drug-related reports she'd read from the BA and SOCA. 'Yes, a few of them did. A bit strange, I thought.'

Jack took out his Swiss Army knife again and scraped along

the outside of one section of the crate and caught the residue in his hand. 'Sniff that.'

Jamila bent down and sniffed hard. She immediately sneezed and looked at Jack in confusion. 'What's that mean?'

Jack sniffed the residue too and sneezed. 'It means that the gang are very ingenious, Jamila. They've coated the outside of the crate with a residue made from pepper. The dogs can't smell the drugs through it.'

Jamila was stunned. 'How did you work that out?'

'I never get hay-fever in the winter,' Jack said enigmatically.

'I don't understand half of what you say,' Jamila said, smiling at him. 'But if they got that through there must be lots more crates out there stuffed with drugs.'

'Yep, this crate is just the tip of an iceberg.'

There was silence as Jamila watched Jack staring at the crate. She had spent a long time studying Jack's methods; if he went silent, he was working something out and he didn't like being disturbed when he was thinking. A minute later, he turned to look at her.

'The only way we'll find the gang is to set a fly-trap. I'm going to see the chief super after Christmas and get his authorization.' But Jack knew that if this dangerous operation was going to be successful, he'd have to ask for help from someone he didn't want to involve: Bianca.

CHAPTER 38

24th December 2012

Angelica had been lying in bed since she had told Mark that she had given her brother away. The admission had made her withdraw from the world; Mark couldn't reach her any more. The woman lying on their bed wasn't the woman he married and loved so much. It tore tiny fragments from Mark's heart each time he looked at her pale, porcelain face. He still couldn't believe the things he'd been told about her could possibly be true. How could someone so beautiful be capable of such callousness? Such cruelty?

He'd called their private doctor and asked him to come to the house urgently to see his wife. When the doctor had asked what was wrong with her, he didn't know what to say. How could he tell him that she simply wasn't there? Each day she picked at her food and washed herself if Mark told her to; but that was all the interaction she had with the world, except for her occasional ramblings which made no sense to Mark. He'd rung the owner of the newspaper after the police had left and told him that he needed to appoint a temporary editor as he was ill. He'd invented an illness that would lay him low for weeks. But he really was ill; not physically, but mentally; he was in torment, trying to replay every conversation he'd had with Angelica;

trying to work out how many times she'd been with that bastard when he had thought she was busy with her charity work. He wasn't a stupid man, so when had he become so gullible? The thought of her making love with Cellini made him feel like vomiting, but he couldn't; perhaps because he couldn't eat. He suddenly noticed that Angelica had gone to sleep and crept out of the bedroom. Perhaps the doctor would arrive soon. He wandered down the stairs and sat in the hall and waited.

Angelica was running with her parents along the street and her mother was crying hysterically. They didn't seem to notice that she was being left behind. Suddenly, they ran into a large building and disappeared. She had a stitch in her side, but Angel carried on running after them, terrified that she might never see them again and entered a large noisy room. It was packed with people shouting in Italian. Her parents stood in front of two policemen in black uniforms who didn't seem interested in the shouting people. But everyone stopped shouting when her father bellowed: 'Mio figlio è stato rapito!' at the top of his voice. He ordered the police to get a search party out immediately. Everyone looked shocked and started shouting again. One of the policemen blew a whistle and ordered everyone out of the room, except the signore and his family. Everyone went out shouting at each other. The policemen kept asking Angelica's father question after question while her mother wailed over and over again. Her father didn't want to answer the questions. He kept shouting that they must start a search immediately, but the policemen just continued asking questions. Angelica tried to block out all the terrible noise. She wanted her mother to hold her, but she didn't seem to notice her at all.

'Find my baby. Find my baby,' she kept sobbing over and over again.

But the questions went on. *What was their exact location when the baby disappeared? What was the baby wearing? How old was he?*

Did Signore da Carrara have any enemies who could have committed such a terrible crime?

Angelica looked at her parents. Couldn't they see that she was there? Couldn't they see that she needed them? When the policemen started writing a report her father hit one of them and her mother's wailing got louder and louder. Angelica put her fingers in her ears to cut out the sound, but it didn't work. The noise went on and on and on.

A man with a black bag came and put a needle in her mother's arm and she stopped wailing. Angelica tried to cuddle her, but she didn't even look at her. 'Mama, I'll look after you. Don't be sad. Angel's here.' But her mother ignored her; everyone ignored her.

Something was pressing different parts of her body. She looked down and saw another man with a black bag staring down at her. Why were there two men with black bags? He was talking to her, but she didn't want to talk to him; she wanted her mother to cuddle her.

'How long has she been like this?' the doctor asked Mark when he'd finished testing her reflexes.

'A couple of days. This is going to sound strange I know, but...it's almost as if she's living somewhere else.'

He glanced at the doctor quickly to see if he thought him mad.

The doctor looked worried. 'Mark, Angelica doesn't need a G.P. She needs a psychiatrist.'

CHAPTER 39

24th December 2012

As Jack drove towards Chief Superintendent Ian Dunmore's house, he hoped their encounter would be better than the last one. It had been after the siege and the CS had shouted at him that it was incredible that a DCI with his experience had botched an operation. It should have been straight-forward, and then he'd been stupid enough to admit he'd made a mistake in front of an undercover reporter! Jack tried to explain that it had been impossible to move quickly enough to stop the extreme actions of an Islamic husband who wanted to destroy his wife for committing adultery. He had doused her in petrol and set her alight in front of their son before Jack could rescue her. *But you were in charge, Jack – you should have gone in earlier!* The CS had shouted. Two days later, Jack had handed in his resignation.

His satellite navigation system guided him to Hampton Wick, down the A 310; then told him to turn right into Park Road. Concentrate on the present, Jack, told himself, stop living in the past. The chief super's modern house was halfway down the road; Jack was surprised; he'd expected an old-fashioned man like Ian Dunmore to be living in a Victorian villa. Claire Dunmore opened the door and smiled at him.

'Happy Christmas, Jack. Something must be important for you

to come all this way to see Ian on Christmas Eve. But how lovely to see you again.'

Jack smiled back at her; they'd only met twice before, but she sounded as if she'd really meant it. She showed him into a large bright lounge where Ian Dunmore sat in front of an inviting log fire, enjoying a drink. He turned and smiled at Jack.

'We were just having a Christmas drink, Jack. Will you join us?'

'Better not, sir. I've got to drive home and I'll be drinking later.'

The chief super sipped his drink; then put the glass down on a small table beside him. 'Sit down. It sounded urgent on the phone.'

Jack glanced at Claire. He didn't want to speak in front of her. Years of being a policeman's wife had obviously given her special powers; she smiled at the men and left the room.

Jack had spent a long time working out exactly what to say to the CS to get clearance for his idea. He told him concisely what he'd discovered and mentioned that a member of the drug ring was prepared to cooperate with them in exchange for police protection and a lighter sentence. He didn't want to mention Bianca but had to; she'd need police protection too.

'She's a good friend of Batas. She trusts me and she's the only one he trusts, sir. If I work with them, I think we can catch the gang that's been running rings around the BC, the SOCA and the Met for months.'

Ian Dunmore had been only mildly curious when Jack had started his story, but by the time he'd told him about the ingenious method they used to smuggle in the drugs, coupled with the fact that one of them was blackmailing Mark Logan's wife because she was the hit-and-run driver they were looking for, he was staggered.

'How did you find all this out?' Dunmore said in amazement.

'I've been working undercover for weeks, sir. I knew there

was something suspicious about Paolo Cellini's death and it all led back to him. You know what I'm like with leads.'

'Yes, they always seem to go somewhere unlike Alan Saunders'.' Dunmore got up and put another log onto the fire making the sparks shoot up the chimney.

'I'd like to come back, sir,' Jack said quickly before he lost his nerve. His body was tight with tension as he looked to see how the CS would react.

He turned to smile at Jack. 'I've been waiting for you to say that for a long time.' He sat back in his chair. 'I shouldn't have accepted your resignation, Jack, but we have a problem.' He picked up his glass and sipped his drink. 'Alan Saunders has got your job. I can't have two DCIs in one division.'

Jack stared into the fire, feeling deflated. It was his own fault Alan had been given promotion.

'But there could be a solution,' Dunmore continued, finishing his drink and pouring himself another.

Jack looked at the CS and held his breath.

'I'm telling you this in confidence. I think DCI Saunders could be transferred in the New Year, so I'll need an experienced senior officer.'

Jack felt light-headed from holding his breath.

'I'd like you to continue working under-cover on full pay,' the chief super continued, and who knows, if you crack this case, there could even be a promotion. This is strictly off the record of course.'

Jack could hardly remember driving home he was so euphoric; from Chauffeur to DCI and perhaps more in a month! All he had to do was set up the fly-trap with the help of the SOCA, get all the information he could from Rico and try not to get killed.

Chapter 40

24th December 2012

Jack found it difficult to concentrate on family conversation; he kept thinking of the crate lying in the basement, full of cocaine. What if the gang discovered it before they could plan the fly-trap? He had to get Bianca to find out as much detail about them as she could, but, then, life would become dangerous for her and she'd had enough trouble in her life already. But he knew Rico Batas wouldn't open up to him.

'Dad?'

Jack turned to see Tom looking at him quizzically.

'Do you want one?'

'What?'

'A drink.'

'Sorry, just thinking of something I have to do.'

'Not over Christmas, surely, Jack,' Mary said, looking at him with disbelief.

Jack glanced at Lucy before saying, 'No, not over Christmas, Mary. I'm on holiday. I'll have a beer, Tom. Anyone else fancy a drink?'

'I'll have a G& T,' Tom said.

Jack smiled at Lucy; their son had actually made a joke.

'He heard someone ask for that on an old film we were

watching,' Mary said, smiling. 'I'll have a glass of white wine, Jack. Only one day left.'

Jack frowned at her. One day to what?

'It's Christmas day tomorrow, Dad, remember.' Tom looked at him.

Jack groaned silently; he'd forgotten to buy any Christmas presents. He jumped up. 'Just need to pop out. Back soon.'

They looked at him, startled as he hurried from the room.

He raced around the shops before they closed, buying anything he thought the family would like without even looking at the prices. Then just as he was paying for the presents, he glanced up and noticed a short, stocky man staring in one of the shop mirrors; Jack's heart lurched; he'd seen this technique used hundreds of times to stop people noticing that they were being followed. He wondered how long the man had been tailing him. Why hadn't he noticed him before? He was getting careless. Gathering up his gifts, he ran up one of the escalators. The man looked at him startled; he obviously expected him to walk out of the shop. Jack glanced back; there were lots of people on the escalator behind him; he'd never reach him. Jack raced around to the other side of the shop to the descending escalator and ran out of the back entrance of the shop and into the car-park. Sweat dripped down his face as he started the car; not from exertion, but fear: the man must have followed him home from the hospital. He reversed the car and suddenly saw 'his tail' coming out of the department store, laden with last-minute shopping; walking with him was a woman and two excited children. Jack started laughing. He was becoming paranoid. The man must have been startled because of the manic way he had raced up the escalator laden with presents. How could the gang link him to Rico? he thought, as he drove past Kentish Town Tube station.

The Prince of Wales Road was unusually light in traffic for a Christmas Eve so he managed to drive down it without the normal stops and starts. He turned into Grafton Road and drove up to their semi-detached house which Lucy and he had bought twenty years ago. Today, they wouldn't be able to afford it. He put the Ford in the garage and picked up the presents. As he closed the garage door a light rain descended and he hurried towards the front door. It was Christmas and his family was waiting for him. He glanced through the lounge window; they were laughing at someone on the T.V. For a moment, as Jack stood in the drizzle, staring at them, everything seemed perfect.

He was so absorbed that he failed to notice a black saloon car parked on the opposite side of the road. A short, squat man sat in it, talking into his mobile. He watched Jack open the front door, wipe his feet and walk in.

Chapter 41

27th December 2012

The hospital reception area was festooned with Christmas lights and decorations; it was almost like a celebration of illness, Bianca thought as she walked past it towards Rico's room. She was exhausted by stress and it was arriving in bucket-loads. A couple of nights ago, Jack had phoned her and told her to move out of her flat; she was the gang's link to Rico. She was frightened by what he asked her to do; it was dangerous. But if she didn't, Rico would rot in prison. She told Jack she'd stay with one of the band, but within minutes of cutting the call, she'd fallen into a deep sleep. Her taxi-driver told her on the way to the hospital that a car had followed them all the way from her flat. All she wanted to do was to be able to live without worrying if she or anyone she cared about was going to die. Was that too much to ask? She instinctively looked up at the hospital ceiling as she traipsed down the familiar corridor. Rico was staring up at the ceiling too as Bianca opened the door to his room.

'Hi, Rico. How'd you feel today? I forgot to bring you this.' She put a gift on his bed for him as she sat down. He didn't look at it.

'Christmas – what a joke,' Rico croaked. His throat was still painful. He tried to smile at her and winced with the pain. 'You look tired, Bi.'

Bianca leaned over and kissed his cheek. 'I am, but we've got to work fast. Jack Bradley, the undercover cop I was telling you about needs more info on the drug dealers. What the fuck were you doing with them, Rico? What were you thinking of?'

'Mostly of you, Bi.' Rico pressed his hand in hers.

Bianca sighed. 'You should have kicked him in the nuts when you had a chance.'

Rico smiled at her, then leaned back in the bed – speaking was exhausting. 'What am I going to do, Bi?' He turned to look at the young PC outside his room. 'He's not going to stop them.'

'I've told you. Jack is going to help us, Rico.'

'Why?' Rico snapped.

'It's not like that. He loves his wife and son.'

Rico made a dismissive sound. 'Yeah, so did Ferdinand Marcos.'

'If you help him, Rico, perhaps you could get out of prison in two or three years. If you don't...' Bianca shrugged her shoulders.

'I don't want you coming here again. It's too dangerous.' Rico tried to get out of the bed in agitation. There wasn't any hope for him; he knew that they'd find him before the police did and he didn't want her to be there.

Bianca pushed him back onto the bed. 'And what would happen to you if I did?'

'It doesn't matter what happens to me, Bi. It's only you I worry about.'

Bianca blinked rapidly. She was sitting beside a guy whose face looked like it had gone through a meat-mincer; a guy who thought a gang would kill him one night in the hospital and all he cared about was her. She'd never had that much love in her life before and suddenly she was sobbing. 'Rico, why did I go with a bastard like Paolo?'

Rico touched her face; there was no answer to that question. Perhaps she was right; perhaps this man Bradley would help him. He decided to tell her what little information he had about the drug ring, then asked her to leave the UK and go far away, where they couldn't find her.

She promised him she would, but she knew, even as she promised, she would never leave. Her life was in London now and nowhere else.

The car park outside the hospital was in shadows. Bianca shivered as she hurried towards her car. *I must have a death wish,* she thought as she got into the car; she was being followed and yet she was still going to see Rico. She was just about to start the engine when she heard a click behind her. She screamed as she saw a man's face in the rear mirror.

'Cut the screaming now!' he shouted in her ear.

She stopped screaming immediately and started shaking.

'I'm a reasonable man, just tell me where the fucking drugs are and you can go home and have a kip. How's that sound?'

Bianca tried to stop shaking so she could speak. 'Rico doesn't know.'

He pressed something hard against her head and screamed again. 'Stop wasting my fucking time and tell us where they are or I'll shoot the top of your fucking head off!'

Tears poured down her face, soaking her coat. 'I don't know, I don't know.'

'I'm counting up to three, then say goodbye to your head.'

'One! Two! Three!'

There was a sharp click, then nothing. Bianca was paralyzed with fear; she couldn't feel her body. There was complete silence in the car. Then she heard another softer click. What was he doing?

'Just testing, love,' the man said in a quiet voice. 'Okay, so Rico don't know where that bastard Cellini hid the stuff, but your boyfriend do, don't he?'

'My boyfriend's dead.' She held her arms tightly around her body in case she fell apart.

'The dodgy ex-copper, love. The one who took you home...remember him? He's been nosing about Cellini's place. But we been nosing an all. Nothing there, but he's a bit of ferret, so here's what you gonna do.'

Chapter 42

31st December 2012

Angelica had been taken into police custody after they had taken a statement from Rico Batas of his account of the events leading to him being assaulted. Jack's old team worked through the entire database of tires and compared them with another database to determine the brand and model. They passed the results to the Forensic team who analyzed them on a powerful computer with Autodesk Revit software. All the tests confirmed that the tires had belonged to a vehicle owned by Angelica Logan. Other members of the team studied a database of garages in London; they eventually found a garage that had worked on the Lexus the day after the Albanian boy had been hit. The repairs were consistent with the vehicle hitting something or someone at high speed. But the most conclusive forensic evidence of all were the spots of blood on the underside of the car. Forensics studied a slide of Ramiz Agani's blood and compared it to a slide from the blood spots on the car and discovered they were a perfect match.

Alan Saunders was ecstatic; he had all the evidence he needed to charge Angelica Logan with first-degree vehicular manslaughter and attempted murder. But when she was brought into the police station in a completely disorientated state, the custody sergeant had immediately called a police surgeon and

Alan Saunders wasn't allowed near her. When she was sent to a medium secure psychiatric unit to be medically assessed, DCI Saunders knew he wouldn't be able to charge her with either crime if she was declared unfit to stand trial. He was incandescent with rage. She'd wriggled out of her sentence, he'd shouted to Jamila, by claiming she had mental-health problems. All criminals had to do these days was plead insanity and they could get off with murder! Where would it stop? After listening to him ranting for hours, Jamila thought she'd have to ask the chief super for a transfer; she really couldn't work with such a bigoted man.

She rang Jack to tell him what had happened but he was more interested in informing her about the fly-trap operation they were planning in two days' time. He wanted her to go to the chief super's room for a briefing tomorrow. Jamila felt her heart racing; the operation was going to be dangerous, but it was an opportunity to prove that she was a good officer. She was suddenly bumped back to earth when he told her that she wasn't experienced enough to be on the front-line of the op; he wanted her as back-up. How could she get promotion if she wasn't given any opportunities? He knew that she was one of the best shots in the Met.

Chapter 43

2nd January 2013

Jack had made an enormous effort over Christmas to seem bright and cheerful and Lucy's parents had been deceived, thinking that whatever was worrying him had now been resolved, but Lucy and Tom knew it hadn't. Tom came up to him when they were alone to ask what was happening. He wasn't a child any more he told them. Jack suppressed a smile, but Tom did look mature at that moment. How could he be prepared if something went wrong, he asked his father, if he had to live with so much uncertainty? In that moment, Jack realized that Tom had lived with far too much uncertainty since Lucy's illness. When Colin and Mary had gone out for a walk, the three of them went into the study to talk.

Jack looked at Lucy. 'I think he's mature enough to cope, don't you?'

She blinked once.

Tom sat tensely on his chair as his father spoke.

'I'm working undercover on a drug-smuggling case. I found out where one of the dealers has hidden a stash of drugs. Tonight, we're going to catch the gang. That's it in a nutshell, Tom.'

Tom's eyes were enormous as he looked at Jack. 'Will it be as dangerous as the last drugs op?'

'I'll be working with the same SCD7 team I worked with before. You know how good they are.'

'Is Jamila going with you?'

Jack knew he was trying to make the work more personal; he liked her. 'No, she's not experienced enough yet, but she'll be one of the back-up team.'

While Jack was speaking Lucy was typing. They looked at her laptop.

yr dad is a great dci trust him i do

Jack smiled at Lucy. 'Thanks, Luc.'

'What are you going to do?' Tom asked; his voice tight with tension.

Jack and Lucy knew exactly what he was thinking. He could lose both parents.

'You know I can't tell you the details, but remember how many ops I've done. I never take unnecessary risks, Tom. I bet I'll be home before you come back from your Batman film.'

how much Lucy typed

'A grand,' Jack said, smiling at her.

'I don't want to go,' Tom spoke in a flat voice.

Jack looked at his vulnerable son and wanted to hug him, but he knew that if he did, Tom would break down and he wanted him to be strong.

'You can't let your grandparents think that's something's wrong, Tom. I'm relying on you, remember.'

'Hello. Where is everyone?' Mary called out from the hallway. They heard the front door close.

'Are you ready, Tom?' Colin shouted. 'We don't want to be late.'

'He's coming, Colin,' Jack called back, smiling reassuringly at his son.

'Be careful, Dad. I can buy a lot of Batman books and games with a grand.'

'No chance,' Jack said, getting up and ruffling his son's hair.

'Now get going.'

Jack waved to Colin and Tom from the lounge window, thinking about the night ahead. He'd been liaising with his friend and colleague Bob Cooper, the Head of the SCD7 since Jack had got the go-ahead from the chief super. Some of the team would be waiting at the pub. The rest of them would be entering Palladian Mansions via the tradesman's entrance at the back. Both men had been worried by the lack of time they'd had to plan the op, but they didn't have a choice; it was too dangerous for Bianca and Rico if they didn't move tonight.

But it wasn't only the lack of time to organize the op that was making Jack edgy; Bianca hadn't been in contact about her whereabouts after her initial phone call. Something had happened. He tried not to think of the worst scenarios. He should never have allowed her to become involved. What was he thinking of? These guys were drug dealers; she was a nightclub singer. How could she know the depths to which drug dealers could sink? But even as he was thinking such thoughts, he knew he was being disingenuous. How could he have got any information about the dealers from Rico without her? He thought of all the kids he had seen dying from overdoses. He didn't have any choice, did he? If Bianca hadn't become involved, they would have killed Rico and Jack would never have flushed them out. But he could have made contact with the gang himself, couldn't he? He *could* have done it without her. His thoughts were driving him mad. It was the waiting that was a killer; it was always like this before an op. Bianca wanted to help Rico, he reasoned. It wasn't his fault she was involved. She could have said no. He didn't force her. *God, you're doing it again – trying to justify involving an innocent person.*

He turned to look at Lucy. She was very pale; he couldn't tell in the lamplight whether she was nervous for him or it was caused by her illness. He went over and sat beside her wheelchair and held her hand.

Mary peered over her reading glasses at them and got up. 'I'm going to make some tea. Like some, Jack?'

'No, thanks. I've got to go out soon to see someone.' He gave her the same reassuring smile he'd given to Tom. It seemed to work. She smiled at him before going into the kitchen.

'I'm working with the best team the Met has, Luc. You know that, so there's nothing to worry about.'

youre speaking 2 me not tom she typed

'Sorry. You know the nightclub singer I told you about? Since she rang me to say that one of the gang contacted her, she's not been in contact again. They want to meet me at a pub near Cellini's apartment. I asked her if she was okay and she sounded odd. Christ knows what they're doing to her or planning for the team. But I'm the one with the trump card, Luc. They won't get to the drugs without me. I've not told her a thing.'

is she wired Lucy typed.

'Too dangerous. I hope to God she's okay. You know what they're...' Jack didn't need to finish the sentence. Lucy had worked long enough at the Met to know what drug dealers did to people who crossed them. 'I've got to leave, Luc. Everyone is getting into positions by 20.00 hours.'

They both looked at the clock over the desk. It was 6.30 p.m.

'I'll withdraw a grand from the bank before Tom gets home.' His joke fell flat as she typed.

luv u

He kissed her quickly; then walked out before he broke down.

The pub was half empty when he arrived. Jack was surprised, then realized that people were still probably hung-over from New Year's Eve. He glanced over at the three members of the team playing a game of pool in the corner and went over to the bar. His eyes were focused on the front door; he was desperate to see if Bianca was okay. He looked at his watch and glanced at the guys at the pool table; one of them glanced over towards him briefly. Jack tried to slow his heart rate; he had to remain very calm.

'You're holding up the queue, mate!'

Jack looked at the man behind him who pointed at the barman, waiting to take Jack's order. 'Sorry, small lemonade, please.' He had to order something, but couldn't drink before an op.

The door of the pub opened bringing in a flurry of wind and freezing air.

'Close the bleedin' door!' someone shouted. Bianca walked in with a short squat man. The man closed the door carefully. Jack looked at the terrified expression on Bianca's face as they walked over and joined him.

'Are you okay?' he said to Bianca as they all sat down at a small table.

She nodded briefly without looking at him. Her eye make-up was smeared as if she'd been crying. Jack breathed slowly and looked at the thug with her.

'Where is it?' The squat man gave him a look that Jack had last seen on one of the faces in Tom's comic book; it was evil.

'If you follow me. I'll show you. It's not far away.' They all got up from the table. The man held Bianca's arm in a vice-like grip. Jack resisted the urge to chop down on it hard and break it. He had practised aikido for many years and could have done it easily.

'Don't play any games with me,' the man said, giving Jack a look that spoke volumes. He was much shorter than Jack, but there was no doubting that he was capable of killing him.

'I've no intention of playing any games.' Jack glanced at Bianca, but she wouldn't look at him.

The three of them went out into the icy night and walked towards the Palladian Mansions. The man turned to him in surprise. 'We've searched Cellini's apartment.'

'It's not in his apartment,' Jack said, looking carefully around the street; he knew that they were being watched by the gang, but he couldn't see them; they were good, he thought.

'Where, then?' The man tightened his hold on Bianca's arm. She winced in pain.

Jack couldn't stall any longer. 'It's in the basement.'

'Where's the exit?'

Jack hesitated for a second.

'Don't be stupid, Mr. Bradley.'

'Drive around the corner, there's a small entrance around the back of the Mansions.'

'Did you get all that?' The man said into his wire. 'Move in positions now.'

They walked in the foyer of the mansion block. One of the SCD7 team was sitting there, dressed immaculately as a concierge. He looked at them suspiciously. 'Who are you going to see?'

'Mrs. Montgomery. 5th floor,' Jack said. He'd worked with this man on the last drug haul. 'Just say it's Jack Bradley and friends.' He'd already told Mrs. M that a new concierge would be ringing up, but he wouldn't be arriving. He'd explain later.

They walked over to the lift and got in. Jack pressed the button for the basement and they descended.

The man looked at Jack.' Where's the back exit?'

'In the basement,' Jack said impassively.

The man's eyes narrowed as he gave Jack a chilling stare. 'I told you – don't play games with me. Show me,' he said as they got out of the lift. 'We're walking over to the back exit,' he said into his wire, then looked at Jack. 'Open it.'

The large exit door had three bolts; Jack glanced at Bianca as he opened the bolts, but she seemed too frozen to notice what was happening. The SCD7 team was waiting in readiness, but he needed to know how many of the gang would be coming through the door. Suddenly, the room was full of people in grotesque masks holding Kel-Tec P11's and Glock 17's; small, neat guns that were easily concealed. *Jesus Christ*, Jack thought; he hadn't expected so many of them would be armed. He glanced at Bianca; she was on the point of collapse. The small squat man stared at him.

'Show us.'

Some of the masked men ran around the basement, checking that all the rooms only had stored items in them, not realizing that the team had discovered many ingenious places to hide. Jack strolled over to Cellini's store-room, needing time to work out exactly when to give the signal. He had to get it right this time.

One of the masked men hit him over the back. 'Stop fucking around! Move!' he screamed at Jack.

Jack winced against the pain and opened the door of the store room. The masked people crowded into the room and stared at the empty crate, then stared at Jack. One of them cocked back the hammer of his Glock with his thumb and pointed it at Jack. Jack exhaled deeply before he pulled back the board in the crate he'd removed earlier and exposed the cocaine. There was a loud whoop as they saw a life's dream of wealth in front of them. Within seconds, the men were ripping the crate apart; Jack was forgotten in the excitement of the find, except by one man in a mask that reminded Jack of the Elephant Man. He was holding Bianca in front of him; one arm tight across her throat. The man's gun and eyes were totally focused on him, while Bianca stood frozen with shock beside the remnants of the crate. Jack stood helpless in the gun's focus while the gang loaded up the bags they'd brought until all the cocaine had been removed. The men were striding towards the exit. Elephant Man glanced over to them and walked backwards with Bianca, not taking his eyes off Jack. If he gave the signal now he was likely to get killed, but he couldn't wait much longer.

'Now!' he shouted.

The store-room doors burst open and the basement was

suddenly full of the SCD7 team and the sound of gunfire. Jack dived as Elephant Man fired his Glock at him. He hardly registered the pain in his arm as he rolled over bringing up his SIG in a single movement and firing into the man's chest. Elephant Man collapsed onto the concrete, cork-screwing his mask into grotesque shapes. The team raced off after the masked men and Jack heard a rapid succession of shots outside the exit. He glanced at Bianca; she was slumped on the concrete, moaning softly.

'It's okay, Bianca. It's okay. It's over.' He looked down, surprised to see blood pouring down his arm. As he did, the small squat man moved out of the shadows, his gun pointed at Jack.

'Throw the SIG towards me,' he said in a quiet voice as he dragged Bianca up off the floor and held her in front of him.

Jack's head snapped up. The man in the pub. Jesus – he'd forgotten him.

'I won't tell you again, Mr. Bradley. I haven't got a lot of patience.'

The man's voice sounded ominous in its stillness and far more educated than before. Jack threw his gun towards him and groaned silently; he'd cocked up another operation.

'Now I want you to tell the SCD7 team to back off. Do that now.' The man pulled Bianca towards the exit, his gun pointed at her head.

Jack fell to his knees, wondering how much blood he was losing. He kept hearing gunshots outside. 'Coop? Can you hear me?' Jack shouted into his wire. More gunshots in the distance, then a crackle.

'What's happening?' Bob Cooper's voice was faint.

'A hostage situation in here. You need to back off.'

Jack heard Coop's voice shouting to the team in the distance. The gunfire stopped.

'Thank you, Mr. Bradley. You've been very helpful.' The squat man smiled as he pointed his gun at Bianca. 'It would have been interesting getting to know you, but there's never enough time to do every—'

A single shot sliced the air; Bianca was thrown aside as the man collapsed onto his stomach. Jack lay on the concrete, looking up at the ceiling. Not the best place to die, he thought as a fuzzy face hovered over him and he lost consciousness.

Chapter 44

5th February 2013

The newspapers had been awash with accolades for the Metropolitan police for weeks after their dramatic capture of one of the biggest drug-smuggling rings in Europe. Chief Superintendent Ian Dunmore had issued numerous press statements praising the superlative teamwork of DCI Jack Bradley and DCI Bob Cooper's team at the Serious and Organized Crime Command. He deeply regretted the deaths of two members of the squad during a barrage of gun fire, but he would personally ensure that the deceased's families would be well looked after. The public had been fascinated by the fact that everyone in the drug-smuggling ring had thought that the leader of the gang was called Capote. No one suspected he was, in fact, a short squat man who posed as the messenger boy. Not one member of the gang even knew his name. Sir Barnaby Morgan-Hughes, the police commissioner, awarded a commendation for bravery to DS Jamila Soyinka who shot the leader of the gang and saved the life of DCI Bradley by her quick thinking. The ACPO National Drugs Committee Award was going to be given jointly to DCI Bradley and DCI Bob Cooper.

Everyone told Jack how lucky he'd been. If DS Soyinka hadn't put a tourniquet on his arm quickly he'd be dead; the bullet had hit his brachial artery. He *had* felt lucky. After a short stay in hospital he'd made a quick recovery because of his fitness and was recuperating at home. During his convalescence, Jack, Lucy and Tom had searched avidly on the internet and had eventually discovered that the leader of the gang had gone to primary school with Paulo Cellini in the East End of London before Cellini's father had become wealthy and moved Paolo to a public school and had paid for Paolo's friend to go too. So that's why the man had been able to move from East End slang to educated English so easily, Jack thought.

There was a ring of the doorbell and Tom raced out of the study. He had been transformed by Jack's recovery. All his resentment and anger against his father after Lucy's illness had gone. Jack turned to look at Lucy, as usual shocked by her deterioration; both he and Tom pretended it wasn't happening.

They'd been having a steady stream of visitors since Jack had been shot and Tom had become a good host. They could hear him in the lounge talking to someone and went to join him. Jamila smiled as Jack and Lucy came in, but she couldn't hide her shock quickly enough as she registered the change in Lucy. She went over to kiss her.

'Ah, the lady with the lamp returns,' Jack quipped.

'Dad, that's *so* not funny.' Tom made a face at his father. 'Do you want a drink, Jamila?'

'Coffee would be great, Tom.'

He bounded out of the room. Jamila and Jack glanced at each other briefly as Lucy's labored breathing filled the room.

Jamila got up and stood awkwardly in the center of the room. 'I'll come back another time when you're not...' Her voice trailed away.

'I'm taking you to bed, Luc.' He looked at Jamila. 'No, stay and talk with Tom. It'll take his mind off...'

Neither of them seemed capable of finishing a sentence, Jack thought as he pushed Lucy's wheelchair out of the room.

Lucy was gasping for breath as he lifted her frail body into the bed and went to hook her up to the oxygen cylinder. She blinked at him twice. His hands shook as he put the oxygen mask over her mouth. She blinked at him twice again. Her eyes had always been so eloquent.

Jack's tears dripped onto her as he held her face. 'I can't, Luc. I haven't got the courage. Forgive me. Please.' He watched her painful breathing gradually become easier and soon she was asleep. Jack leaned his head against a wall and suddenly he was sliding down it. Seeing the silent desolation in Lucy's eyes was infinitely more traumatic than facing a man with a gun.

CHAPTER 45

15th February 2013

Tom's hand was tight in Jack's hand as they looked down at Lucy's coffin. In his other hand he held a drawing of the bird table he'd made for his mother. He looked up at his father and Jack nodded. The mourners watched the drawing flutter down on top of the coffin. Neither Jack nor Tom had cried since her death; Jack knew that if they did, they might never stop. All evidence of Lucy's illness had been removed from the house by Lucy's parents; all that was left was evidence of the vibrant wife and mother she'd once been in her numerous photos, books and scientific journals. Jack hadn't spoken to Lucy's parents much since the night she had died. It was too painful for them all. Tom and he had started jogging together. They had a daily routine to keep them both fit. When they returned, hot and sweaty, one morning, they'd looked at Mary's face as they entered the house and immediately knew.

Jack had put his arm around Tom's shoulder and they'd walked together into the bedroom. Lucy lay in bed with an expression on her face Jack hadn't seen in three years; it was peaceful. All the pain had been removed and left his lovely girl behind. Mary had combed out her brown hair and dressed her in her favourite blue dress; the one she always wore when they were going to the theater. What a labor of maternal love, Jack thought. He and Tom stood looking at Lucy for a long time without speaking.

Jack felt someone touch his shoulder. The vicar was looking at him expectedly. They were waiting for him to place something in the coffin. He opened his hand and he watched the pressed rose that Lucy had kept from the night of their engagement flutter down on top of her.

The reception after the funeral was surreal. He watched everyone moving their mouths but had no idea what they were saying. It was like watching a black and white television screen with the sound turned off. He and Tom sat side by side on a settee without speaking to anyone; both buried in grief. For the first time in his adult life, Jack wished that he believed in the after-life; he wanted Lucy to be waiting for him somewhere.

It was weeks later, when Jack was clearing out Lucy's desk that he discovered that she had copied one of Keats' poems into one of her notebooks.

When I have fears that I may cease to be
Before my pen has glean'd my teeming brain,
Before high-piled books, in charactery,
Hold like rich garners the full ripen'd grain;
When I behold, upon the night's starr'd face,
Huge cloudy symbols of a high romance,
And think that I may never live to trace
Their shadows, with the magic hand of chance;
And when I feel, fair creature of an hour,
That I shall never look upon thee more,
Never have relish in the faery power
Of unreflecting love;- then on the shore
Of the wide world I stand alone, and think
Till love and fame to nothingness do sink.

At last, Jack laid his head onto her desk and wept.

Chapter 46

14th June 2013

Jack stared out of Mrs. M's window at the tangle of ivy that was torturing the beech tree on the opposite side of the street. Ivy always reminded him of Alan. Everyone at the Met had cheered when they heard he'd been transferred to a back-water job in Norfolk. He was glad he'd gone back to work soon after Lucy's funeral; his colleagues and work had helped him cope. He hoped that it had helped Tom to go back to school; at least he wasn't embarrassed by his father's job anymore. Thank God for Lucy's parents, Jack thought. He couldn't have coped with Tom without them.

Carla came in with a tray of tea and put it down.

'I know how to make the British tea, Signore Bradley,' she said proudly.

Jack turned to smile at her. 'Your English is improving, Carla.'

'Mrs. Monty – she good teacher. She come now.'

As if on cue Mrs. Montgomery hobbled into the room and beamed at him. 'Sorry I'm late. My chauffeur is useless in heavy traffic. I ought to sack him, but I'd only have to get someone else.' She slumped into her chair in relief. 'How are you, Jack?' She studied him as he poured the tea out for them.

'Better, Mrs. M. I thought it was all rubbish, but time does help.'

'I read a quotation the other day. "If time heals all wounds, why don't they make clock band-aids."'

Jack smiled at her. He liked being with her; she didn't swamp him with unwanted sympathy. He passed her a cup of tea.

'Now tell me what you're working on at the moment.' Her eyes lit up. She loved Jack's visits. 'Is it another murder? I like murders.'

Jack laughed. 'You're incorrigible Mrs. M. Wasn't Paolo Cellini's murder enough for you?'

'Strange that Angelica never confessed, isn't it? She confessed about her other crimes, so why not Paolo's? You know Mark Logan has resigned from his job. It must have been appalling for him to read all those dreadful things about Angelica in the newspapers.'

'Well, she did some dreadful things, Mrs. M.'

'Yes, I know, that's why it's niggling me that she hasn't confessed. Catholics like confessions, don't they?'

'Perhaps she's confessed to a priest. We don't know.'

'Perhaps she can't, Jack. I hated all those media programmes about how she escaped justice by pleading insanity. People don't choose to have schizophrenia, do they?' Mrs. M sipped her tea as she waited for Jack's answer. She knew that he felt responsible for the Albanian boy's trauma after his mother's death. Perhaps he felt no pity for Angelica; perhaps he just wanted retribution.

'It must be a living hell, Mrs. M,' Jack said, then realized he had no idea what it would be like to have schizophrenia. Perhaps it had been far worse for Mark Logan, than her.

'I wonder if anyone goes to see her now that the media frenzy has died down. Apparently her husband doesn't anymore. I wish I could, but I can't face visiting a psychiatric hospital.'

'Frightened they won't let you out, Mrs. M?' Jack said, smiling at her.

She roared with laughter.

Jack stopped his car outside St. Bernard's Hospital in Ealing, wondering why he'd come. Paolo Cellini's death was old news. He was working on another case of organized crime. But Mrs. M had given him the nudge he needed. He liked every part of a puzzle completed and she was right. It was strange that Angelica Logan hadn't confessed to Cellini's murder.

He got out of the car and asked the way to The Orchard; a medium secure mental-health unit. He was surprised by the clean, contemporary lines of the building; he'd expected something Gothic and oppressive. He smiled as he walked in; his thinking was pure nineteenth-century lunatic asylums. The corridors were light and whitewashed; the walls full of contemporary posters. The whole atmosphere was designed to be uplifting. As he looked around for a nurse, one magically appeared at the end of the corridor. When he explained that he'd come to see Angelica Logan, she smiled at him and showed him her room.

'She doesn't get many visitors. Don't expect too much of her,' the nurse said enigmatically, before she opened a door and popped her head into Angelica's room to announce his arrival. She smiled at him briefly again before striding off.

Jack crept in, not knowing what to expect. She was sitting in a chair, staring at the window and looking as insubstantial as a shadow.

'Hello, Mrs. Logan. I came to your house once with Margaret Montgomery.' His voice sounded too loud; there was a long, embarrassing silence. He stood nervously in the center of the room, not knowing what to do.

She suddenly turned to look at him. 'Do I know you?' She frowned as if trying to search her memory banks. 'Shall I ring for tea?' She looked around as if the room was bugged and whispered. 'Actually, I don't think the service here is very good. I've rung a number of times in the past and no one comes, but don't say anything. Did I tell you I can't be redeemed?'

Jack was thrown by the sudden shift in conversation. 'No, you haven't mentioned that,' he said, sitting down opposite her.

'You can't be redeemed if you deprive a mother of her child. No Madonna can forgive you for that, can she?'

'What child are you talking about?' Jack whispered. Perhaps she would tell him something important.

'I had hundreds of lovers. Perhaps you didn't know that.'

Jack held his breath. Her mind was fire-working in all directions. So was this was what schizophrenia was like? He wondered how much medication she was on; her eyes held no light.

'Paolo was one of many, but I've done worse things than that.' She rang a small bell at her side and listened to it tinkling. 'I like that sound, don't you?'

'What things?' Jack desperately wanted her to concentrate.

Angelica got up from her hard chair and stared out at the uninspiring view of a courtyard full of weeds. 'I wish they'd put me in the room with a better view. I like trees. My mother was put away too. I didn't see her much.' She turned to look at him. 'Do you know my husband?' she asked as if she was making social conversation at a dinner party.

'Only by reputation,' Jack said, disturbed by her desperate lurches in conversation.

'Everyone in London knows Mark. He's a very good editor. Did you know?'

'Yes, so I've heard.'

'Now what can I do for you?'

Her tone was almost regal, Jack thought; amazed by how complex the mind was.

'I wondered if you could tell me about the night that Paolo Cellini died,' Jack spoke casually as if his question wasn't important.

'That's a long time ago, Mr... What *is* your name?'

'Jack Bradley.'

'Paulo. He was very beautiful. A woman came that night. I don't know why. I thought she looked... I wish they'd bring the tea. It *is* tea-time.'

'What woman?' Jack tried to keep the irritation out of his voice. She couldn't help the way her mind worked.

'How could I be redeemed if I prayed to a plaster copy?'

She looked at him as if he knew the answer. It suddenly came.

'Paolo Cellini had the real Madonna and you needed it.'

'Of course I did.'

'Who was the woman you mentioned? It wasn't the Madonna, was it?'

She frowned at him, trying to remember. 'She was jealous. She shouted at me.'

Jack's heart started to thump hard. 'Was her name Bianca Vella?'

'She said I went to school with her as if I could remember.' She smiled at him. 'I went to school with hundreds of girls.'

So Bianca and Angelica were both with Paolo Cellini the night he died! 'What happened, Mrs. Logan?'

She turned to look at him as if she'd only just seen him. 'When? Oh, I'll have to ring again. It's so irritating.' She rang the bell and listened. 'Are they coming?'

'What happened the night Paolo Cellini died?' Jack whispered. If only she could concentrate long enough to give him an answer.

'At last,' she said as the door opened and a nurse came in with an arsenal of tablets on a tray. Angelica Logan suddenly turned to Jack and said clearly. 'I destroyed him, you know.'

Chapter 47

15th June 2013

It had taken Bianca a long time to recover after the drugs raid; she'd had recurring nightmares for months, but Rico was right; she was a fighter and fought she had. She had decided two months ago that Angelica Logan wasn't going to destroy her life as she'd destroyed other people's.

She sat in her new dressing room and put the finishing touches to her make-up; she was an expert on knowing exactly how each audience wanted her to look like; tonight she was going for exotic sophistication. Everything had been altered since Paolo's death; she didn't want any reminder of him in her club. A large colorful Maltese rug covered the parquet floor; a burgundy velvet-covered settee was angled in the corner, giving the room the comfortable feel that had been lacking from it before. Her large oak dressing table was surrounded by soft lights; here she could store hundreds of bottles of lotions and make-up so all the clutter was gone. She sat back and smiled; she too was uncluttered. The trauma of the past was buried; at last, she could appreciate the present.

A knock on the door.

'Yes?' she called out.

'There's a gentleman at the bar, Miss Vella. He'd like you to have a drink with him,' Sam, the new manager called through the door; he'd learned never to walk into her room.

She frowned. 'How many times do I have to tell you, Sam? I never drink with the customers!' She was only hiring him until Rico came out of prison; Rico's organization was meticulous.

'He says he knows you. Jack Bradley.'

Bianca smiled in the mirror. She'd been waiting for him to come for a long time. 'Tell him I'll be out in five minutes.'

She stood up and placed a gold necklace around her neck, then put her burgundy evening gown on; she'd discovered the elegance of burgundy after Paolo's death. She studied herself in the mirror and smiled; she looked like the sophisticated owner of an up-market nightclub.

Jack sat in the bar looking around in amazement. The club had been transformed; from a seedy jazz club to a sophisticated night-club. Gone was the glitzy lighting and cheap-looking stage; now the stage wouldn't have looked out of place at a top London theater and the decor was state-of-the-art. The only thing that was the same was the band and the barman. Like the decor, the band had improved. When Bianca had rung him to say how sorry she was about his wife's death, she'd told him she was opening a new club called *Number One* and when he was feeling better, she'd like him to come. He'd thought the name too ambitious at the time, but he didn't now. He'd read online reviews which raved about the excellence of the food, the superlative quality of its wine list and the sexual allure of its resident singer's voice. Obviously, everyone else had read the reviews as the place was packed. Jack got up and glanced at the menu which was placed in front of the dining-room. He sat down quickly; if he ate here he could say goodbye to a month's salary. Where on earth did Bianca get the money from to buy the place? The newspapers said that Cellini had left all his money to Catholic Convents in Italy; nothing for his girlfriend or father. He looked at the clientele and suddenly felt under-dressed in his lounge suit; all the other men were wearing dinner suits.

He glanced up and saw someone who resembled Bianca sashaying towards him, but this woman was far too sophisticated. He almost choked on his cocktail when he realized it actually was her. 'Good God. You look like a different woman.'

She leaned forward and kissed him on the cheek. 'Thanks, Jack. I am. The woman standing before you would never have gone with a bastard like Cellini.' She looked over to Pierre and mouthed champagne. He smiled at her and went to get it.

Jack noticed that she now called her dead lover by his surname. *Interesting*, he thought.

'You look good, Jack. Being a DCI suits you better than being a chauffeur. How are you both coping?'

'Better now. I'm trying to remember all the good times, not the bad. I think it will take Tom a little longer, but he's getting there.' Jack smiled at her. 'And how are you? Stupid question, you look stunning.' She gave him a coquettish smile. She was a very alluring woman, Jack thought.

'I was in a bad place for a while. Lots of bad dreams, but...' she shook her head. 'I'm here now. What do you think of *Number One?*'

'Amazing, it must have cost a fortune.' He looked at her questioningly.

'It did.' She glanced up at Pierre as he hovered near her.

'I've put it in ice by your table, Bianca.' He walked over to her table and waited for them.

'Come and join me, Jack. I'm not singing for a while and I always sing better after vintage champagne.'

She got up and people waved or smiled at her she oscillated towards a table near the stage. Jack watched the motion of her hips and felt himself becoming aroused for the first time since Lucy had died.

He heard a man at the nearby table say, 'You think that's hot.

You wait until you hear her sing.' The men at the next table looked enviously at Jack as he sat down beside her.

'You've got a fan-club, Bianca.'

Pierre showed her the bottle of champagne and she nodded. He opened it in his usual expert manner and poured them two glasses.

'I've always had fans, but in the past they were sad losers; now they're all wealthy winners,' she said, touching his glass with hers as Pierre walked off. 'Cheers, Jack.'

'Cheers.' Jack sipped the most superb champagne he'd ever tasted. 'This is amazing.'

'I know. Cellini gave me expensive tastes. Now I can indulge them.'

'How?' Jack asked bluntly.

'He gave me a flawless emerald necklace. The only thing of any value he ever gave me. I had it valued. It was worth a great deal of money so I sold it and now I'm enjoying life in the fast lane, Jack. It's good. You should try it.'

'My salary forces me to live in a slow lane, Bianca.'

She smiled at him suggestively. 'That could be changed.'

Jack smiled back. 'I'm too old to be a gigolo and I like my job.'

'That's a pity. I've not met a man who's so good with a gun before.' She laughed as she poured some more champagne.

'I wanted to see you, but there's another reason I'm here tonight. I went to see Angelica Logan in the psychiatric unit recently.'

Bianca went very still and put down her glass. 'Why?'

'I hate unsolved puzzles. I couldn't understand why she'd never mentioned switching Cellini's heart tablets.'

Bianca shot him a look. 'What did she say?'

'That you were at his apartment the night he died. What happened?'

Bianca drank more champagne, then stared at him for some time before she spoke. 'Paolo Cellini was a bastard who had a heart condition, Jack. When I found Angelica with him, I shouted, threw a few things and then left. It made me sick seeing them together.'

The band started to play and Bianca turned her attention on them. 'You must always listen to good music, Jack.' She put a finger across her mouth in a gesture of silence.

Jack stared at her as she listened to the band, wondering what really *had* happened that night.

Bianca was back in Paolo's apartment again on that horrific night; the night that was knitted into her dreams.

She'd found him with the woman who'd almost destroyed her life. They were standing close together in his bedroom and the emerald necklace was fastened around her neck; Bianca's face flooded with blood.

'You bitch!' she screamed at Angelica. 'You fucked up my school-life and now you're fucking my man!' And suddenly she was hitting her with years of suppressed anger. Suddenly she felt a searing pain in her arms as they were wrenched behind her.

'What the fuck's wrong with you?' Paolo screamed at her.

'Wrong with *me*?' Bianca screamed back at him. 'Nothing's wrong with me! What's wrong with you? We've been going out for two years and you're fucking her!'

Paolo released her arms and smiled. 'No, I'm not. I'm fucking a woman called Stella.'

Bianca looked at him confused; who was Stella?

'I'm going,' Angelica drawled as if she was bored.

Bianca gasped as she saw the vulnerability on Paolo's face; she had never seen him look like that ever before. He held Angelica's shoulders in an effort to stop her leaving.

'No, don't, please. I've got something to show you.'

Bianca felt a sharp pain in her chest. He was pleading with Angelica to stay, not her. And Angelica looked at Paulo with sudden disdain as if she hated his need of her.

'You really ought to choose women more carefully, Paolo.' Angelica glanced briefly at Bianca if she'd found her under a stone. 'I'll leave you lovebirds together.'

She sauntered off into the lounge and Paolo hurried after her as if Bianca didn't exist. A knife lodged in her chest as she slumped on the bed. They were speaking about a statue as if she wasn't there! As if a religious icon was important when she had been betrayed by a man for whom she would have sacrificed her life! She sat still as Paolo told Angelica that her Madonna was a fake. Bianca heard her groan loudly. She suddenly shot up; she wasn't going to let that bitch win a second time.

She stormed into the lounge and found Angelica staring into a crate with look of horror on her face. 'You don't even remember me, do you?' She poked her to get her attention.

Angelica turned to her as if she'd never seen her before in her life. *How can she have forgotten what she's done to me?* Bianca thought. It was unbelievable.

'We went to school together in Italy. You got me expelled. You must remember me!' Bianca fought to stop herself crying.

Paolo looked at them in surprise. 'You know each other?'

'No,' Angelica said.

'Yes,' shouted Bianca at the same time. 'I caught her fucking the gardener's son and everyone thought she was so pure.'

For the first time, Paolo looked at Angelica in confusion. 'Angelica?'

'Neither of you know anything about each other. Does she know you were adopted, Paolo?' Bianca enjoyed the look of horrified surprise on Paolo's face. 'He was abandoned as a child, Angelica, his father told me. Perhaps that's why you're such a bastard, Paolo. You've just never felt loved since your mother's death, have you?'

'Abandoned?' Angelica turned to look at Paolo. Her face was suddenly very white. 'When?'

Paolo stood in front of Bianca shaking with anger. 'How dare you pry into my life, you fucking tart!'

Bianca was amazed that she wasn't upset by his anger; for the first time she felt that she was in control. 'He was left at a Catholic Convent in Italy and the only thing he had with him was a blue rattle.'

Angelica collapsed onto the carpet, moaning. 'It's not true. Paolo, tell me it's not true.'

Paolo looked down at her, totally confused by her reaction. 'What happened to me has nothing to do with us. Why are you so upset?'

Angelica lifted the Black Madonna out of the crate and started praying to it, tears pouring down her face.

"Forgive me my sins, Holy Mary; forgive me the sins of my youth and the sins of my age, the sins of my soul and the sins of my body, my secret and my whispering sins, the sins I have done to—"

'Stop praying!' Paolo shouted. 'Tell me what's wrong!'

And suddenly Bianca knew. There'd been rumors in school about her brother being kidnapped. Angelica had given her brother away! She gasped. It was monstrous.

'You've been fucking your own sister, Paolo. That's why she's so upset. She's the one who abandoned you and now she'll go to hell for all eternity.'

Paolo was frozen in horror; one hand clutched to his heart as he stared at Angelica. 'Tell me she's lying. Angelica! Tell me she's lying.'

But Angelica kept on praying to the Madonna and Paolo groaned. 'Oh, mio Dio! Oh, mio Dio!' He staggered into his bedroom. 'My tablets. My tablets,' he kept shouting.

Bianca looked at Angelica. 'Where are his tablets?'

Angelica kept praying as if she hadn't spoken.

'Where are they?' Bianca shouted to Paolo.

'In the bathroom cabinet – quick!'

She raced into the bathroom and opened the cabinet and

found some bottles. She scooped them up and raced back into the bedroom. Paolo was slumped on the bed, holding his chest. She gave him the bottles.

'Jesus – you stupid tart! These are vitamins! Get the Metoprolol!'

She raced back into the bathroom; then suddenly stopped, noticing two pairs of wet footprints, the wine-stained bathwater, the empty glasses and bottles of wine. All the time she was singing in the club, he was lying in a bath drinking wine with the person she hated most in the world. She found the bottle of Metoprolol pills hidden behind more vitamin tablets. She took the pills out of the bottle and put them in her pocket. She replaced them with white vitamin tablets and went to the door of the bathroom.

'What was the name again?'

'Metoprolol! Can't you fucking remember anything?' He got off the bed, wincing with pain.

'Sorry, Paolo. I'm a bit like you. Can't remember things.'

Paolo staggered into the bathroom. 'Stop playing fucking games. I'm in pain! Give them to me!'

She passed him the bottle and watched him fumble to open it.

'You bitch! Open it!'

Even now, he's abusing me, Bianca thought as she opened the bottle for him. She put some tablets in his hand. He swallowed two in one gulp and waited for them to kick in. Nothing. He looked down at the tablets in his hands as an agonizing pain tore through his chest and along his arm.

'These aren't Metoprolol!' His face was covered in sweat. 'Jesus Christ. What the fuck are you doing?' He clutched his chest in agony.

She suddenly realized what a dangerous game she was playing and fumbled to get Metoprolol out of her pocket. 'Take these, take these!' she shouted at him.

But Paolo just held his chest, his face contorted with pain.

Suddenly he lurched towards her, scattering tablets everywhere. Bianca watched in disbelief as he collapsed onto the floor. Terrified, she crouched beside him, trying, too late, to push the Metoprolol tablets between his teeth. But even as she was doing so, his eyes glazed over and his body went limp.

She started rocking back and fro. 'Oh Holy Mary Mother of God. I didn't mean you to die, Paolo. I didn't mean you to die. I only wanted to scare you. Don't leave me. I can't live without you.' She gathered his body in her arms and held him for a long time, tears streaming down her face. The love of her life was dead and she'd helped kill him. Panic suddenly swept over her – Angelica was in the lounge! She'd tell the police and then she'd rot in prison for the rest of her life. She laid Paolo's body back on the floor and ran out of the bathroom. She had no idea what she was going to do when she saw Angelica, but when she got to the lounge, there was no sign of her or the Black Madonna. All that she'd left was the emerald necklace lying on top of a marble table. Obviously she couldn't take it home. A huge wave of relief swept over Bianca. She stood still, thinking what to do. She wasn't prepared to go to prison; how was she supposed to know that Paolo needed the tablets so quickly? But no one would believe her in a court of law. *There must be a way out. There must be a way out,* she kept chanting to herself. The solution suddenly came. She rushed back into the bathroom, steeling herself against seeing Paolo again. He looked incredibly vulnerable, lying naked on the rug. Taking a soft white towel from one of the rails, she laid it carefully over his body, then collected all the Metoprolol tablets and put them back in the right bottle, then did the same with the vitamin C tablets. She wiped the bottles carefully with some tissues, pressed Paolo's hand around the Metoprolol bottle and put both bottles back in the bathroom cabinet using the tissues. She wasn't going to be accused of his murder when she hadn't killed him. She went back into Paolo's bedroom and opened the drawers. She didn't want any of her clothes to be left here. She opened the drawers where she left her underwear and was stunned to see them empty. Paolo had thrown them away! He obviously didn't want her coming to his apartment again. What a bastard the man was. She opened the bottom drawer and found a pair of silk panties that had Angelica stamped all over them. She picked them up and put them behind a radiator in the bathroom. She felt no guilt. Look what the bitch had done to her life and she couldn't even remember her. The thought held her together as Bianca wiped all the surfaces, checking the apartment for any sign of her presence there. Taking one last look around, she picked up the emerald necklace and left.

Jack watched Bianca all the time she was listening to the band, wondering what she was thinking. As they stopped playing, she looked at him as if she was going to say something. But just at that moment, there was a drum-roll and the saxophonist started introducing her to the audience. Everyone clapped loudly and waited for her to sing. Bianca got up and sashayed onto the stage. The lights dimmed and there was silence as she smiled at the audience.

'Good evening, ladies and gentlemen. Tonight, I'm going to start by singing one of Bessie Smith's songs called: "A Good Man Is Hard To Find". But I'm sure that doesn't apply to the gentlemen in this audience tonight.'

The audience laughed as the band played the intro; then fell silent as Bianca sang in a seductively poignant voice.

"A good man is hard to find
You always get another kind
Just when you think that he's your pal
You find him fooling round with some other gal
Then you rave, you almost crave
You wanna see him down in his grave."

And at that moment, Jack knew that she'd been the one to switch Cellini's tablets, not Angelica Logan. Why hadn't he thought about the significance of the lack of fingerprints on the vitamin C bottle before? Two tablets couldn't have fallen behind a radiator if no one had opened the bottle. And only a woman who loves a man covers his body. Angelica Logan didn't love Paolo Cellini. Of course, he could never prove what she'd done and he suddenly realized that he didn't want to.

She would always relive the night when she'd allowed the man she once loved to die, while he had to live with the knowledge that he'd allowed the woman he loved to live.

Bianca bowed to the enthusiastic audience; then looked across the room at him.

We all have our secret crosses, Jack thought as he smiled at her. She smiled back.

Author's Footnote

Baby hatches like the one I mentioned in the novel, are the modern version of the medieval foundling wheels where Italian mothers placed their unwanted offspring in revolving cribs that spun them safely into the confines of convents. Many of the abandoned babies born then were born out of wedlock or through adulterous liaisons. But the use of modern baby hatches is growing rapidly across Europe; mainly because parents are unable to financially support their children. However, these modern hatches now have a weight sensor alarm which alerts people to an abandoned baby's presence. Italy and Greece both have clauses under which women can give birth anonymously and are granted immunity from prosecution if they leave their babies at the special hatches in hospitals.

I have changed the ownership of the two paintings Angelica loved for the benefit of this story. Correggio's *Madonna and Child With The Infant Saint John The Baptist* was indeed sold at Sotheby's on 6th July, 2011. [The day that Paolo and Angelica first met.] However, it was purchased by the National Gallery of Victoria, Australia for $5.2 million; the highest price they have ever paid for any acquisition to date. *Madonna and Child* by Giovanni Battista Salvi owned by the National Gallery in London. If you are in either country, I hope you will go to see them.

Roundfire Books, put simply, publish great stories. Whether it's
literary or popular, a gentle tale or a pulsating thriller, the
connecting theme in all Roundfire fiction titles is that once you
pick them up you won't want to put them down.